LOVE AND MONSTERS

BOOK CLUB BOYS
BOOK 1

MAX WALKER

WALKING PRESS

Edited By: ONE LOVE EDITING

Cover designed and illustrated by Camille Pagni.

Noah Barnes

A trip to the grocery store changed my life.

That's where I bumped into my 'straight' co-worker and good friend, Jake Perez.

I decided to invite him to my book club night, not realizing the chain of events that invite would kick off.

Immediately our chemistry became too explosive to contain, making our friendship and work relationship complicated. That same night, a bloody package addressed to me lands on my doorstep.

Falling for Jake was never in the plans—then again neither was being targeted by a dangerous stalker.

This was going to be interesting.

Jake Perez

We were supposed to stay just friends—but how was that going to happen when all I wanted to do was kiss the guy?

Joining his book club sounded like a perfect way to spend more time with him. I wasn't counting on liking him more and more with every passing second.

Then came the targeted threats, throwing a wrench in our budding 'friendship'.

One thing was certain, though. Well, maybe two.

I was going to help Noah figure out who was behind

making his life a living hell and I was going to do it while staying as just friends.

Friends who liked to hold hands and kiss and...

Yeah. This was going to be harder than I thought.

ALSO BY MAX WALKER

The Rainbow's Seven -Duology

The Sunset Job

The Hammerhead Heist

The Gold Brothers

Hummingbird Heartbreak

Velvet Midnight

Heart of Summer

The Stonewall Investigation Series

A Hard Call

A Lethal Love

A Tangled Truth

A Lover's Game

The Stonewall Investigation- Miami Series

Bad Idea

Lie With Me

His First Surrender

The Stonewall Investigation- Blue Creek Series

Love Me Again

Ride the Wreck

Whatever It Takes

Audiobooks:

Find them all on Audible.

Christmas Stories:

Daddy Kissing Santa Claus

Daddy, It's Cold Outside

Deck the Halls

———

Receive access to a bundle of my **free stories** by signing up for my newsletter!

Be sure to connect with me on Instagram, Twitter and TikTok **@maxwalkerwrites.** And join my Facebook Group: Mad for Max Walker

Max Walker

Max@maxwalkerwrites.com

1

NOAH BARNES

HE WAS WEARING those khaki pants again.

The ones that hugged his bubble butt and bunched up between his legs when he sat. They were the pants that turned me absolutely feral. Like a cat in heat, yowling at anything close by that could potentially fuck me. A tree branch? Sure, yowling. A pair of muddy sneakers? Yowling.

A delicious-looking bulge offered up by my straight coworker and friend? *Absolutely* yowling. Loud enough to pop a couple of eardrums and break a few windows.

I adjusted myself in my seat, hiding just how excited those damn pants made me by rolling my chair further under my desk. Somehow, I managed to pry my gaze away, keeping my creeper tendencies in check while I tried to focus on the spreadsheet in front of me. Numbers swam, columns danced, rows rearranged themselves all into the shape of a thick pen—

"Hey, Noah, you have lunch yet?"

"Nope, not yet."

So if you'd like to serve me some sausage, we can just get started.

Damn... I was thirsty. And not just for the half-drank Gatorade bottle on my desk (blue, because that was the superior flavor according to anyone with taste buds). It wasn't exactly a new state of being for me. I'd been boy crazy ever since my hormones kicked into overdrive—likely the exact moment I witnessed the star quarterback of our high school's football team changing in front of me, nearly causing an extremely embarrassing and trauma-tizing mess in my towel. Luckily, I held it together that day, but the boy-session never left. I embraced it in my senior year when I came out to two of my best friends in an empty Taco Bell parking lot after we had snuck a (minuscule) amount of vodka out of my parents' fridge and got drunk at the playground nearby.

I remember being scared shitless. Eric and Tristan had been my best friends since elementary school. We'd been through some crappy times and some over-the-chart incredible times, always sticking together through it all. But this? Well, this was different. It wasn't about who cheated in Super Smash or Tristan choosing to go on a date with Sarah Miller over their usual Saturday night hangout.

This threatened to shake the very core of our friend-ship. Being gay—especially back in the early 2000s—was something that many people still didn't understand, and high school boys weren't exactly revered for their ability to fully understand and empathize with the world around them. Not only that, but kids were mean as shit. My friends might have been okay with me being gay, but would they have been okay with being gay by association? It all stacked up on my shoulders and made the words a mission to get out, likely not helped by the slight slur I had from taking my sip of vodka and orange juice.

"I'm...well, I'm—"

"What? Scared of butterflies? We know that," Tristan said, pushing his glasses up his nose and flashing that thousand-watt smile of his.

Eric took a bite of his taco, speaking through the crunches. "You're going to be competing on the next season of *Big Brother*?"

"No, yeah, right, I wish. Imagine me on—" I shook my head, getting off track. I just had to let the words out. Two simple yet galaxy-sized words:

"I'm gay."

There was no taking it back once I said it. The truest part of myself was laid bare, right there next to my half-eaten Crunchwrap Supreme. And, as I always should have known, there was no *need* to take it back. In fact, there wasn't any need to be scared about coming out to Eric and Tristan either. Not when Eric spoke up and came out himself that same night, Tristan joining the rainbow mafia a month later.

Turned out that I'd been the first bedazzled domino to fall, but I wasn't the last.

"Want to go for some Cuban?" Jake asked, drawing my attention up to his inhumanely blue eyes. Seriously, there should have been some law against having eyes that beautiful. *Especially* when you were straight. It was way too much power for one person to yield. Pretty privilege *and* straight privilege? It made me sick to my stomach.

Not sick enough to say no to a *medianoche*, though.

"Sure," I answered, locking my computer and reaching for my wallet, still under the stacks of papers I had left it under. My office wasn't exactly the picture of cleanliness and organization, but it worked for me. I'd only been in this position—accounts payable manager for a large construction company here in Atlanta—for about a month now, and in that time, I'd been way more focused on getting myself settled than on organizing my office.

Jake arched a skeptical bushy brow as I dug in a chaotic cabinet for my keys.

"What?" I asked. "I've got a system."

He chuckled, which slightly annoyed me. Was he laughing at me? And why did his chuckle sound so damn cute? "Yeah? What system is that? Windows 95?"

That got a genuine and surprised laugh out of me. "Alright, let's go," I said, grabbing the keys from underneath a tangle of multicolored rubber bands and jingling them in the air. "Before I end up having to re*boot* you in the ass."

Jake turned and gave himself a slap on the ass.

Damn him.

Damn him to gay-baiting hell, and damn me, too. Send me on my merry gay way right down there with him, because *damn* I wanted to bury my face in that juicy a—

His phone started to ring, startling us both and knocking me right out of my horned-up daydream. He dug in the pocket of his khakis and pulled out his phone, a flash of concern crossing his blue eyes as he read the name on the screen. When he answered it, I could hear a woman's voice on the other end, but her words were muffled.

"Okay, okay. Don't worry. Just stay where you are. Yes, yes, I'll be right there. Okay, bye, love you."

He hung up, the concern staying in that aquamarine gaze of his.

"Everything okay?" I asked as we stepped out into the windowless hallway lit by a row of fluorescent lights.

"Not really, no. Sorry, I'm going to have to rain check on lunch today."

"Totally fine," I said. "Go handle whatever you need to handle."

"Thanks, Noah." He held me in place with that infinite sea of blue. It felt almost as if he was about to say something else. Like he wanted to explain his situation further. I tried reading his thoughts, wondering what the hell rattled around inside that big (and admittedly handsome) head of his. Was it drama back at home? Maybe his girlfriend needed help with something, or maybe she was calling him home for an afternoon quickie.

Whatever it was, I figured I'd find out tomorrow when we bumped into each other. Jake reached out and gave me a friendly pat on my arm, the pat turning into more of a slide as he dropped his hand, his fingers grazing my elbow. He opened his mouth again, but no words came out. He pursed his lips and gave a wave before turning and walking toward the elevator bay, leaving me behind to watch as his perfectly perky bubble butt reminded me just how hungry I'd been.

Gah damn it.

I went to lunch by myself, eating my sandwich and sipping on my Cuban coffee and wondering how the hell I was going to stop myself from salivating over a man who'd never want me, at least not in the way I wanted him.

Whatever. I'll just get drunk with the book club tonight and find someone to hook up with after. That should keep Jake off my mind.

————

"AND YOU'RE sure he's straight?" Eric asked, opening the bag of chips and dumping them in the big red bowl. I squeezed between him and Tristan and opened my fridge, grabbing the queso and guac dips.

Clearly, I hadn't stopped thinking about Jake, which was why I had accidentally let his name slip when the boys asked me why I looked so pensive.

"Maybe bi? Pan? I don't know. I just know he had a picture of him and his girlfriend on his desk. Unless he has a sister that he kisses on the cheek in front of the Christmas tree."

"Girlfriend or sister, neither options are really ideal for you if he's kissing her like that," Tristan helpfully noted.

I rolled my eyes as I transferred the dips from their plastic containers and into smaller ceramic bowls. "It's fine, guys. Even if there was a shot, I don't think I'd take it. Especially not if he really is in the closet. Not after Franky. He made me cross off anyone that could hurt me like that again." I grabbed the dips and walked back into the living room, setting them down on the coffee table as Eric brought out the chips. There was a stack of labeled notebooks and a cup full of pens and pencils sitting in the center of the table.

"What Franky did to you was fucked-up, but everyone's situation is different. I'm not saying there's even a chance with Jake—"

".Thanks."

"—*but* if there was, then you can't assume that he'd act the same as Franky. That guy was a huge dick, and I think he would have been a dick whether he was closeted or not."

Tristan walked in, a bowl of grapes and strawberries in his hand. "Who's got a huge dick?"

"Stand down, size queen," Eric quipped. "We're talking about someone *being* a huge dick, not having one."

"Although," I said, raising a finger in the air, "Franky did have that too."

"Was that why you stayed with him for that long?" Tristan asked as he dropped onto the couch, nearly knocking over the book he had left on the armrest.

"No, I stayed with him because—when he wanted to —he knew how to be wildly romantic, and I'm a naive little lamb that's watched way too many rom-coms and thinks one of those happy endings can happen to me. I just have to find and possibly fix my Prince Charming before that happens." I shrugged, bare feet on the carpet as I trod back to the kitchen. "But there's no fixing someone who doesn't want to be fixed... and yes, the dick did help."

"Truth," Eric said as he followed behind me. "Franky likes playing with people. It had nothing to do with him still being in the closet. If someone is truly struggling to come out because of family or whatever else, then yeah, I get it. But Franky didn't have an excuse. He was just a self-hating queer dude that wrapped you up in his toxic web."

I took a deep breath, leaning against the counter. Everything Eric said was right. Per usual. Eric always had the read on people and knew someone's intentions before they even shared introductions. He'd called out Franky from the moment I brought him around, saying that there was an off-putting energy around him. I ignored the warnings and red flags so that I could dive headfirst into a messy yearlong relationship instead that left me with some heavy-duty emotional scars and a heaping of shitty memories. From being cheated on (multiple times) to being left stranded in Cabo after an explosive argument on vacation, I didn't really have much to fondly look back on.

But I had stayed with him. The brief moments of bliss I experienced with him were enough to keep me coming back for more. That trip to Cabo started with him renting out an entire villa for the two of us, the outdoor bathtub already full and covered in rose petals when we arrived, my name spelled out in ruby-red petals on the floor.

Little did I know he had a similar setup two streets down for the other guy he was flying in that same day.

"You're going to find your prince," Eric said, hand falling onto my shoulder. He smiled, dazzling me with that trademark grin of his.

"I'm fine with a duke. Hell, I'll even take a viscount. A court jester? Who-the-fuck-ever, so long as they have a penis and a pulse."

Eric snorted, shaking his head. "We gotta work on your standards."

"Yeah, clearly," I replied, laughing with Eric as I opened the fridge to grab the most important ingredients for a successful book club meeting: the wine... shit. Where was the wine? I moved aside the half-drank milk carton on the brink of expiring, hoping bottles of chardonnay would magically appear in between an empty bottle of orange juice and a stack of peach yogurts.

None did.

"*Fack*," I said, closing the fridge. "I'm out of wine."

"Want me to text Yvette or Jess? See if they can grab some on their way here?"

"No, that's fine. I'll run over to the grocery store real quick." I grabbed my keys from the crystal bowl on the counter and slipped on a pair of sandals. Tristan looked up from his phone, arching a recently plucked and shaped brow.

"Aren't we starting soon?" he asked.

"I'm just grabbing some wine real quick. I'll be back. If the girls get here before me, you all can start."

I left my friends in the living room, walking down the steps of my townhouse and jumping into my car. It was supposed to be a simple trip to the Publix around the corner; little did I know that my entire life course would be altered just because I forgot to restock on twelve-dollar bottles of wine. I could have stayed home, asked the friends who were on their way to pick up some wine for us. We could have had a dry night, sipping on water and Pepsi instead. I could have gone to the gas station or ordered it through a delivery service on my phone.

There was an infinite number of possibilities on how such a simple predicament could be solved. But only one of those possibilities pushed me directly onto a collision course with destiny.

2

JAKE PEREZ

"AH, FUCK," I said to myself, looking in the rearview mirror and seeing the driver behind me distracted by something in his lap.

I let out a preemptive honk, which seemed to do the trick.

The car that nearly rear-ended me swerved to the left and pulled up next to me. The man started yelling and flailing his hands around. I had a sudden urge to Red Shell his ass and knock him off the road like we were in a game of Mario Kart. He was acting as if the red light we were both stopped at was my fault and forgetting all about the phone he had his nose buried in moments before he slammed on his brakes.

Instead of turning Peachtree Avenue into a bumper car arena, I sucked in a deep breath and did my best to ignore the still-yapping guy next to me. I already had too much shit on my mind to worry about some small-dicked driver forgetting the rules of the road. It had been way too long of a day, one I was more than ready to put behind me.

And this Grindr date would hopefully do just that.

I was tempted to slam down on the gas and leave this guy yelling into my dust but decided that I didn't have the burning need to prove myself to a complete and utter stranger. Not when I was on my way to do something else with a complete and utter stranger.

Besides, my piece-of-shit car would likely brake down before the next red light.

This wasn't something I was used to. Not at all. I had bounced from monogamous relationship to monogamous relationship for the last five years of my adult life. It left no time for random hookups and fiery flings. No desire either.

But things were different now. Very, very different.

I'd only just downloaded the app that morning, my picture being approved a few hours ago. It didn't take long at all to find a guy less than five miles away from me, his dick pic landing in my inbox minutes after I asked him "what was up."

It was a good dick pic, too. Really good. He was lying down on his bed, legs dangling off the edge, hard dick aimed up at the ceiling with his thumb pressed at the base. The floor-length mirror leaning against the wall helped paint the full picture.

Plus, his room was clean, which gave him major bonus points.

I sent Mr. Anemone a picture of the growing bulge in my khakis and had him sharing his location moments later. He lived in Midtown, not very far at all from the quiet suburb I'd recently bought a house in. It would take me ten, fifteen minutes tops to get to him.

Shit. Did I need to bring beer, wine, tequila? Was it rude to show up at someone's house without anything with me? No matter how anonymous this someone might be?

I had a feeling that most guys prowling through the app didn't care about anything except the dick I walked in with. Still... I should bring something. If not as an offering, then as a way to get myself drunk for the night ahead. My nerves were starting to ratchet up the more I thought about the fact that I hadn't been with a guy in a while. I started thinking back to my first time. It was in college when one of my fraternity brothers and I had to share a bed. We never talked about it again, even though I often thought back to it, remembering how it felt to have our two bodies sliding together, our arousal so intense that we both came twice that night.

It was the night I realized I was bi.

I dated around and got with guys and girls but my next serious relationship wasn't until I was with Heather. Dated her for a while, planned on proposing, found out she was meeting up with her ex-boyfriend on her "business" trips, and broke up with her shortly after. One of my good friends, Ashley Lamb, was there to help me pick up the pieces.

Except she did such a good job of it that we ended up together.

About a year into our relationship was when I

dropped down on one knee, ring in hand. I had felt pressured by our friends and family to lock things down. I thought Ashley wanted the same thing. Except, up until then I could sense something had been a little askew. I thought maybe a ring might be able to fix it.

Wasn't the smartest idea I ever had, but it also wasn't the worst.

Imagine my surprise when she said no.

(I wasn't actually that surprised).

She sat me down, teary-eyed and shaking, and she came out to me. It was an emotionally wrought moment that had me crying with her. Not out of sadness or anger, but more so out of a surprising swell of happiness. I understood the hurt and stress having such a big secret could cause, and I didn't want that for Ashley, even if it meant our romantic relationship was effectively ended the moment she spoke her truth. It made me realize that our connection had always been lacking a certain spark.

I returned the ring the next day.

So there I was, sitting in a grocery store parking lot, wondering when the hell it was going to be my turn to be happy. I wasn't the kind of guy that liked to bounce from person to person. I enjoyed the idea of finding someone and throwing my anchor down, building an unshakable foundation of trust and love between us. It's all I really wanted.

Well, maybe not *all* I wanted.

My notifications dinged, the Grindr sound echoing inside my silent car. I took out my phone and opened it to another dick pic and a message asking me to "hurry up and milk this load." I sent back a couple of drooling emojis and adjusted my boner so that it was held down by the waistband of my khaki pants. I knew there'd be no way I'd find my "one" tonight, but at least I could have a little fun.

I got out of my car, the late-spring breeze carrying with it the sting of an extra-hot summer waiting in the wings. The sun was just beginning to set, throwing a bucket of orange-and-purple paint all over the cloudless sky. The clean glass facade of the modern grocery store reflected some of the colors and made it seem as if I was walking directly into an impressionistic painting. The bright fluorescent lights and chorus of high-pitched beeps and casual conversation washed over me. I'd never been to this store, so I had to orient myself first, scanning the aisle markers and stopping when I spotted the liquor aisle, along with the familiar face that walked out of it.

Noah.

It was my smile-prone and slightly messy coworker who was quickly turning into a good friend of mine. I always enjoyed our lunches together, which would usually devolve into a fit of laughter over our half-eaten plates of food as Noah recounted some viral video he'd watched or a crazy story of the trouble he and his group of friends got themselves into.

It certainly didn't hurt that Noah wasn't bad to look at.

At *all*. His grin came easy and never failed to light up that handsome face with his lopsided dimple and honey-gold eyes. He had a great sense of style, blowing my basic khakis and gray polo shirt out of the water with his stone-gray pants rolled up at the ankles and a floral black-and-blue button-up half tucked into the waist. His sleeves were also rolled, and a thin golden necklace shone around his neck, gleaming brightly against his tan skin. He was a little shorter than me—which I liked—and was blessed with an ass that could double as two basketballs if the NBA ever found themselves in some kind of dire shortage.

Noah spotted me and offered a friendly wave, walking over with two bottles of white wine in his hands.

"Hey there," I said, moving aside as a determined grandpa pushed past me with a cart full of Lunchables and toilet paper.

"So you do exist outside of the 9-to-5," Noah quipped, reaching out and poking me with a finger and nearly dropping one of his bottles.

"Do I? Or am I just in your head?"

"Don't do that to me right now, Jake. Grocery stores are already hellish enough. I don't need to have an existential crisis while I'm in here."

That got a laugh out of me. "Good choice of wine," I said, pointing at the bottles in his hands. "I'm a pinot grigio kind of guy, too."

"It's not just for me," Noah clarified. "It's for my book club."

"Oh, you've got a book club? What's it called?"

"Reading under the Rainbow. It's a bunch of queer people getting together and reading mystery and thriller books. We talk about the chapters we were assigned that week, get drunk on wine, and end up talking shit about one thing or another. It's fun times."

"Sounds like it," I said. "What book are y'all reading now?"

"*Just Beneath Her Bones.* It's about a girl who—"

"Who's being stalked by someone, and then she finds out the jewelry she's been ordering online is actually made of human bones."

"You've read it?" he asked, his eyes lighting up.

I nodded, feeling a spark of something in my chest at how impressed Noah appeared to be. "Just finished it last week, actually."

"I didn't know you were a reader."

"I think there's a lot about me you don't know," I said, cocking my head.

Noah licked his lips. Nodded. Looked down at the floor before pulling his gaze back up to mine. I couldn't tell if it was just in my head or not, but I could have sworn his eyes lingered a moment on my crotch before jumping up to my face. "You know, we've got an open spot in the club. I don't know what your plans are for the night, but if you're free, you can come join. You don't have to be gay or anything to read under the rainbow. We accept the straights."

Internally, I winced at Noah's categorization of me. I didn't blame him or feel offended. I understood that I presented as a typical heterosexual dude in society's outdated terms, and Noah had likely seen me with Ashley at some point, further cementing his idea of me. It wasn't his fault or his burden to carry. It was something that repeatedly occurred to me as a bisexual person. The assumptions and erasures of entire identities solely because of the way they present and who they're with at the time. It was like assuming someone who ordered fish at a restaurant was a strict pescatarian and not just craving a little bit of salmon and capers.

But it wasn't the time to go into all that with Noah. Maybe that conversation would come up some other day, but for now, Noah was expecting an answer. Did I take him up on his offer and crash his book club, or would it be better if I stuck to the original plan and headed off on my dick appointment with a bottle of wine and a condom in my back pocket?

It was an easy choice.

"Yeah, sure, I'll join you guys if your friends don't mind."

I'd message the guy when I got back into my car. Hopefully he wouldn't be too upset, but then again he likely had three other guys lined up in his chats, so I wasn't too stressed about it.

Noah's grin widened. "Perf. I'm sure they won't mind. We're a pretty chill group of people."

That made me even happier with the choice I'd made. Ever since the breakup with Ashley, I had quickly realized that most of my friends had been her friends, and even though our breakup was amicable, they still remained a text away for her and were nearly nonexistent to me, none of them reaching out to see if I was doing alright or if I needed anything, even just a chat. As I got older, creeping toward my thirties now, I also came to find that making friends was way harder than it used to be back when you were forced together through similar classes or clubs.

"Come," Noah said, turning toward a checkout lane. "Let me pay for these, and you can follow me back home. I'm just down the street."

"I'll take one." I reached for a bottle, grabbing Noah's hand instead. He straightened as if a shock of electricity jolted through his spine. Was it the same bolt of lightning that crashed through me the moment my hand closed around his? What the hell was that? Why were my toes tingling, my heart fluttering, and my thoughts suddenly tangled up like a pair of wired headphones lost inside of a coat pocket?

"I, uhm," Noah started, moving his hand back so that mine fell down to my side. "No need. I've got it."

"No, seriously," I said, making a grab for the bottle again, closing my grip around glass and not Noah this time. "I don't want to show up empty-handed."

Noah nodded and let the bottle go. Was there a blush on his cheeks? I couldn't quite make it out, Noah turning and walking to the cashier with his back to me.

The tingles and flutters continued until I pulled up behind Noah in his driveway.

And then the flutters and tingles only got more intense, mixing with the nerves that sprouted like a rose garden inside my belly.

3

NOAH BARNES

DAMN, Jake smelled good. No, not even good. He smelled *divine*. Like a mixture of pine trees and leather and sex. Masculine with a soft edge that made me want to bump into his side and start purring like a cat begging to be pet. Maybe that's why I had gotten the genius idea of inviting him over to join the book club, even though he knew none of my friends and barely even knew me. Sure, we were quickly becoming work buddies, but that was worlds away from the type of friendships I'd cultivated with the people currently sitting around my dining room table.

"Ready?" I asked Jake as I unlocked my front door, the sound of laughter and music already leaking out through the threshold.

"Born ready," he answered, smiling a toothy grin that lured me in like a floundering captain trying to make it to the lighthouse before his ship sunk. I blinked away the spell and walked into my house, announcing our presence and being greeted by a couple of happy cheers.

"I come with not just wine," I said as I turned the corner into the dining room, "but also a *man!*"

The gathered group looked past me at a still-smiling Jake, holding up his bottle of wine like he was offering his firstborn to the ritualistic town council. Tristan started a slow clap, which was picked up by the rest of the group. He stood and looked at Jake with reverence in his eyes before they crinkled, and a fit of laughter took his silly ass over. I rolled my eyes as the rest of the group started to join in on the laughter.

"Sorry," Tristan said, sitting back down and rubbing his eyes. "I enjoy the dramatics."

"Clearly," I said, unable to tamp down my smile. "Everyone, this is Jake. We work together, and I bumped into him at the grocery store. He's a big reader, so I offered him a spot in the club." I peeked my head around the corner from inside the kitchen. "That's fine right?"

"Yeah, he's *very* fine," Tristan said, licking his lips. I rolled my eyes again and went back into the kitchen, laughing to myself as Jake continued on with introductions while I poured everyone some wine.

"Hey, Jake, can you help me carry these out?" I asked.

"Sure thing." He entered the kitchen and thankfully looked like he was still in one piece. It was touch and go there for a moment with how ravenous Tristan's gaze had been. I'd half expected Jake to turn the corner wearing a tattered shirt and ripped-up khakis, hickies all up and down his chest.

"Your friends are funny," Jake said, delicately grabbing three glasses in his big hands.

"And ridiculous. Don't take anything they say seriously."

His eyes glittered under my kitchen lights, as if he'd gotten fistfuls of blue stardust and used that as contacts. It was almost surreal. I wanted to paint him—and I wasn't even an artist. The furthest I'd likely get was a blocky stick figure with sapphire eyes, and still, I wanted to grab the nearest stack of papers and pens and go to town.

"Thanks for inviting me," he said, crossing his arms and leaning against the kitchen counter. "It's nice seeing you outside of work."

I cocked my head. A small ember nestled into the base of my spine, warming me from the inside out. Something about the way he said "nice seeing you" fanned the ember and made the flames lick down my back. I tried stamping it out, ignoring the way my briefs started to tighten.

"Yeah, of course," I said, turning my back to him in a futile attempt to break whatever spell this man was beginning to cast on me.

"I love your house, too. You've got a really great style." His eyes roamed around the kitchen, which had been renovated right before I bought the place about a year ago. There was an Italian countryside–inspired backsplash—all clean blues and whites swirling together in an intricate and repeating pattern—with a polished and eye-catching white marble countertop. The island had a leathered black top that matched the black door to the walk-in pantry, currently open and letting in the last dying sunlight of the day through an arching window.

"Thanks. I'll give you a full tour once the book club's over."

"I'd like that," he said, a slight gravel in his voice, the ember lighting into a full-blown bonfire. What the hell was going on with me? Jake was off-limits. I wasn't a hundred percent sure on his sexuality, but the safest bet to make was that he was straight and likely just being nice to me.

Unfortunately, that didn't mean much, considering I had the syndrome most gay men were afflicted with: Hetero-Cockholme Syndrome.

Sure, I'd made that up, but I would bet anything that it was an actual phenomenon.

It occurred whenever an even minimally attractive straight man was being nice to a thirsty gay guy, rewiring the gay guy's brain and creating an explosion of rainbows and dick, making the gay guy think that the friendly and benign gesture (whether it was bringing an extra coffee to work because the barista accidentally made one or holding the elevator door open for you) meant that mind-blowingly great sex would immediately be had.

Somehow, someway, likely by the grace of glittery gay Jesus, I was able to pull myself out of the trance. We went back into the dining room with the wineglasses, the room full of laughter and warmth. I said hi to Jess and Tia, girl-friends whom we met at a Pride parade and became besties with ever since, and Yvette Gomez, one of my close friends from college. They gave me tight side hugs before I grabbed the moderator seat at the head of the table. This week, I'd been the one chosen to lead the discussions, which was usually a fun job since we all liked to get creative (and a little power-hungry) with the role.

Today, I had whipped up a drinking game for the group. "Okay," I said, lowering the music so that it was just background noise. "Today's game is Buzz Word. Each one of us has a secret word that only that person knows. Every time that word is said, you have to take a drink within five seconds. But be sneaky about it because if someone can guess your word, then you lose your chance at winning this twenty-five-dollar gift card."

I pulled out the cards with the words on them and shuffled. I had purposely created over twenty cards so that I could hand one out without knowing what was on there, which made it easy to adapt to having one extra player.

"Alright, should we start?" I asked, taking a peek at my card. "Murder" was my word.

Great. I'm going to be trashed five minutes into this.

We slipped into book club mode, opening up the discussion on chapter ten, where we had last left off. I focused heavily on character, honing in on Gabrielle Munoz, the main character who orders the necklace and becomes the target of the twisted killer. The first murder had just occurred a couple of chapters back, and in this one, Gabrielle ends up ordering one of the morbid pieces of jewelry without realizing it was made of real human bones collected from the victim.

"That's wild," Tristan said, taking a sip of his wine. He picked off a fluff from his black T-shirt and flicked it in Yvette's direction. "Did you make sure your necklace wasn't sourced from a fucked-up murder?"

One, two, three, four. I picked up my wineglass and took a gulp.

"No, I forgot to ask the seller that question," Yvette said dryly.

"When do you think she figures it out?" Eric asked.

Jess chuckled, swirling her glass of wine. "Probably not until the last chapter, duh."

"What about the house?" Jake asked, drawing all eyes toward him. "The way it's falling apart, how it's described as 'showing off its bones' all the time. Do you think—"

"Bones!" Jess shouted, pointing at her girlfriend, who was glaring at her over the rim of the wineglass. "Tia's word is bones."

"Is it?" I asked, smiling.

She flipped over her card. "Bones" was written in bold letters across the center. She threw her locs over her shoulder and rolled her eyes. "Out of everyone here, you're going to get your girlfriend out first?"

"Sorry, babe, I just can't ever keep my eyes off you."

Tia shook her head and smiled, accepting the apologetic kiss on the cheek from Jess. "Don't worry," Jess said, leaning back in her chair. "If I win, we're splitting the gift card anyway."

Underneath the table, just next to me, Jake's knee brushed against mine. I froze, like a meek mouse turning a corner and spotting the salivating house cat. The conversation around me grew jumbled as I realized Jake wasn't moving his leg away. I shot a glance at him, seeing nothing but a neutral expression set amongst those glittering blue orbs of his. I wondered if he felt it, too? The sudden burst of fireworks that lit up the inside of my chest, sparking through my nerves, settling between my thighs.

Of course he doesn't feel it. He probably doesn't even realize he's touching me.

I rolled my neck, cracking a couple of spots loud enough to earn a glare from Eric, who hated the popping noises with a fiery passion. Jake shifted, and his leg separated from mine, letting me bring my attention back to the discussion, even though my thoughts were still being pulled in Jake's direction.

What the hell was it about him that had me so sprung? Yes, he was handsome and funny and smart and kind and tall and just my type and...

Okay. Maybe I *did* know what the hell it was about him that had me so entranced.

"Noah, what about you?" Tristan asked, leaning across the table, his liquid-gold eyes pinning me in place.

"Huh? Sorry, I missed the question."

He cocked his head, eyes darting to Jake before coming back to me. "What's got you so distracted tonight?"

"That was the question?" I asked, looking away from Tristan's pointed glare.

"No," Eric said. "The question was if you thought

there was any importance in how the author describes Archie, the killer's ex-husband, as being as monstrous as 'what lurks in the darkest corners of a soul.' Think that's important? Did he have anything to do with the murders?"

"Yeah, actually, I wrote that down." I flipped open my notebook and skimmed through the pages for my notes. *Four, Five.* I took a drink of my wine, setting it down and feeling good that no one called me out.

"Murder," Jake said, head cocked, eyes drilling a hole through me. "That's your word, isn't it?"

"Ah crap," I said. "You got me."

"Nice job, Jake."

I shot a slicing glare at Tristan. "Don't side with the new guy," I said.

Tristan looked like he was about to say something that likely would have had the entire table blushing, judging by the gleam in his eyes. But before he could get the words out, a shrill and piercing scream cut through the air, coming from the open window just over his shoulder. It was the kind of scream that could have only come from intense fear, born from a terror that instantly transferred to every single person in the room. It wasn't a happy yell or an angry one or an excited one.

It was a horrified scream, and it made us all freeze in shared panic.

What was even worse? That it sounded like it came from right behind the front door.

4

JAKE PEREZ

I SHOT up from my chair, nearly tipping it over. It was an instant reaction. Hearing that scream brought me directly to being in my mom's house, hearing her yell in her bedroom. It was never a shout filled with as much terror as the one we just heard, but still, it triggered a fight-or-flight response in me. I was already at the front door by the time I realized Noah was at my side. The other book club members were close behind, Eric putting a hand on my shoulder before I could open the door.

"Let me. I used to be a cop."

"We'll all check it out," Noah said. There was fear in his eyes, but there was also a swell of courage in the way his jaw set and his brows furrowed.

"Fine, but I'll go first," Eric insisted, his tone taking on an authoritative edge. I stepped aside. It *would* probably be smart to let the tattooed and muscular ex-cop take the lead on this.

The night air was exceptionally warm and sticky,

especially for the very beginning of spring, foreshadowing an even hotter summer in Atlanta. The street was flooded with light coming from an open door, where Noah's neighbor currently stood, haloed by the white light as he clamped a hand over his mouth. He must have heard the same shout we had.

The shout that came from the older gentleman standing on Noah's front steps, his head turned downward toward what appeared to be a cardboard box at his feet.

Eric moved forward, Noah and I right behind him. The rest of the book club stayed inside the house, Tristan already calling the police.

"What happened?" Eric asked the man, "We heard the shout from next door. Are you okay?"

"I'm okay, I'm okay," he said, shock filtering through his voice.

"Mason, you're paper pale. What the hell happened?" Noah asked. His side was pressed against mine, our fingertips brushing together. I had the urge to reach for his hand and give him a comforting squeeze. Not sure where that came from, but instead, I settled for a gentle nudge against his side. He looked up at me and offered a shaky smile.

You're okay. We're good. No reason to be scared.

"That happened," Mason answered, pointing at the box at his feet. It appeared like the sides were soaked through with some sort of liquid. The flaps were open but angled so that I couldn't see what was inside without leaning over Eric. Mason had a plate covered with aluminum foil in his hands. "I was just bringing over some of this cake I baked and, well this package was here, the flap was open. I took a peek inside..."

"Oh, fuck," Eric said. He took a step to the side, allowing me to see into the box.

"Holy shit."

Oh no, we do have a reason to be scared.

It registered immediately. I was looking down at a severed chicken head, upturned so that it looked up at us with empty eyes, its bloody beak opened in a silent shout. Inside of the beak was a Pride flag, the stick impaled through whatever was left of the chicken's throat. The cardboard box was colored crimson red, the blood still fresh enough to drip through and color the steps underneath it. But it wasn't just the chicken head and Pride flag in the box. There appeared to be a necklace around it, blood staining the beads but the rainbow pattern still coming through.

I tried to stop Noah from seeing it, but it was too late. He leaned around me and peered into the box, seconds later turning around and running down the steps, where he reached a bush and threw up everything that was in his stomach. I hurried down to be at his side, putting a hand square in the center of his back and rubbing in slow circles. When he was done, he wiped his mouth and kept his eyes down to the floor, apologizing. His next door neighbor ran hurried down to offer his help with anything, but Noah could barely even get the words out to explain what had happened.

"No need for that," I said, hand now on his elbow. I

couldn't explain exactly why, but I was beginning to grow more concerned about Noah's safety and comfort than I was about what was in that box. "You're good. I was seconds away from doing the same thing."

Noah looked up at me with big, doe-like eyes, fear beginning to dissipate from them. I realized I was still holding his elbow. I let go, stuffing my hands in my pockets.

"It was addressed to you," Mason said from the top of the stairs, causing me to whip around and face him.

"Huh?" I asked.

"It was addressed to you, Noah. Look." He crouched down and touched one of the flaps of the box with the edges of his fingertips.

"Whoa, whoa, don't get your fingerprints on this," Eric said, but it was too late. Mason had already moved the flap downward so that Noah's name and address were clearly visible, written in a thick black marker.

"What? What happened?" His neighbor asked.

Noah turned back to the bushes, but nothing came up this time. I rubbed his back again, but I knew nothing I'd say or do right now would likely help. This was way outside of my accounts payable scope. I really didn't have much of an idea on how to handle this. A blood-soaked threat sent to a new friend who I really didn't know all that much about? Yeah, I wasn't prepared for this at all.

"Robby," Noah said, "did you see anyone leave that package at my house? Anyone walking down the street that seemed a little off?"

Robby, a skinny guy with glasses and wearing a pair

of dark blue scrub pants and white t-shirt, shook his head. He put a concerned hand on Noah's elbow, looking back up at the package,

Tristan came out of the house, phone still held against his head and a look of frustration twisting his face.

"Tristan, what's the deal with the police?" I asked from the bottom step.

"They have me on hold. Can you fucking believe that? I'm not ordering takeout here. What the actual fuck."

I winced. Not the answer I was expecting.

"What happened?" Tristan asked, looking into the box before spinning around. "Oh, hell no. Nope, nope. Not today, Satan. Not today."

He came down the steps, Mason and Eric following him down, the box left on the top step like a bomb ready to detonate at any moment. Noah sat down on the floor, a hand on the back of his neck, his head shaking.

"Why?" he asked. "Who the hell would try and send that to me?"

"It seems like they wanted to send a message," Mason said, holding himself as if he was going to collapse inward. "With the flag and the necklace."

"Plus," Eric said, "what else are roosters called?"

Noah rubbed at his face. I saw tears beginning to form, sliding down his cheeks. I crouched down to be on his level, putting an arm around his shoulder.

"Did you see anyone leaving when you were arriving?" I asked Mason, looking up into his frightened eyes, which were magnified by a pair of thick glasses, the lenses scratched. He was a tall guy with about a dozen different necklaces hanging over his long-sleeve black t-shirt, along with a couple of noticeable scars on his hands.

"No, no one," he said. "The street was empty."

"Don't you have a doorbell camera?" Tristan asked Noah, looking up at his home.

"I do."

That got us all to perk up.

"But it hasn't been working for weeks."

He gave a shrug, arms wrapped tightly together. Noah stood up and rubbed at the side of his temples with his eyes shut as if he were trying to wake himself up from a bad dream. I may have just been work friends with Noah, but that was enough for me to know that he didn't deserve any of this fucked-up shit. Especially not because of his sexuality. It made my blood boil. I could feel it bubbling in my veins, heated by the anger that sat in the center of my chest like fire in a forge.

"Cops are on their way," Tristan said, slipping his phone back into his pocket with an eye roll. "Can't believe I was on hold for that long."

"Alright," Eric said, walking down the steps after taking photos of the box. "No one touch it. Let's wait. Noah, how ya feeling?"

"Not great, I'll tell you that much."

Again, I wasn't entirely sure what drove me to do this, but I reached an arm around Noah's shoulders and pulled him in for a side hug. For a moment—brief enough to make me second-guess if it even happened—Noah seemed to melt into my side, his body going limp, his head resting against me, and his body leaning into me. Then the hug was over, bodies separated, the space between us feeling miles long even though I could reach out and hold his hand in mine.

"Thank you," Noah said, looking up at me and offering a shaky smile. "This never happens at our book club, I promise. You just picked one hell of a night to join us."

"It's all good," I replied, returning the smile, trying to radiate confidence and strength even though the contents of that bloody box *did* actually shake me up.

Sirens sounded from down the street, followed by a splash of red and blue lights, painting the entire street of townhomes in stark colors. I already spotted a couple of neighbors looking out from the corners of their blinds, curious to see who was getting in trouble. They parked directly in front of us, two officers climbing out of the car and doing an immediate scan of the area, looking us all up and down as they walked toward us. My heart rate picked up—as if it could get any higher. Even without doing anything wrong, cops still made me nervous. I glanced down at the guns holstered on their hips, hating how close we were to them.

"What happened here?" the closest officer asked— Officer Hallston, according to his badge.

Noah started to explain, but Mason soon jumped in, finishing off the story with tears still welling up at the corners of his eyes. He almost appeared more distraught than Noah did, and the threat wasn't even directed at him. I didn't really blame Mason, though. I'd probably feel the same if I were the one to open that box, knowing that whoever set it there had been feet away from me.

The two cops took down all of our accounts, no matter how short they were, and walked up the steps with gloves and plastic wraps going over their shoes. They looked things over, neither of them seeming the least bit fazed. Sure, they'd both probably seen much worse, but not even a flinch came from either.

"We'll take this into evidence," Officer Hallston said as he came back down the steps and went toward his car, coming back with a bag big enough to fit the box inside. He handed it to his partner and gave Noah the rundown of what happened next, which basically boiled down to sit and wait. They couldn't do anything without going through forensics first.

"Can't you look through any red-light cameras around the area?" Eric asked. He crossed his arms against his chest, the colorful sleeve tattoo on his left arm appearing to swirl.

"We'll look into it."

"It was a yes-or-no question."

"And I gave you an answer."

Tension thick as an ancient oak tree sprung up between the two men. Tristan sensed it and put a hand on his friend's shoulder. Eric shook his head and walked back up into Noah's house, saying something under his breath. Tristan followed close behind, walking past a worried Yvette, who was perched on the threshold with a glass of water held high in both hands. Noah seemed tired. He nodded to the officer and thanked him, the words sounding hollow as they came out of his mouth.

The cops got inside their cruiser and sped off, leaving us alone with a still-frightened-looking Mason and Robby. At least Mason had one hand in the pockets of his khaki shorts, still holding the cake in his other hand. I'd been scared that he was about to break one of his own ribs with how tight he was clutching himself.

"I'm sorry about all this," Noah said, directing the apology to the three of us.

"None of this is your fault, Noah." Robby put out a reassuring hand, grabbing Noah's in his and squeezing. He smiled, nodded. At least he got along with his neighbors. If it were mine, they would have taken pictures and reported the bloody threat to the HOA president before they would have told me, likely hoping there was a clause in the rulebook somewhere about chicken heads and evictions.

"You know, if you don't want to stay alone in your place, you're more than welcome to sleep over in mine. The guest room is currently a mess, but I've got a real comfortable couch."

"Thanks, Robby, but I've been fighting some bad knots in my neck all week. If I sleep on a couch, I may not end up getting back up."

"Oh, no worries. Just thought I'd offer."

"Thank you, though." Noah opened his arms and took Robby into a warm hug. Robby told him to call if he needed absolutely anything and then turned to hurry back up his steps, the door closing and the lock loudly clicking shut. Mason dipped his head, shaking it and holding out the aluminum foil covered plate.

"I doubt you're still in the mood for a slice of lemon bundt cake, or maybe it's exactly what you're in the mood for."

Noah took the plate and offered a thin smile. "You know I can never turn down your baking, Mason. Thank you."

"Of course. If you need anything, you know where I live. Just knock on the door or send me a text."

Mason took his leave, giving one last sympathetic look at Noah before heading down the street and climbing up the steps of another townhouse on the corner.

Only the two of us left. The street was dark, the moon already finding its place in the center of the night sky. I hadn't realized how late it had gotten. Between the fun we were having with the book club and the terror that soon followed, time seemed to have flown right on by.

"What a fucking mess," Noah said, rubbing the bridge of his nose. "God, I hope they can find fingerprints or hair or *something*. I need this figured out like yesterday."

"They'll find whoever did it," I reassured him. "You know, my guest room is fully functional. Plus, the mattress is memory foam, so if you want to crash at my place tonight, you're more than welcome to."

Noah seemed to consider this offer much more than he had considered Robby's. "You sure?"

"A hundred percent," I said.

"Oh, thank God, because I was pretty nervous about going to sleep alone tonight. Not that we're going to sleep together or anything, obviously. That would be weird. But yes, I mean, if that's alright, I don't have—"

"Come on, let me go grab my keys." I was smiling. Even with the macabre shadow that hung over tonight, I still managed to find a cheek-splitting grin, and it was all because of Noah and his rambly ways. I was about to mention how I thought sleeping together wouldn't really be weird at all but figured that had the potential of permanently frying his circuits, so I kept it to myself.

Oh, Noah. Noah, Noah, Noah. What am I going to do with you?

The second I asked that question of myself, about a hundred different answers appeared, almost all of them involving a naked Noah unraveling at the touch of my fingertips.

5

NOAH BARNES

FEAR WAS A WEIRD EMOTION. It could be exhilarating in the right circumstances, controlled, like on a roller coaster or inside a theatre. It could also be debilitating. Strong enough to seize your muscles and make your heart feel like it was three rapid beats away from splitting in half. It could be fleeting—like nearly tripping down the stairs but catching yourself at the last second—or it could be lifelong, the invisible scars of trauma cutting across your brain and fueling your nightmares every time you closed your eyes.

I sat in Jake's car, gripping the seat belt tight, eyes set forward as my thoughts spun like a broken top, wobbling back and forth over who the hell could have sent that to me.

"Do you have any exes that turned a little psychotic after the breakup?" Jake asked, his voice somehow remaining calm, cool, and collected.

"Yeah, actually," I answered through the pile of sand

that had been dumped into my mouth at some point. I swallowed, trying to wet my throat and instead just gulping loudly.

"Who?"

"Franky. He was one of my first boyfriends. He didn't want to come out of the closet for me, though. We broke up—it was pretty nasty. He said some fucked-up shit, but nothing as fucked-up as that box."

Jake made a "hmm" sound as he drove us down a tree-lined street, a neighborhood of flipped homes surrounding us, looking like they'd all been plucked out of the same HGTV makeover catalogue. White stone, black trim, bright doors. All of their blinds shut, TV light showing through the cracks. Everyone winding down after a day of routines and responsibilities, completely unaware of the chaotic storm of crap that was currently driving past their homes.

"When's the last time you two spoke?"

"Like a year ago."

"And he lives around here?"

I nod, fidgeting with the A/C vent so that the cool air blew directly into my face. "Down in Midtown. He's got a wife now. I don't know why he'd all of a sudden do this."

"Do you know his wife?" Jake asked. He slowed down as he took a right, pulling into the long driveway of a home that had still managed to retain some of its original bones without being copy-and-pasted from the houses next door. There were long windows and an awning that came out over a wide porch, a variety of potted plants hanging from the railing. It seemed very well taken care of, reminding me of just how badly my own home needed a pressure washing and a couple of paint touch-ups.

"I've only met her once. She was one of his friends when we were dating. Of course, she had no idea Franky and I were together at the time. She comes from a big televangelist family, tons of money, and probably an equal amount of skeletons in her closet... There was one time, though. I think she found a text or something between Franky and me. We were already broken up, but he kept our messages for some reason. I woke up to five missed calls from her and two extremely angry voicemails telling me to stop corrupting Franky. I never returned her call."

"Good," Jake said, parking his car and turning off the engine, silence filling the space. "Do you still have the voicemails?"

"I do."

"Give them to the police, then. You never know."

"And what about that Mason guy? What's his deal?" Jake asked.

I shrugged. "He moved into the neighborhood about four months ago. Nice guy, always baking and always giving me something. He's apparently from Philly. He's gay, too. I think his partner passed last year from cancer."

Jake nodded and cracked his knuckles.

I sucked in a rattling breath. The fear slowly faded, but the anxiety remained, quivering inside me like a razor-sharp wire being held taut, ready to snap and slice me in half. I took in another breath. And another. Nothing was really working. The wire was twining through my ribs, making it harder for my lungs to expand. My head started feeling light, my eyes having a difficult time finding focus.

Jake must have noticed. His hand falling on mine was the equivalent of dumping a bucket of ice water over my head. I turned, finding his eyes, finding a focus.

I could breathe again.

"It's going to be alright, Noah, I promise. Life never runs in a straight line. Bad times come, but good times follow, and those are sometimes the *best* of times. My mom used to tell me that all the time. It helped remind me that whatever I was going through had a way out, and whatever was on the other side gave me something to look forward to." His hand squeezed mine. When had his fingers slipped through mine? Why wasn't I moving away? This wasn't a "friend supporting friend" kind of handhold. This was something much more—intimate. As intimate as two hands could get.

Beyond that, though, Jake's touch worked as a salve. It unwound the tightening razor-sharp threads of anxiety that were threatening to cause a full-blown panic attack.

Another breath. This one came with a smile, matching the one that inched across Jake's face.

"Your mom must be related to Aristotle. That's a really good way to look at things."

His smile flickered, his hand slipping from mine, moving back to his lap.

"Come, let's get inside," he said, taking the keys from

the ignition, the smile back in full force. I could get used to that smile. Even if I much rather preferred that smile to be pressed up against mine, something that had a very low likelihood of ever happening.

I got out of the car, following Jake up the steps and onto his porch. I got a closer look at the flowers, all of them thriving. He had bright ruby-red roses and thick bushels of pastel purple lavender. Two large blue pots of prehistoric-looking ferns flanked his door. He unlocked it and stepped inside, welcoming me in with a flair of his arm and a tiny bow, as if I were some kind of royalty.

"Wow, it's bigger on the inside," I said without really thinking.

"Huh?"

"Oh nothing, just a *Doc*—"

"*Doctor Who* reference? You watch it?" Jake asked, eyebrows raised.

"Are you kidding? I worship it. Favorite doctor?"

Jake cocked his head before nodding with a slanted smile. "David Tennant's doctor, hands down. You?"

"It's a tie between Matt and Jodie. I'm leaning more toward Jodie, though."

He nodded, and I tried not to show how happy I was at letting my inner-geek flag fly. "How about companion?" I asked.

"Donna Noble," he answered without missing a beat. "And Rose."

"I'm going with Amy. I just loved her entire storyline. She and Rory are my favorite fictional couple. The crap they go through is intense, but they still get their HEA."

Jake licked his lips, smiled. Fuck. Did he realize how sexy he looked when he did that? Now his lips were all shiny and shit. I looked down at my hands, trying hard to focus on the topic and not on the fact that I could feel myself getting hard.

"Want a tour?" Jake asked, kicking off his shoes and placing them neatly on a rack next to the door. I followed his lead, taking off my socks, too, and leaving them bundled up inside my sneakers. The hardwood floors were cold against the soles of my feet, matching the chill in the air. I peeked at the digital thermostat and saw he kept it at a brisk sixty-nine.

Straight boys and their overheating bodies. Hopefully, evolution helps them out at some point.

Jake spoke a command, and the rest of the lights slowly came on, bathing his living room in a warm golden tone, highlighting the soft browns of his leather couch and the rich beige of his entertainment stand. A massive TV hung on the wall, framed by a strip of lights taped behind it, currently set to a shifting rainbow pattern.

Huh. Interesting choice.

"You've got a green thumb, huh?" I asked, noticing all of the thriving plants around the room. There was a row of succulents on the windowsill, a couple of large tree-looking things potted in massive black clay pots with rubbery leaves, and a few trailing plants that let their vines hang down a bookshelf packed with an assortment of books.

"I do," Jake said, looking around with a glint of pride in his eyes. "Got into it pretty recently, actually. I used to kill even the fake plants I had. One night, I had an edible and a glass of wine and went to town, researching and ordering things online. Turns out, I really like being a plant guy."

And imagine how much you'd enjoy being a plant gay.

I made my way over to the fireplace, where a couple of framed photos of Jake and people who I assumed were his close friends and family sat. One of them showed only two people: Jake and his girlfriend, perched on the ledge of a jagged rock formation, backpacks strapped to them and smiles plastered wide. She was the one I'd seen come into the office a couple of times.

"You two look happy here. Where was that?" Asking as if I didn't know what the hell the Grand Canyon looked like.

"Letchworth State Park."

Hmm... maybe I didn't know what the Grand Canyon looked like.

"It was a fun trip. They call it the Grand Canyon of the east."

Oh, thank God.

Jake came over, grabbing the photo off the ledge. "This was two weeks before we broke up, actually."

"At least you—wait, what? Broke up? You two aren't together anymore?"

He nodded, smiling. "That's usually what happens in a breakup."

I slant my mouth, arched a brow. The shock was still

filtering through me. "What happened? If you don't mind me asking."

"I don't mind at all," he said, placing the photo back in its place. "Ashley came out to me. Realized that she was a lesbian, which made our relationship just a little complicated."

"Just a little," I echoed, chuckling, still in a slight haze of disbelief.

"We're really good friends, though. Thankfully. I love that girl to death. I helped usher her into the queerdom, so I think that means we're friends for life."

Hold up. Did I hear that right? What the hell was Jake doing ushering anyone through the pearlescent rainbow gates if he was a straight dude...

Unless.

Fuck. I'm such an idiot.

"I'm bi, by the way. In case you hadn't figured it out yet."

I winced.

"Damn, you're that upset?" he asked, sounding slightly hurt.

"What? No, no! Oh crap, no. It's just—well, I feel like such an asshole. I had assumed you were straight, but I should know better than to assume anyone's sexuality." I didn't have to look into a mirror to know my cheeks were firehouse red, burning with embarrassment.

Jake chuckled. "Listen, it's fine. I get it. It happens to me all the time. Especially when I'm dating a girl. It's hard for people to see all sides of a situation."

"And that's exactly why it's *not* fine. I don't think bierasure is appropriate in any scenario, and yet here I was holding a big-ass eraser. I'm sorry."

"I appreciate the apology, Noah, but I don't need it. You weren't the one that created the heteronormative blueprint we all function under—consciously or subconsciously. I've lived it. I've been told I must be gay when I'm seen dating a guy or that I have to be straight when I'm holding a girl's hand. It's rare for someone to see past the binary, even after I come out.

"But I definitely see past it. I know who I am, I'm confident in who I am, and I'm glad I get to fuck whoever I want. So at the end of the day, I guess I'm the one that's winning."

I tried to hide the quiver in my knees when the word "fuck" dropped from his lips. "That's honestly not a bad way to look at it," I said, cheeks still warm but the embarrassment fading away, being replaced by something else. A growing spark inside my core, catching on my nerves and shooting through every inch of my body.

Jake shrugged, leaned back so that he was perched on the arm of his couch. "It took me a little bit of time to get there, though. It's hard when you come out and people either think, 'oh, he'll be fully gay soon' or 'he'll be back to being straight' as if being bi is just a stopover point and not a full-ass identity. And honestly, hearing that all the time started making me doubt myself, which is pretty wild since I'd always been confident and headstrong about who I was."

"As if coming out wasn't already complicated enough."

"Pfft, you're right about that." Jake licked his lips again and smiled, his eyes pinned to mine, his head slightly craned so that I could see the gentle rise and fall of his pulse.

"Alright, so are we continuing with the tour of my TARDIS?"

"Let's do it, Doctor."

He gave me a wink and turned, leaving me and my goofy cheek-to-cheek smile staring at his back, wondering what kind of magic this man must have had to be making me smile on such a shitty, messed-up night.

Maybe it's not magic. Maybe it's his sonic screwdriver...

6

JAKE PEREZ

THE HOUSE TOUR ended with us in my kitchen, floating around the island and chatting about what kind of food we loved.

"Definitely *ropa vieja*," I said, grabbing a bottle of pinot grigio from the fridge and setting it on the counter with a clink.

"What's that?" Noah asked.

"It's a Cuban dish my grandma would make all the time. It's basically shredded beef soaked in a tomato sauce with tons of peppers and onions and other good stuff. It translates to 'old clothes,' which always gave me a kick when I was a kid. I loved asking for a dish of old clothes."

"It sounds delicious," Noah said, his eyes glittering under my kitchen lights. I wasn't entirely sure how he managed to do that under such drab lighting, but I certainly didn't mind. Looking at him was like looking at a rare crystal inside a museum, always shifting and glowing differently depending on which angle you looked at it from.

"What about you? What's something you can eat every day?"

"Besides ass?"

That got a surprised snort out of me.

"Sorry, sorry," Noah said. "It's getting late, and my brain is malfunctioning."

I was about to tell him something along the lines of "dinner being served," but he cut me off, a strawberry-pink blush coloring his cheeks.

Good, I thought as Noah described his favorite dish (a double-decker cheeseburger from a nearby diner). *I shouldn't be flirting so much with my coworker. We're just friends. Let me not mess anything up.*

"You've got my mouth watering," I said.

"We should grab some food there sometime. After you cook me some of that *ropa vieja*."

I smiled at Noah's butchered attempt at speaking Spanish.

"I don't think I can make it as good as my grandma used to, but I'll try." I pressed the wine opener to the top of the bottle and pushed the button, the whirr of the machine filling the kitchen, followed by the pop of the cork as it was lifted off. The glug-glug of wine being poured came next as I filled two glasses up to the brim.

"You've got a heavy hand, there," Noah said, smiling and mouthing a "thank you" as I handed him his glass.

"I think we've earned this after today."

"I agree." He delicately brought the glass up to his

lips and sipped, some of it dripping down his chin. He wiped it with the back of his hand, lips glistening. I swallowed, looking away, focusing instead on recorking the wine bottle and placing it back in the fridge.

Just friends. Just friends.

We left the kitchen with our wineglasses in hand, moving to the living room, where we sat on opposite ends of the couch. I put down two coasters—one from a trip to London and another from a trip to Austin—and settled in, the soft, plush leather feeling like a cloud against my back. Noah sat with his legs underneath him, hands on his knees, smile on his face. I noticed that he was the kind of guy with a perma-grin, which was the complete opposite of my sometimes severe resting bitch face.

"So where are you from, Noah?" I asked, avoiding the hypnotizing effects of his toothy smile. If we were going to keep this friend thing going, then it was important to know a little more about each other. Book club may have been over, but I was still excited to read up on Noah's history, flicking through the chapters and figuring out what made this golden retriever of a man tick.

"I was born in North Carolina, in a small town about an hour from Asheville. My parents own a dairy farm. They wanted me to stay and take over the reins, but I'm *really* not about that life. I wanted to work indoors, with air-conditioning, and I also wanted to live in a city that had more than four gay people in it. Hence, Atlanta."

"When did you come out?" I asked, reaching for my glass, giving it a swirl, and drinking.

"When I moved to Atlanta after high school. I actually came out to my parents on the phone—yeah, I know, not the greatest, but it worked. They kind of already knew, especially my mom. Moms *always* know. It's like a sixth sense. A homo-sense, if you will."

I laughed, feeling relieved that Noah's coming out story was on the lighter side of things. A stark contrast to my painful experience.

"How 'bout you?" Noah asked. My smile wavered, the buoyant mood in the room being drained out as if someone took a pin to the balloon we were currently floating around in.

I decided to start with the simple stuff first. "Well, both my parents are Cuban. My mom came when she was twelve, and Dad when he was sixteen. Both of them ended up in New York—that's where they met, at some nightclub. They danced salsa all night and never stopped."

"Aww, that's sweet."

"Yeah, my dad loves saying that story. They really were a loving pair, never scared to hold hands or kiss each other, even when other parents never seemed to be that touchy-touchy. They really did teach me what love meant." Memories flooded back: my parents driving and my mom playing with my dad's hair, us walking through the mall and my dad wrapping my mom up in a random hug and dipping her down for a kiss.

My dad, red-faced and shouting, cracked through the glossy memories. Vitriol, anger, fear, all directed at me.

"Then I came out to them, and it changed everything."

Noah's eyebrows shot up, nearly disappearing under a swoop of dark brown hair. He ran a hand through it, setting it messily back in place. "Ah, crap, I'm sorry. What happened?"

"I came out to my mom first. She was okay, but she knew my dad wouldn't be. He came from a very traditional Cuban family, with all the toxic bullshit that sometimes comes with that. He was extremely masculine, followed the traditional roles down to a T. My mom would have to serve him at parties, always cook, always clean, that kind of stupid shit. And rolled up in that was an intense anger toward anything queer.

"When I told him I was bi, he blew up. I'd never seen him so angry. I thought he was going to kick me out of the house, and I was only seventeen. I was scared, crying, shouting. My mom was doing the same. It was a fucking disaster. But I didn't get kicked out, and the next day came, and he acted like nothing ever happened. I never forgot that night, but I never brought it up again either. And we won't get the chance... he died three years ago. Heart attack." I pulled in a deep breath. I hadn't talked about this with anyone.

"Jake— I'm so sorry. I'm sure he loved you, like you said, but you also didn't deserve that reaction from him," he said after swallowing a gulp of the white wine. "No one does."

"I agree, on the flip side though, it was a moment that taught me who I really was and who I never wanted to become. It's so weird how love and monsters can live so closely together under the same roof. Because I'm sure my dad *did* love me, but the claws and teeth were only one wrong word away from coming out and shredding me to pieces."

Noah nodded. When had we gotten so close on the couch? No longer was I even able to lean on the armrest. Instead, my only option would be to lean on Noah's knee, inches away from mine. I decided not to make things weird and kept my hands to myself.

"I'm glad it didn't break you, though," he said, sucking in a deep breath. "You made it through all of that and turned into a better man because of it. That's something that would make any dad proud of their son." His smile flashed, warm and bright, like a warm winter sun thawing away a thin layer of powdery snow. Bright and pure and fresh. He raised his arms in a stretch, his T-shirt lifting up and showing a flash of soft skin highlighted by a dark trail of hair that went down from his belly button and disappeared under his shorts. He swallowed down a yawn. "Sorry, I don't think I've been up this late in years."

I glanced at the clock on the wall, the big blue hands pointing to one in the morning.

I made a move to stand. "Yeah, maybe we should get to bed."

"I don't mind staying up a little longer," Noah quickly said, stopping me from getting up. "I'm having a good time."

"I am, too," I said, my heart hammering in the same way it had when I was on the precipice of getting my first kiss.

Fuck.

The wine was getting to me. Not only did my muscles start feeling like they were infused with Jell-O, but my thoughts started to swirl down the drain faster than I realized. I *should* probably be excusing myself and getting ready for bed, but instead, I moved closer to Noah on the couch, using a reach for my wineglass as an excuse.

I couldn't help it. I didn't want to call it a night. I was having too much fun, and judging by the glint in Noah's green eyes, he was telling the truth when he said the same.

And those lips... *fuck*. He had such sexy lips. Slightly pouty but easily turned upward for that thousand-watt smile of his. Pillowy, too, with a dip at his cupid's bow.

"Do I have something on my mouth?" Noah asked, bringing a thumb up and rubbing his bottom lip so that I could see his teeth.

"What? Oh no, no, I was just, uh..."

He arched a brow, cocked a smile.

"Staring?" he said, completing my sentence.

"Not really staring. I think I blinked a couple of times."

He narrowed his eyes. "So that doesn't count as staring?"

"No, I don't think it does."

Noah's eyes dropped to my lips, and he made a show of blinking before bringing his gaze back up to mine. I couldn't hold back the laughter. It spread to Noah, the walls between us quickly crumbling, chipped away at the base and turning to dust with every new belly laugh.

"You're too much," I said, setting my wineglass down, my thoughts turning into a hazy and lusty mess. I kept trying to remind myself that Noah was just a friend, but that was becoming increasingly hard to believe when nothing about this felt "friendly." There was a much more thunderous undercurrent that pounded against the boundaries of friendship.

It was an undercurrent that carried me forward.

My body moved on autopilot, as if a horny little green man had landed inside the folds of my brain and taken control of things himself. I closed my eyes, leaned in, lifted an arm over Noah's shoulders, took a breath, felt his on me.

I pulled him in, felt him melt against me.

Our lips met. What followed was a kiss that unraveled reality. A kiss so strong it was responsible for the Big Bang part *dos*, creating entire galaxies between our skin, a kiss that made me feel drunk and high and blissed-out all at once. It was warm and soft at first, tender, the both of us exploring this new land with an eagerness that was barely able to be contained.

And then it wasn't. Tongues whipped together, teeth nipped at lips, the sweet taste of wine and man swirled together, same as the stubble from our five-o'clock shadows. My skin scratched, my body thrummed. Heat expanded in me as if a star had been dropped in the very center of my chest. It took everything I had in me to not throw a leg on him and straddle him down into the couch, showing him just how wild this kiss drove me, how hard it made me.

Somehow, someway, I managed to regain control. I pulled back, even though Noah's hand on my neck made me feel like I was minutes away from making a sticky mess inside my briefs, which I could already feel were wet from how excited Noah's taste had me. If I didn't break the kiss now, then it would be game over. We'd both be naked and writhing on this couch, and that would forever change whatever track this friendship was on—possibly for the better but also maybe for the worst. I didn't want to risk it.

Not tonight.

Not yet.

"That, uhm," Noah said, speechless, his jaw slightly dropped. "I should probably get to bed."

"Same," I said, standing up and making a show of bending to grab the wineglasses, buying time for the blood in my body to rush elsewhere. By the way Noah's eyes dropped to my crotch, I didn't think I was very successful.

"Ah, crap," he said as I disappeared into the kitchen. "I didn't bring any sleeping shorts. You've got any I could borrow?"

"I think so. Hold up." I set the wineglasses in the sink and ran the cold water, splashing some on my face before wiping it off with the checkered hand towel. A deep breath did nothing to calm my racing thoughts. Part of me said—no, *shouted*—to throw caution to the window and throw Noah on the bed. But that part of me had gotten in trouble before, landing in bed with people that later gave me more regrets than orgasms. Not to say Noah would be one of those people, but we'd already proved to have similar interests and endless conversations that were actually entertaining. Why risk derailing things so soon?

Noah was already in the guest room when I finished rooting around my bedroom. I leaned on the doorway and lifted up a pair of red-and-white boxers. "It's laundry day, which means all my clothes are sitting in a hamper waiting to be organized. All I've got are these boxers. I swear they're clean."

"I wouldn't mind if they weren't."

"Huh?"

"Nothing," he said, grabbing the boxers and smiling.

I laughed, that part of me shouting even louder. All I had to do was kiss him again. Guide him down onto the mattress. There, I could kiss his neck, touch his chest, grind against his cock. I could have my way with him. Make him mine. Have him yelling my name, making me do the same. Rattling the headboard so hard that I was sure I'd need to buy a replacement by the time the sun came up.

"Alright," I said instead, turning before my bulge poked out one of Noah's eyes. Lord knows he couldn't keep them off it. "Have a good night, Noah. If you need anything, you know where to find me."

"Night, Jake. Thanks for having me over tonight. It means a lot."

"Don't worry about it."

I closed his door and went to my bedroom, where I immediately dropped my shorts and took myself in my hand, resting against the door as I shut my eyes and imagined Noah down on his knees, lips wrapped around me. I blew in minutes, my toes curling against the hardwood floors as I shot ropes of come, the sound of the splatter mixing with Noah's name falling in whispers from my lips as my eyes rolled back.

And even with that release, I *still* had a sex dream starring Noah and me on a yacht in Greece.

7

NOAH BARNES

I WOKE up to the delicious smell of scrambled eggs and sizzling bacon. Confusion soon followed as I wondered who the hell was in my kitchen cooking breakfast? It took a couple of sleep-dazed seconds to remember that I wasn't actually in my house, nor was I still dreaming. This was Jake's guest bedroom, and I was wearing Jake's underwear, which he had been so gracious in lending me and I'd been so fucking horny in wearing them. Seriously, I think I slept the entire night with a boner, judging by how I woke up with my hard dick poking out from the slit.

I gave myself a couple of tugs but figured I should drag myself out of bed before I had to explain to Jake why his bedsheets needed a quick wash.

I changed out of the boxers, putting on the shorts I wore yesterday along with a simple T-shirt. Jake had set up the guest bathroom with toothpaste and a toothbrush still in its plastic container. I tore it open and brushed my teeth, looking around at the clean white subway tiles and claw-foot bathtub with its brushed copper handles, a small and opaque window letting in just enough morning light.

Aside from looks, the man also had style. He knew how to decorate so that everything fit together and nothing was overwhelmingly gaudy or tacky. It was impressive and attractive... not that I should even be thinking along those lines. There was nothing between Jake and me but a solid friendship.

Well, and that heart-stopping kiss he planted on me last night. I still felt tingly all over just thinking about it. The passion that drove our bodies together, it was undeniable and uncontrollable. I didn't know how he managed to break the kiss because I was ready and willing to go all the way. The dam had broken, and my basement had flooded. Maybe it was a good thing he'd stopped the kiss, or we would need Noah and his big old boat to come and save us from the flooding.

Just friends, that's all we are, I tried reminding myself as I left the guest bedroom and walked down the hall, following the mouthwatering scent of a fresh breakfast being served.

Friends who make out and wear each other's underwear...

Just friends.

"Morning," I said, turning the corner and spotting my *friend* with his back to me, his focus on the frying pan in front of him. He wore a light blue tank top with the sides cut to be wider, showing off the rippling muscles that went down his side, leading toward a delicious-looking V-shaped dip that disappeared under the gym shorts he had on, cut about three inches above the knee so that his meaty thighs were on full display.

Friend, friend, friend, friend.

"How'd you sleep?" he asked, turning to me and giving me the warmest damn smile I'd ever gotten. As if his morning was made just by seeing me.

"Like a baby," I answered, shuffling over to his side. "Need any help?"

"Nope, just pour yourself some coffee or orange juice, and take a seat. I'll have this done in a couple minutes."

"Smells great," I said, reaching for the coffeepot and pouring it into a mug he must have gotten from a trip to Disney. I slipped my fingers through the Mickey-ear handle and went over to the fridge, where Jake mentioned his creamer would be. Next to the fridge, Jake had his iPad propped up with the morning news playing.

A grim headline took over the bottom portion of the screen as the reporter interviewed a police officer, yellow crime-scene tape surrounding the home behind them.

"Another one?" I asked, slightly shocked as I read the headline: *Third murder in Atlanta leaves residents fearing a serial killer.*

"Yeah, I've been watching all morning. Crazy shit."

I sucked in a deep breath. Not exactly the best news to wake up to the day after receiving a bloody threat at your doorstep.

"I'm sure they'll catch whoever it is," Jake said,

tapping on the screen and switching over to a playlist of chill pop songs. I appreciated the change. My anxiety was already running on overdrive. I felt like I'd chugged the entire coffeepot, and it wasn't all because of the threat either. There was something else on my mind, making it all infinitely more complicated.

That kiss. *The* kiss.

Holy shit was that a kiss. I'd never felt such an intense explosion of chemistry before, and I'd kissed my fair share of boys in the past. What happened between Jake and me was almost paranormal. Yes, I was partly being dramatic, but I was *mostly* being honest. It was the kind of kiss that made you want to do extremely dirty things for. I was ready to give it all last night; I didn't care that we'd be going to work in the same office come Monday.

All I really cared about was coming before then.

But—thankfully—one of us had more sense than the other. We stopped before any more bodily fluids were swapped, as frustrated as that made me. I knew it was the right thing to do.

But fuuuuuck, that kiss. I wanted to shoot up from my seat, grab his face in my hands, and go in for round two.

Instead, I grabbed the Mickey Mouse mug and sipped on my hazelnut-infused coffee, the cream swirling in light honey-gold circles.

"You know, I was thinking about your, well, situation—"

"Situation," I said with a chuckle. "Good way of putting it."

"I was thinking that I wanted to help you get to the bottom of it. I'm not a professional detective by any means, but I think we might have a better shot than the people that had us on hold for forty-five minutes last night. I know it's nothing like the books we like to read, but I've had to have absorbed something from the Fletchers and Hawkins of the world."

I leaned back, looking up at the thunderstorm of a man who'd come crashing into my life from a random trip to the grocery store. "Jake, you really don't have to get involved. You were already nice enough to let me crash here for the night. That's honestly more than I was ever expecting."

"So don't expect anything, then. Consider whatever I do from here on out unexpected."

I arched a brow, licked my lips. Honestly, the smell of buttered toast and cheesy, garlicky eggs wasn't the only thing that made my mouth water. He set the plates down on the table, sitting down across from me, a smile playing on his lips.

The same lips that had cast an unbreakable and unexplainable spell on me.

"I wouldn't even know where to start," I said, deciding to play along with this. If he wanted to cosplay as Sherlock and Watson for a little bit, then fine, especially if it meant getting to hang out with him more often. And if we ended up figuring out who was behind that box, then it would be a win-win situation. Well, maybe not for the sick fuck who'd sent me that threat, but I knew *I'd* definitely be winning.

"I was thinking about that, too, actually. I think we need to make a visit to the police station first. I want to put in a request for any evidence they may have collected. I did some research, and apparently, we can also request to see the police officer's dash cam footage from when they were dispatched. It's a long shot, but maybe you can spot a familiar car or face. Maybe whoever did it stuck around to see your reaction and fled once the cops got there, putting them in front of the dash cam."

"It's worth a shot," I said. "I'll tell Eric to come with us. He might know some officers there. Maybe that'll help us get some good info."

"That sounds like a solid plan to me."

"Perfect," I said, feeling a surge of hope swell up inside me. The sooner we could figure this out, the sooner I could get back to my normal life. I returned Jake's smile before stabbing a fluffy yellow puff of scrambled eggs and cheese, biting into it, letting it practically melt in my mouth. "Damn, this is good."

"Breakfast is my specialty," Jake said, a little bit of pride slipping into his tone. "Wait until you try my famous french toast."

"Does that mean I get another night at the Perez Bed and Breakfast?"

Jake winked at me. He bit into his toast, leaning back on the chair with an arm thrown over the back, his leg crossed on top of the other. "You've got an open reservation. Stay however long you like."

I put on the voice of an older man and bent downward in my chair. "Fifty years later," I said with a flair of my hand.

"Damn, well, you look great for—how old are you fifty years from now?"

"Thirty-two."

Jake narrowed his eyes, the math not mathing in his head. I started to laugh, straightening in my chair. "I'd be seventy-six," I answered truthfully this time.

"I'd be seventy-nine. Probably less hunched over than you. I've got good core strength."

I cocked my head, lifting a finger. "Is that... I don't think... whatever, fine. You'll probably have a straighter back than me, but at least I'd have the bigger dick."

Jake nearly spat out his orange juice. *Yes.* I'd timed it just right.

I started to laugh, Jake joining in the chorus. "You don't even know if that's true or not," he said when the laughter died down.

"Alright, well, prove it to me, then." I placed my open palm on the table and wiggled my fingers. "Let's see it."

Jake stood up and started to lower his shorts, far enough for me to see some pubes. I snatched my hand back and started to laugh again nervously. "Oh my God, I was joking. It was a *joke.*"

That I very much wanted not to be a joke, but I wasn't about to say that part out loud.

Jake sat back down, holding his stomach from the laughter. "Unexpected, remember?"

"Unexpected," I repeated, chuckling through my bites of eggs and toast, deciding in that moment that yes, this was in fact one of the best breakfasts I'd ever had, and not just because the food was perfectly cooked, but mainly because of the handsome company currently sitting across from me, keeping the giddy laughter going and the good feels flowing.

Unexpected. Pretty much sums this all up perfectly.

8

JAKE PEREZ

THE POLICE STATION smelled faintly of rotting eggs mixed with an overpowering pine cleaner. There was a small waiting room where the people that weren't wearing handcuffs got to sit and get offered some of the most watered-down coffee in the entire world. The three of us turned it down, sitting next to a window that looked out at the cop-car-filled parking lot. It was a cloudy day with a near constant threat of rain, making it all the more gloomy inside these four walls.

Noah sat with his legs crossed, eyes bouncing around the room. Eric radiated a bit more confidence, which made sense, considering his past occupation. He'd already said hi to a couple of the officers and had one of them go speak to his captain for us. We were told we'd only be waiting for a couple of minutes, but it was already reaching half an hour without anyone calling us over.

I stood and stretched, deciding to go ask the uniformed man sitting at the desk if there was any movement on our case.

"Nothing," he said, answering without barely looking up from the computer screen.

"You sure? We just need dashboard cam footage and a cha—"

"I know what you need. I don't have it." This time, he did look up from his screen, a look of frustration twisting his bushy brows and scarred upper lip.

I wasn't the confrontational type, especially not when it came to the law, but *damn* did I want to ball up a fist and send it flying across this guy's jaw. He was so nonchalant about this. Meanwhile, my boy—my *friend* was sitting back there chewing his nails down to the bed because of how scared he was.

Friend. All we are.

Eric got up from his chair, the thin metallic legs scratching the already scuffed green tiles. He wasn't coming to the front desk, though. Instead, he walked right over to a side door, where a smiling man waited with an arm held out, receiving Eric's shake.

"Nice to see you again, Eric."

Eric pulled the man into a tight side hug. "You too, Julian. These are my friends Noah and Jake. Noah's the one that the threat was addressed to."

Julian, a captain according to his badge, looked to Noah, his big brown eyes appearing sympathetic as opposed to the icy-cold glare I got from the guy at the

front desk. "Sorry you're going through this, man." I
noticed a rainbow wristband attached to his Apple
Watch, popping against the black-and-white forearm
tattoo he had. It made me feel noticeably more comfortable, knowing that Julian likely understood firsthand the
kind of bullshit Noah was going through right now.
Granted, he could just be a guy who liked colorful wrist-
bands, but I decided to err on the everyone's-queer side
unless proven straight, at least for now.

"Come, let's go to my office. I can go over what we
found with y'all."

Eric and Julian walked lockstep down the bare hall lit
by a stark fluorescent light. There were offices on either
side of us, some of them larger, others appearing as
cramped as broom closets. Noah stuck close by my side.

"Did you ever tour one of these for school?" I asked.

"No, it was never on the agenda. We got field trips to
Disney World and Six Flags, not the county prison.
Where the hell did you go to school? Alcatraz?"

I chuckled, enjoying the ribbing when it came from
Noah. He had a way about him—it allowed him to say the
snarkiest and shadiest comment known to man but pull it
off with a smile that buried itself directly into the center
of your heart.

"I think they wanted to scare us into never getting in
trouble."

"Did it work?"

I shrugged. "For me, it did. But then again, I was
always a Goody Two-shoes. I only started rebelling in
college, once I was out of my parents' house."

"And what did rebelling consist of?"

That got another chuckle out of me as memories started to rush back, some of them more blurry than others. "Getting drunk and blowing closeted frat guys. And some uncloseted ones, too."

Noah nearly tripped. He looked like he was about to say something but was too tongue-tied to get it out. If he managed to untangle his thoughts, I'd never know since we made it to Captain Julian's office at that very moment.

I walked past him, bending and whispering, "Unexpected," in his ear before entering one of the more spacious offices we had seen. Playing around with him like that made me giddy, reminding me of the early stages of a blossoming... something. A blossoming friendship.

Captain Julian took a seat at his clutter-free desk, the notepads organized in a stack by increasing size. Behind him was a rectangular window that had a much nicer view than the parking lot, this one looking out to a wooded area that blocked the highway on the other side. A photo of Julian and his husband kissing at their wedding took up a large portion of the sturdy desk, confirming my suspicions and making me that much more comfortable.

"Alright," he said, hands on his desk, "so I'll start with the bad news first since there's a bit of that: we didn't find any prints. Forensics is still going through, but they aren't expecting to find any DNA either. I've got a handwriting expert looking at the address, but without samples to compare them to, they won't get us very far."

From the corner of my eye, I could see Noah deflate,

sinking in the chair. My instinct was to reach out and hold him, rub his knee, tell him it would be fine. That move would have likely confused the majority of people in the room, so I held myself back, offering him a pursed frown instead.

"Now, here are the things we *do* know. One, it was hand-delivered. That box did not go through any kind of postal office. I have officers canvassing the area and asking everyone if they spotted someone or something that seems suspicious."

"Have they found anything yet?" Eric asked. If he was disappointed with the direction this was going, then he did a great job of hiding it.

"Nothing. But they haven't finished. I expect a full report by tomorrow afternoon."

I cocked my head, a thought striking me. "So someone hand-delivered the box and *still* managed to avoid detection? How the hell did that happen?"

The captain shook his head, empty hands opening over his empty desk before fitting back together in a loose fist. "That's a good question. Maybe they know the neighborhood well, or maybe the person who sent the threat wasn't the one who delivered the box. There could have been a third-party involved."

Noah rubbed a hand over his face. His eyes were shut, his mouth tight. There was tension clear in the way his shoulders practically touched his neck. Maybe I could offer him a massage later, work out some of those knots. Friends did that all the time, right?

"What about the dashboard camera for the officers at

the scene?" Eric asked, throwing me out of my Sean Cody fantasy. "Is that available?"

"It is. I'm getting someone to get it on a USB drive for you, but I can play it now if y'all wanted to see it."

"We do," Eric said as the three of us leaned forward. Julian turned his computer screen so that it faced us. He clicked through a couple of screens and found the video, an entire display appearing, showing everything from how fast the officer was going to whether or not his lights and sirens were on. It was nighttime, and the video was a little grainy but serviceable. The footage began from the moment the cop left the station, which was approximately six miles away.

Captain Julian sped the tape up, slowing it down once the officer was only a few blocks away from Noah's house. We all watched with hawk eyes, even though I wasn't entirely sure what I was looking for. I still didn't know Noah's social circle well enough yet to spot a suspicious car hanging around his neighborhood.

We watched it all the way up until the police car pulled up to Noah's townhouse. I could sense the last wisps of hope slip out of the room through the air vents. Noah asked to watch it one more time. The captain obliged, pressing Play and leaning back in his chair, eyes just as intent on the black-and-white footage as ours were.

Again, the tape was nearing the end, the cop car making a left and entering a side street attached to the neighborhood. The captain was about to exit out of it when Noah jerked up. "Hold on, rewind."

The captain did, the footage skipping backward in five-second increments. Noah watched as I held my breath, wondering who he saw. All I could tell was that there was an older-looking Honda Civic driving down the opposite side of the street, one of its headlights busted. It wasn't very clear as to who the driver was, their face concealed by shadows that flickered under the streetlights.

"That's Franky's car," Noah said, a hand moving to cover his mouth. "He has that same exact window decal."

Noah pointed at the screen to a tiny corner of the car window that showed a lightning bolt sticker. I wouldn't have spotted it if I wasn't looking for it.

"Franky who?" Captain Julian asked, taking out a notebook from the bottom of his stack and clicking the top of a pen.

"Franky Gorga. An ex of mine. He's married with kids now, and we haven't talked in years. I don't know... it doesn't really make sense for him to leave that threat, but why is he driving around my neighborhood at night anyway?"

"Do you think that's him behind the wheel?" the captain asked.

Noah shook his head, chewing on the inside of his cheek. "I can't say for sure."

"Alright, well, it's something I can look into, at least."

Noah sat back with a sigh. I could feel his frustration. I shared in it. This meeting didn't provide many answers; if anything, it offered up more questions. And whoever was twisted enough to send a severed chicken head to

Noah's doorstep was still out there, walking around, possibly planning their next move. Every second felt crucial, and I realized then that I couldn't leave it to chance. I couldn't leave it down to an already strained police department, where cases went cold for decades, if not longer.

I decided that I'd have to do some digging myself.

The captain stood, the meeting coming to an end. He offered his hand again and apologized for not being further along. We shook, Captain Julian offering his promises, saying that he had the best of the best working on it. Noah's smile appeared genuine, his thanks just as honest. He was a good guy, there wasn't a doubt in my mind about that.

It made this situation all the more baffling. Who the hell would want to torture someone with such a kind heart? Like a predatory cat toying with a defenseless mouse, living off the thrill of it. Off basic and bloody instinct.

It made my stomach churn.

We found ourselves outside of the station, the spring breeze rattling a couple of branches in a nearby oak tree. Eric stepped aside to make a call, leaving me and Noah standing as if we'd just gotten out of a film. None of this seemed quite real.

I decided to ask him a question that had been on my mind since that morning. "Do you want to crash at my place again?"

Noah looked up, eyes catching a bit of the sun, nearly knocking me off my feet. How did he always manage to do that? Look so damn effortlessly ethereal... and I never described someone like that. But that was Noah. Capturing this otherworldly kind of glow even when we were standing feet away from a dirty police station, an overflowing trash can too close for comfort.

And yet *still* Noah made this all feel like some kind of movie. The good ones. The ones you watch over and over again, even if it's just by leaving it on in the background, because occasionally tuning in feels like a warm hug while you handle mindless chores.

"No, that's okay," he said, the light disappearing from his eyes as he looked down at his sneakers. "I should sleep in my own bed tonight. I appreciate it, though. I really do."

"You sure?" I asked, wanting to press but not be pushy at the same time.

"Yeah. It's probably best."

I tried not to let my disappointment show, swallowing it like the bitter pill it was, feeling it bounce down my throat and leaving an acidic trail in its wake.

"Okay, no worries."

"But you should come to the next Reading under the Rainbow. It's going to be at Yvette's for, well, obvious reasons. She lives in Decatur. If you want to, I can officially add you to our email chain."

"I'd love that," I said, the disappointment quickly replaced by something else, something brighter.

"Alright, perfect. Same email as your work email?"

"No, here, use this one." We traded private emails

and realized we didn't have each other's numbers. Those got added in, too.

It didn't take me a whole two hours before I was texting him, which resulted in me smiling myself to sleep that night as we shared silly memes and viral videos.

9

NOAH BARNES

I DROVE through the gates of Yvette's community, taking a right and going past the pool, going toward the end of a large cul-de-sac, where Yvette's two-story farm-house-style home took up most of the corner. I parked behind Tristan's car, spotting him and Eric through an open window, the two of them laughing up a storm.

It was book club night, and honestly, it couldn't have gotten here fast enough. Our bimonthly meetings were often the highlights of my weeks. Getting to hang out with my friends, talking books and playing games, was seriously more effective for me than therapy, and after all that had happened recently, I was in dire need of a session.

And of course, seeing Jake outside of work was another big perk to book club. We'd been texting a ton and were having lunches alone together when other colleagues didn't invite us out to eat. Seeing his smiling face and ocean-blue eyes always helped make the day go by that much faster. Watching him walk past my desk to grab some water or take his fifteen-minute break usually guaranteed that I'd lost my spot in whatever Excel sheet I was working on at the time. Daydreams of our kiss would constantly float through my mind, distracting me with thoughts of Jake and his soft lips against mine, his hand moving to grip the back of my neck. It might have been a short kiss, but it had already proved to be one of the best I'd ever had.

I didn't even want to think about how good everything after that kiss could have been.

I was (slightly) grateful Jake had the willpower and wherewithal to stop us before things got out of hand. I didn't want to ruin this budding friendship; I didn't want to complicate things. It happened to me before, getting close to someone and thinking we'd make great friends, only to end a drunken night hooking up together and waking up to awkward texts and an entirely derailed friendship. Twice already, I had ended up having sex with a friend, and both times ended in sporadic messages and brief interactions. One of those guys was actually Robby, who quickly went from trustworthy neighbor and reliable friend to relatively distant acquaintance after our awkward night together. We had zero chemistry, and the sex wasn't all that great, which likely attributed to the new dynamic between us, but still, I just didn't want to risk it with Jake.

Even though I was positive our sex would be tectonic-plate-shatteringly good.

But Jake was a good soul and proving to be an even

better friend. The last thing I wanted to do was mess up the solid connection we were building, which meant the kiss would need to stay in the past, confined to my daydreams and spank-bank fantasies. I had to think about him in the same way I thought about Tristan and Eric. They were practically brothers to me, which meant any kind of romantic interaction was completely off the table.

Speaking of, I could still see Eric and Tristan through the window, both of them currently trying to teach Jess and Tia some kind of viral dance, their hips swaying and hands clapping in unison. I chuckled to myself as I got out of my car and walked over to the already unlocked door. I stepped inside, the sound of music and laughter greeting me before any official hellos had been traded.

"You're the last one to get here," Yvette said when I turned the corner into her living room. She held up a shot glass, bright blue liquid filling it up to the brim. "That means this one is yours."

I gave her a playful glare and took the shot. Blueberry and vodka swirled down my throat and earned a shoulder-shaking shiver from me. She took the shot glass back and went to the kitchen, leaving me to make my rounds, ending the hellos with Jake, who stood up from the couch and wrapped me up in a tight hug. A good one, where our bodies just kind of fit perfectly together and I could sort of feel the slight rise of his crotch.

It was a *really* good hug. "Mmm, you smell great," I said as we separated, unable to help myself.

"Thank you. It's a new cologne."

"Well, keep buying it."

"I will," he said with a smooth wink.

Yvette's living room was cozy and well decorated, the main sitting area compromised of seven modular couches that were cloud white and just as soft. They were able to be rearranged however Yvette liked, so there were three love seats and one singular seat, where Yvette came and sat cross-legged, book in one hand and wineglass in another. Jess and Tia were on one of the love seats, and Eric and Tristan were on the other, so I plopped down next to Jake. He was also double fisting a book and a colorful can of beer, matching the colorful blue and pink stripes of his polo shirt, a pair of black shorts tying it all together. His light brown hair looked like it had just been cut, cleaned up down the sides and trimmed at the top.

"Everyone settled in alright?" Yvette asked, pushing a rogue curl out of her hair. There was a stack of tarot cards sitting on the side table next to her, a bed of purple velvet fabric falling down onto the floor. She was big on reading them and would often do it for us whenever we needed that little extra guidance.

"Perfect," she said with a clap of her hands. "There's plenty more drinks in the fridge, and I ordered us pizza— should be getting here soon. But in the meantime, let's get this show on the road. Everyone caught up on their reading?"

A chorus of yups and yeses came from the group. I set my book down on my lap, the surrealistic painting of a sinister girl and a suburban house staring back up at me.

Yvette sat back in her seat. There were two large watercolor paintings of her two cats that bordered either side of her, their curving gold frames making the cats look even more regal than the two kings they'd been in real life. "Perf. Okay, so for tonight's game, I wanted to pull out a card every time we start on a new chapter, but the cards aren't for us. They're for the characters. I'll pull one out, say what it means, and we can all decide which character it's for. Sound good?"

"Ooh, sounds really fun to me," Jess said, her girlfriend nodding in agreement.

"Let's get it started, then."

And so our book club night officially began. We started it off by talking about the insinuation that the murderer started making the macabre jewelry because of her obsession with her Archie, the main character's ex-husband, who had a wide collection of rare and expensive jewelry. There was a chapter where Archie and the murderer talk, although the murderer's POV or name isn't revealed, so it was clear a link was there between them. It was also insinuated that the murderer was becoming fixated on Gabrielle and targeted her jewelry store ads specifically to bait Gabrielle into buying from her.

Yvette grabbed her deck and gave it a shuffle, closing her eyes before pulling off the topmost card and flipping it over, setting it down on the long white coffee table in the center of the room. It depicted a woman and a man huddling together against a strong and snow-filled wind, the snow flecks glistening silver against the matte background. A silver-and-golden border surrounded the card like ivy growing along its edges.

"Okay, so I asked what are the driving factors behind a character's motivations. And we got the Five of Pentacles. This card represents extreme financial stress or at least a fear of financial failure. Who do you guys think is scared of that the most?"

Jake perked up, and all eyes turned toward him. "That's probably Matt, Gabrielle's brother."

"Isn't he the richest one out of all of them? He owns his own handyman company," Tristan noted.

"Right, but look at how he jumped in and helped his sister's soap business when she mentioned it might fail. He didn't think twice about giving her what she needed and doubling it. He was desperate to keep her succeeding because even the proximity to failure scares him."

Tristan nodded, reaching for the bowl of chips and crunching his way through agreeing with everything Jake said.

"But Archie was scared, too, right? Didn't he lose a lot of money in the divorce with Gabrielle?" Jess asked.

"I think Archie definitely has some skeletons in his closet," Jake said. "And I also think he's still pretty obsessed with Gabby."

Yvette nodded and grabbed the card off the table, placing it back in the deck and giving it another shuffle before tapping it on the palm of her hand three times and setting them back down. "I've got to agree with Jake. I think there's something going on with Archie. He seemed to go overboard in complimenting her on the necklace when they bumped into each other at that restaurant. Almost like he knew it was made of bones or something."

A cold shiver crawled up my back. Wearing a necklace made of bones without even knowing it. The book was only fiction, but that didn't mean the idea of it didn't send a physical chill through my body. It's what I loved so much about reading. The different thrills and sensations that could come from any page, delivering a jaw-dropping twist or some cheek-blushing steam.

"I think that's a good place to break," Yvette said, standing up and collecting a couple of empty glasses. Eric got up and helped her with the refills, the two of them disappearing into the kitchen.

Tristan stretched out his legs and covered his mouth as he yawned.

"Next club meet is the annual retreat, right?" he asked to no one in particular.

"A retreat?" Jake echoed.

"Mhmm," I said, nodding. "Every year, we rent a cabin up in Blue Ridge and spend the weekend there, reading and drinking and soaking in the hot tub. I was going to send out an email tomorrow to the group."

Jake's eyes lit up. His smile widened so that they crinkled the corners of those sapphire-blue orbs. "I love a good mountain vacation. I used to spend every Christmas in the mountains with my parents. Haven't been in a little while."

"Good, it should be fun. Always is," I said, realizing that the cabin we booked was already short one room, and that was before Jake joined our group. I made a mental note to try and get that fixed. "I need this escape more than ever."

"Is everything okay?" Tristan asked, catching on to *why* I felt like I needed the escape. "Has anything popped up?"

I shook my head and tried not to let the disappointment or fear enter my voice. "Nothing so far, but I'm staying hopeful."

Yvette and Eric came back into the room with drinks topped off. "Hopeful about what?" Yvette asked as she sat down, now with a plush gray blanket thrown over her legs.

"About the cops figuring out who the hell sent me that box."

"Maybe we should Drew Barrymore this shit?" Tristan asked, looking around the room, which had suddenly fallen completely silent.

Yvette's pencil-sharp eyebrows rose in unison. "You mean *Nancy Drew* this shit?"

"Whatever. Same Drew, different day," Tristan said with a wave of his hand.

The entire crew started to bust out in laughter, Tristan included. That's one of the things we loved about him. His grasp of the English language was the strongest out of all of us, considering he had a successful career as a reporter and an author, but sometimes a wire or two would get crossed, and he'd say the most off-the-wall thing, but what made it even funnier was the conviction he'd say it with.

"I do like where you were going with that," Tia said when the laughter died down. She patted the corners of her eyes where a couple of tears had collected.

"Same," Eric said. "I miss working cases sometimes."

I shook my head, already thinking of about a dozen ways this could go wrong. "No, I don't want anyone else getting dragged into this."

Jake sat up, head cocked, eyes drilling through mine. "If it means figuring out who's behind this, then I don't care at all about being dragged in. I just want you safe."

I swallowed, the gulp audible.

"Maybe we can set aside some time at the end of our meetings to toss around a couple of theories," Jess suggested, moving her glasses so that they sat higher up her face, the tiny diamond stud glittering on her nose.

"Yeah, I'll bring a whiteboard next time," Eric offered. He looked the most excited out of all of us. "We can list out possible suspects along with potential motives, try to figure out any links we may be missing."

It made my heart warm, even though the cool tendrils of anxiety clamping around my chest were trying hard to snuff that warmth out. I always felt loved and appreciated by my friends, but this just brought it up to an entirely new level. I wasn't just looking around at friends; I was looking around at my family, each of them ready to do whatever it took to keep me safe.

It nearly brought tears to my eyes, but the emotional train of thought was abruptly derailed by a ringing cell phone, the couch underneath Jake and me beginning to vibrate.

He pulled his phone out and looked at the screen. I could instantly sense a shift in his demeanor. He looked worried, his brow furrowed and his jaw clenched tight enough to show a twitching muscle that went down his neck.

"Sorry, guys, I have to take this."

He stood and excused himself, phone to his ear before the door was even shut. I could have sworn I heard him say, "Hi, Mom," but I wasn't entirely sure. All I knew was that whoever called had sent him into a panicked frenzy, and I had no idea why.

The conversation in the room shifted back to the threat, but my mind remained with Jake, wondering if he was okay out there and if there was any way I could help my friend as much as he wanted to help me.

10

JAKE PEREZ

"JAKE, please hurry home. *No se.* I don't know. I can't remember how I got here. Ay, Jake."

My mom's voice was like taking a shotgun blast to the chest. Hearing how fearful she was and how pained she felt at not being able to remember made me feel like I was dropped into a wood chipper. It hurt. I hated this with every fiber of my being. A disease that took away your loved one little by little but only taking their mind and leaving their body seemingly intact. It was twisted, and the fact that there was no cure, no way to hold on to hope except by hoping for a miracle— *that* was one of the most fucked-up things about Alzheimer's.

"It's okay, Ma. I'll be there in ten minutes."

"Okay, Jake. Okay. Thank you." She started to cry as she hung up the phone—I could hear the sniffling before the line went dead.

I turned away from the house and leaned on my car, and I started to cry, too. Silent streams of tears went down my cheeks as my chest heaved while I tried my hardest to control the sobs that wrenched themselves free from somewhere inside of me. Like bats falling from the shadows of a dark cave, rising up through my throat, rattling against my lips. I put a fist up to my mouth.

Why? Why her? My mom was one of the kindest, most caring, most warm people to ever exist. All she did was work to make sure everyone around her was happy. She donated her money, and she volunteered her time, and she was an incredible mother, even when my father seemed intent on breaking us both down. When they divorced—about five years ago—I thought my mom would have a hard time, but she took it in stride and blossomed even more, finding a group of friends in a local gardening club. She and her green-thumbed gals would go on movie dates and beach vacays and throw big birthday parties. I didn't think I'd ever seen my mom so happy before.

And then she started to forget things. Little things at first. Where she left the remote, where she left her keys, what she was making for lunch. Then it got worse. She'd forget where she parked her car, why she was at the grocery store, which turn to make to get home. That one was the tipping point—when my mom called me in gasping tears as she pulled over at an intersection just down the street from her home. We went to the doctors that day and got the official diagnosis soon after.

It did more than rattle my world. It destroyed it. Sundered it. Split it in half and crushed it between a planet-sized boot. And it created a dark haze over my head that clouded my thoughts, snuffed out any enjoyment, dragging me down in a seemingly endless well of depression.

But I was pulled out of it. Not just by Ashley, who had entered my life around this point and really helped keep my mind off things, but also by my mom herself. Vivianne Perez, even with the odds stacked high against her and her memories slipping away like water through a sieve, stayed positive. Somehow, someway, my mom figured out how to keep a smile on, even when her son could barely keep his eyes open. All I wanted to do was sleep and dream about a better world.

But my mom kept my head up, and I slowly learned the best way to help her cope with this debilitating and just plain old fucked-up disease.

We can figure out how to send billionaires on field trips to space but can't figure out how to cure this. Make it make sense.

I let out a sigh, pushing off my car. I didn't want to go back inside. Not so that everyone could see my puffy eyes and start asking me what was wrong. Instead, I grabbed my phone and shot off a quick text to Noah.

"Family emergency, sorry, I've got to go. Tell everyone I say bye."

I hit Send and took another breath. I got in my car and looked out to the house, the gang gathered around in the living room clearly visible through the open window. I could see Noah get the text and read it, shoulders slumping. He must have said something to the group because their conversations appeared to have stalled.

I decided to go before they looked out the window and saw me still sitting there.

The key turned. The ignition clicked on, the engine thrumming. It rattled and wheezed, and then my entire car went dark, the battery giving out on me at the most inopportune time I could imagine. I dropped my head against the steering wheel, feeling the hard leather smack into my forehead and not even wincing.

Fuck.

I could call AAA, but that would require waiting. Maybe one of the book clubbers had a jumper cable, but amongst a group of queer millennials who likely didn't even know how to lift their hoods, I figured the chances of that weren't very high.

I grabbed my phone and dialed. Noah answered with a confused "Hello?"

"Hey, Noah, I didn't want to go back in and interrupt, but my car's not starting, and I really need to get to my mom's place. Mind giving me a ride?"

"Oh my God, absolutely not. Hold on, I'll be right out."

Noah shot up from the couch, scaring Eric and Jess, who were sitting next to him on the couch. Noah explained something quick with his hands, running over to the door and out of sight from the window. Seconds later, he was opening the door and hurrying down the path toward his car. I got out of mine, giving him a genuine thanks.

"Don't even worry about it," he said, jumping into the driver's seat of his fancy new Tesla.

"Wait... how the hell do you open this?" I asked under my breath, not seeing a door handle before noticing the imprint on the door. I pushed randomly and managed to flip it open before Noah noticed me struggling.

"Ready?" Noah asked as I got in.

"Yup, let's go." I gave him the address, and we were off, silent at first, until Noah asked, "Is she okay? Should I be driving faster?"

I managed a chuckle, shaking my head. "She's not in any immediate danger, no. She has early onset Alzheimer's, and it's progressing pretty fast. She still remembers me for the most part, but she's starting to forget her own home, so she gets scared sometimes and calls me. At least she remembers enough to call me." I felt my throat tighten but managed to hold back any rogue tears.

"Oh, Jake, I'm so sorry. I lost my grandmother to it three years ago, and yet I still can't even imagine the pain you've both been in."

Noah's words were sincere and carried with them a punch that landed somewhere between my left and right ventricle, directly in the center of my heart.

"It's been hard," I said, unable to sugarcoat it. "Really fucking hard. But we're doing our best, handling it day by day. What else can we do?"

Noah reached across the center console and grabbed my hand, squeezing it. A gesture that meant more support than anything else and one that knocked down another wall between us, turning it to rubble. He let go almost immediately, but the brief touch was enough to put a smile back on my face.

"You've got a superpower, you know?"

Noah looked at me as he slowed to a stop under a red light. "What is it?"

"Making people smile. You do it all the time. At the book club, at work, probably even at the DMV."

"I did make the lady taking my photo laugh at a joke I said," Noah said proudly.

"Called it."

He laughed, the sound filling the car like music from my favorite artist. "I just give back the energy people give me. Or at least the energy I *want* them to give me. Keeps things positive and usually rubs off on everyone else."

"It does," I said, still smiling as we drove onto the highway, effortlessly accelerating. The white leather seat seemed to wrap around me. I stretched out my legs, massaging the tension in the back of my neck. "The book club was great tonight. I love being a part of it—sucks that I couldn't stay. I'm excited about the retreat, though."

"Same," Noah said, his grin growing. He drove with one hand on the wheel, the other in his lap, relaxed and comfortable. "It's always a shitshow, but in a really good way. There was one time that Tristan got so drunk he thought the neighbor was a brown bear coming at him. He yelled bloody murder and ran into the cabin, tripping over himself and locking the door. Emily shows up minutes later wearing this big fur coat, knocking on the door and asking if everything was alright."

That story resulted in more laughter filling up the car.

"She looked a little offended when we told her what really happened. I never saw her wear that coat again," Noah continued, his eyes crinkling at the corners. He was focused on the road, which gave me a moment to focus on him: sharp jawline, soft nose, softer lips, long and curly lashes, a couple of perfectly placed beauty marks, a subtle scar that ran at the edge of his left brow. Poetry on skin. That was Noah. Everything flowed together like lyrical prose, creating someone that was equal parts captivating and welcoming. He drew me in unlike anyone else in my life had.

Like magic. Something about Noah put me under a deep spell, and it was growing harder and harder to shake it off. To remind myself that I was sitting next to a friend — a friend that was quickly proving to be one of the best I'd ever had.

So there was no need to mess things up with thoughts of lips and jawlines. No matter how tempting they might have been, how badly I wanted to run my tongue along them, tracing them with a finger while I used another to explore him...

Noah pulled off the highway and drove a few more minutes before reaching my mother's neighborhood. She lived in an older community that lacked landscaping and maintenance but was only a couple of blocks away from the hospital, which made things easier for her. I wanted to try and save up to get her into another place but was beginning to wonder if moving her to a brand-new area would only make things worse.

"This the one?" Noah asked, slowing to a stop in front of a quaint one-floor home. Its awnings were in need of a pressure wash, and some of the white trim needed a touch-up, but other than that, it was the nicest one on the block.

"This is it," I said, unbuckling and taking a breath. "Thank you. Seriously."

"And *seriously*, no problem. I'd do this anytime you need."

"See you tomorrow?"

Noah cocked his head. "Huh? No, I'm waiting here for you. How else are you going to get home?"

"That's fine. I can—"

"Nope." He crossed his arms. "I'll wait."

I arched a brow, sensing that I was running directly into a brick wall with this conversation. And I kind of liked it.

That's when I relented but also when I got another idea. "Instead of staying out here, then, why don't you come in?"

Noah—perma-smile still on his face—answered with a nod and turned off his car, as if he had been waiting this entire time for me to ask him. "I'd love to," he said, making my heart flutter for no reason other than because he was Noah Barnes, and the promise of his presence alone was enough to make me happy.

It's a superpower. He's a damn superhero.

11

NOAH BARNES

I WASN'T EXACTLY sure why, but I was nervous. Not because I was scared of meeting Jake's mom, but more so because I was nervous about making a good impression on her. Silly, considering there was no reason to be worried about that, and yet still, I could feel my hands getting slightly clammy, and my heart started pumping a little faster as we stood outside of her door. She shuffled around on the other side, the sounds of three heavy locks clicking open, followed by the creak of rusty hinges. His mom stood in the doorway with a smile that looked a whole lot like Jake's.

"Hey, Ma, everything okay?"

Jake's mom took him into a tight hug, the kind reserved for a mother and son, before letting go, one hand still on Jake's elbow. "Yes, thank you. I had a moment back in my bedroom. I feel a little better now."

"You sure?" Jake asked, looking her over.

"*Sí, sí.*"

"Okay, good." Her eyes floated to me before Jake realized introductions were needed. "This is my friend Noah. We work together. Noah, this is my mom, Vivianne."

She held out a hand, soft in mine as we shook, brown eyes bright even under the dim light of the setting sun behind me. "We haven't met already, have we?"

"No, no, this is our first time."

"Well, it's great to meet you, Noah." She let go of my hand and opened her arms for a hug instead. She gave me one of the warmest embraces I'd ever felt before stepping back, opening her door a little wider. "Did you both eat dinner already? I've got some chicken and rice left over?"

"Noah should be getting home," Jake said, but I shook my head.

"I've got nothing on the schedule, and my stomach is kind of grumbly."

Jake arched a brow, but his smile diffused any other argument he might be spinning up. Vivianne stepped aside as he entered with me right behind him.

Her home was warm, reflecting the same energy she had given me. The walls were painted a soft beige, and there was a lot of older wooden furniture, freshly polished and cleaned. There was a tall display case showing off plates collected from over a dozen different countries, with other trinkets sprinkled throughout them. She had a couple of plants but nothing like her green-thumbed son. A large blue-and-white rug brought a pop of color, matching the bright blue pillows on the wraparound couch that faced a large television, currently paused on what appeared to be *Big Brother*.

"Who are you rooting for to win?" I asked, pointing at the TV.

Vivianne chuckled, the sound exactly like her son's. Bubbly and infectious. "Krystal, for sure. She's played such a smart game."

I nodded, agreeing, although I wasn't entirely sure there was a Krystal in this season.

"Come, this way. Let's get you boys some food." She shuffled across her living room, walking through the arching doorway into the next room. Jake slowed down and dropped his voice.

"You really don't have to stay if you don't want to."

"Good, because I want to."

His eyes crinkled, smile widening before he tamped it down, even though I wanted him to do the complete opposite. I wanted to see that smile 24/7. Good thing he thought my superpower was making him grin because *he* was the one that looked like Clark Kent whenever he flashed those pearly whites.

I followed him into the kitchen, where a steaming pot of rice sat next to a plate of juicy and tender chicken breasts, appearing to be seasoned to perfection. I noticed Jake grab a jug of milk left behind the sink and open the cap, giving it a quick sniff before deeming it okay and placing it back in the fridge. There were a couple of other items left out, all of them finding their way back to their proper places with Jake's quiet help.

"So Noah, how do you know Jake?" Vivianne asked,

turning to me and handing me a plate filled to the brim with food. Fluffy white rice, perfectly cooked black beans, tender chicken that smelled absolutely delicious covered with sautéed onions.

"We work together," I said, having trouble speaking with how much my mouth watered. "And we're in the same book club."

"Oh, that's great. He was always a big reader. You liked reading more than you liked hanging out with me sometimes."

"Only when I was a brooding teenager," Jake clarified, making his own plate and walking with me into the dining room. "It didn't last too long."

"No," she said with a scoff. "Only lasted about ten years, give or take. Not long at all."

Jake rolled his eyes and laughed, his mom giving his shoulder a loving squeeze before she sat at the head of the table. She had a cup of coffee in her hands, sipping it slowly as Jake and I dug in. My mouth immediately exploded with flavor, and I nearly inhaled the entire plate with a single bite. Somehow, I managed to contain myself and eat like a civilized human being, the conversation between the three of us as smooth and easy as if I'd been part of the family for years now.

It was great conversation, too. I learned all about Jake's childhood obsession with the musical *Cats*, to the point that he'd demand to be a cat every Halloween and knew most of the songs by heart, bursting into spontaneous performances at different family events. I bookmarked that little fact for later, wondering how many more glittering facets this gem of a man had hiding underneath the surface.

He was fascinating, and his mom just the same, telling me stories of her time working as a flight attendant and traveling all around the globe. She did a stint on a few private jets and told us stories about a couple of A-list celebrities she flew with, although those memories were a little foggier than the others. Jake and I were enthralled either way, and before I knew it, the plates were empty, and the clock on the wall was reading nine thirty at night.

I stretched out under the table, accidentally bumping into Jake's feet, but he didn't seem to mind, leaving them right where they were. I grabbed my plate and reached for Jake's, taking it into the kitchen and washing it before Vivianne realized what I was doing.

"You really didn't have to do that," she said, arms crossed and head shaking, her light brown bob catching the kitchen light.

"It was honestly the least I can do."

"Well, you're welcome to come here anytime you want." She pulled me in for one more hug. "It was great seeing you again, Noah."

"You too, Ms. Perez."

"Viv," she said with a flourish of her hand. She walked us to the front door, moving with a bounce in her step that wasn't there before. Her mood had clearly lifted from when we had first arrived. It made me wonder if we should stay longer, but Jake was already stepping onto the porch, and the last thing I wanted to do was overstay my welcome.

"See ya next time," I said, leaving Jake and Vivianne to their goodbyes by themselves. I heard him ask if she needed anything else just as I was getting into my car, his voice cutting off as I closed the door.

My phone buzzed. I figured it was probably someone from the book club wanting to check in with us. Instead, I saw my neighbor's name across my screen.

"Hey, are you home?" he asked.

I shot a quick text back. "No, why?"

"That's what I figured. But I saw a light on in your kitchen, did you leave it on?"

My eyebrows drew together. I racked my brain, trying to remember if I flicked the light on, but why would I do that when I had left my house while it was bright as hell outside?

"No, I don't think that was me. Is it still on?" I texted back.

"Nope, it's not."

"Weird..... thanks for letting me know."

"Of course. I'll keep an eye out."

I texted back two orange hearts and a thanks before stuffing the phone back into my pocket. A sharp chill crisscrossed down my spine. I looked in the rearview mirror, suddenly picturing a masked figure rising up from my back seat with a bag ready to close over my head.

The door opened, Jake getting in, smelling like his mom's cooking.

"What? You look like you saw a ghost."

I shook my head, but that didn't shake the feeling I was being watched. "I just got this weird text from

Robby. He said my kitchen light went on and off, but I haven't been home for hours."

"Shit, seriously?"

I nod, turning my car on and sucking in a deep breath, the oxygen barely making it in before my lungs squeezed it right back out.

"Well, looks like we're having another sleepover, then."

"Huh?" I asked.

"You. Me. Playing Super Smash and drinking beer until we get tired. It's not like you'll be getting any sleep in your own place."

And who's to say I want to get any sleep at yours?

"Are you calling me a scaredy-cat?" I asked instead.

"Not at all. I'm—"

"Because I am," I said, saving him from an explanation. We both laughed, which felt odd considering the potent fear that had a vise grip around my chest only moments ago. "Alright, fine." I pulled out of Vivianne's driveway and headed toward Jake's house, secretly grateful (and excited) about having another night sleeping under the same roof. The thought of going back home and walking through an empty house only to toss and turn in my bed with the lights on really didn't seem appealing to me.

But spending the night with Jake?

Yeah. Yeah, I think I could handle that.

———

"CRAP," I said as I was sinking down into Jake's couch. "I didn't bring any sleeping clothes again."

"I'm starting to think you're doing that on purpose, bud." Jake shot me a wink and disappeared into his bedroom.

Bud?

... Why did that make me kind of hard?

Thankfully, I wasn't left to my own devices for much longer. Jake walked back into the room, having changed into light green shorts that made it extremely difficult for me to keep my eyes above waist level. Was he even wearing underwear? It didn't seem like it with the way he bounced around in there. I took a chug of my beer, needing it to blunt some of the edges of my increasingly dirty thoughts.

And of course, instead of blunting anything, the beer only fueled the fire. My leg bounced, shaking the couch, making me hyperaware of my growing cock.

I stopped the bouncing, but my dick didn't stop growing.

Fuckin' hell, this is going to be an interesting night.

He handed me another pair of shorts. "I already folded all my clothes, so you don't have to wear one of my boxers again," he said, grin on his face.

"Ah, man, really?" I asked, pouting as I grabbed the shorts.

"I mean, I can go grab a pair if you want."

"I'm joking," I clarified, remembering the last time I made a joke and nearly got a handful of meat and potatoes.

He fell down onto the couch with a chuckle, reaching over me to grab his beer that had been left on the end table. It brought his neck *extremely* close to my lips, which made me *extremely* tempted to lean in.

"How'd you like my mom's cooking?" he asked, sitting back out of range of my ravenous mouth.

"It was Michelin-star-worthy. Can you cook like that? Besides breakfast, obviously."

He huffed out a breath, following it with a drink of his beer, setting the can down on the metallic coaster with a clink. "Hell no. Breakfast is as far as I can get. I mean, I'm sure I can get by, but it won't hold a candle to her."

"Well then, we've got to have dinner there more often," I teased, not expecting Jake to answer in the affirmative, asking me when was the next time I could make it.

"I don't know... Saturday?"

"Saturday it is," Jake replied. He had one leg crossed over the other, his knee rubbing against mine. It was a soft, subtle touch but not one that went unnoticed, my body reacting as if the man had pulled out his hard dick and started stroking himself. I was *that* thirsty for him, and yet what the hell was I supposed to do about it? I didn't want to make things awkward between us, and acting on my lusty thoughts could definitely bring a side of awkward if things didn't go right.

But his leg... he was moving closer. It wasn't just our knees touching but a majority of our thighs, the leg hairs rubbing together, the body heat rising and making the room feel a couple of degrees warmer. I swallowed, wondering if the buzz through my veins was the beer already working or something else.

"You know, Noah, I couldn't stop thinking about our kiss from the other day."

Jake's confession nearly knocked me off the couch and sent me flying across the country, landing somewhere in the Pacific Ocean, lost and confused.

"I, uh, well—"

"Is that bad? I know we're just friends, but kissing you felt like kissing the sun. It left a mark on me. And I want more."

My eyebrows darted halfway up my face, my lips parting in slight shock.

"It's not bad, Jake. I don't think so... Honestly? I feel the same exact way; I just wasn't sure how to even bring it up."

He threw me a cocky smirk. "Un—"

"—expected," I said, finishing his thought, a bubbly sensation rising up my chest, like the fizz in an expensive bottle of champagne.

Jake was speaking everything I'd been too scared to put into words, and he was also moving closer, and his hand was on my leg, and it was moving up my thigh now, and his fingers were going under the shorts, and his face was closer, closer, lips on mine.

The rest of that night was history in the making.

12

JAKE PEREZ

FUCK. I tried to stop myself. I really did. I just couldn't help it. My brain had malfunctioned. Melted next to the heat source that was Noah Barnes. Nothing made sense, and everything made sense, all at once. I knew this could end in disaster, or it could end in something totally opposite; this was a way of demolishing our budding friendship or shifting gears in a different direction, and I had no way of knowing what was about to happen.

And truthfully? I didn't really care. Not in that moment. Not when Noah was giving me those big brown puppy-dog eyes, his lips pouting and his cheeks flushed, matching the same rosy-pink color that started climbing up his neck. It made the perfect target, marking the spot I wanted to sink my teeth into.

Fuck friendship. I wanted more. More of Noah, more of him on me, skin to skin, hands exploring every damn inch of him.

Our lips crashed together, his immediate moan giving

me the green light. We'd deal with the aftermath of this later. Right now, all I cared about was tasting Noah on my tongue, his swirling around mine. I reached for the back of his neck, gripped it. Steered our kiss, directing his tongue deeper into my mouth, our noses rubbing and our breaths melding.

It was paradise. I got a taste of nirvana, and I was already addicted to it.

More. I needed *more*. I left his lips, gleaming as they curled into a smile, and I kissed my way down his jawline, running my tongue over his chin. He jerked up on the couch as my lips closed around that throbbing spot on his neck, my tongue swirling and my teeth nipping. He moaned again, louder this time, his hands on my shoulders and fingers beginning to dig for purchase.

From the corner of my eye, I could already tell he was rock hard. The tent he pitched himself in my shorts was big enough to house an entire family. It twitched as I sucked his neck a little harder. I grinned, enjoying this to the nth degree.

So I took my time. I sucked on his neck, moved to a new spot, moved my hands over his chest but left his throbbing cock alone. He gave himself a couple of needy strokes once I had lifted his shirt and started to suck on his pebbled nipples. It was clear he couldn't get enough of this, and I wanted to show him that I felt the same.

I posted up on my knees, my cock pushing hard against my shorts. The light green fabric had already turned a shade darker from the precome that leaked out of me.

Noah's eyes went wide, locking in on my bulge. He reached for it, rubbing it, licking his lips before he leaned in, mouthing me over the fabric. He rubbed his face into it, smelling my scent, moaning as he buried his nose between my legs, my bulge covering half his face.

I leaned down, grabbing his in my hand. It was rock solid, firm, and warm in my grip, radiating heat even through the thin layer of fabric that separated us.

"Fuck, Noah, is this bad?" I asked, Noah already working to pull my shorts down.

"Only if you think it is. I certainly don't."

"So this won't fuck up our friendship?"

Noah licked his lips again, looking up at me as he pulled the waistband over my stiff cock, letting it spring free. "It might do the exact opposite," he said, eyes glued to my throbbing length. He took it in his hands, both of them closing around my shaft and causing me to close my eyes in bliss. I pushed my hips forward, and he knew exactly what to do, leaning forward and wrapping those sexy wet lips around me.

A hiss escaped my chest, like a balloon popping somewhere between my ribs. He encased me in heat, his tongue dancing underneath the sensitive head, flicking across it, tasting me. He opened wider, took more of me down his throat, working what he couldn't get in his mouth with a soft hand, fingers gently massaging my balls.

"Jesus, Noah, your mouth is heaven."

He pulled off me, a string of saliva breaking from his lips and falling to the couch. "Oh, really?"

"Really," I said, pushing my hips forward again, my glistening cock rubbing against Noah's smiling lips. Part of me couldn't believe this was happening, and that made it all the more hotter. I remembered seeing Noah for the first time, sitting behind his desk, looking bored with whatever work he had to deal with, and yet I still found him to be one of the most attractive people I'd ever laid eyes on. Those days unraveled, and I came to know Noah as more than just that bored and handsome guy sitting three office spaces away from me.

And now I knew him even better. Knew how good he could work his mouth and how much of me he could fit inside of it.

"*Fuuuuck,*" I said, another hiss escaping as my fingers threaded through Noah's hair. "That's it, baby. Try to swallow it all. Mhmm, just like that." I pushed down on Noah's head, feeding him my entire size. His nose was buried in my pubes, his eyes looking up at me, watery, his mouth full of me, his tongue massaging me.

I started to fuck him, thrusting my cock into his mouth, down his throat. He took it, swallowing me like a professional circus performer working with swords. He had one hand on the back of the couch and the other on my thigh, pulling me in further. My balls slapped against his wet chin, the sounds of our sex filling the room, grunts and moans and wet macaroni squishing in a pot. All of it.

And it was getting me close. Too close. I hadn't even gotten Noah out of his shorts. I couldn't come yet.

I slowed down, pulled back, Noah sitting back with a gasp of air filling his lungs. I stroked myself, using his spit as lube, my palm gliding up and down. "Take those off," I said, looking down at his straining shorts.

He didn't think twice. Noah pulled down his shorts and kicked them off, his hard dick smacking against his stomach. Pink and firm, uncircumcised, throbbing, a clear drop of precome pooling at the tip.

Fucking delicious. I got off the couch and down onto my knees, parting his legs a little wider and holding him in my hands, holding his cock so that it stood aimed up at the ceiling, pulsing in my grip. I'd never seen a better-looking dick. And it wasn't like dicks were known to be particularly *pretty*, although I personally found them all to be attractive in their own way, but Noah's dick was just... *fuck*.

"Jerk off for me," I said, leaning back just so I could watch.

Noah took himself in one hand.

"Hold up," I said, leaning in and spitting on the head. "There. Go."

His smirk turned lusty as he began to jerk himself off, using my spit as lube, spreading it up and down his shaft. He used his thumb to go over the head, lifting it to show off a clear string of precome. He went back to stroking, mixing his precome and my saliva, closing his eyes and opening his legs. His balls tightened, his free hand rubbing on his chest.

"Fuck, Noah, keep going. Just like that."

I spit into my own hand and started to stroke, my core wound as tight as a spring about to snap. Watching Noah pleasure himself was one of the hottest damn things I'd ever laid eyes on. Seeing him thrust into his hand, his head falling back with his eyes shut and his lips shaped to form an O, it drove me wild. I jerked myself off harder, biting into my lower lip.

Part of me wanted to get up and sit on his lap, taking him inside me inch by inch. My hole clenched, my cock throbbed. I wanted him, so fucking bad. I needed him inside me, needing that beautiful cock stretching me open.

"God, I'm so fucking close, Noah."

I kept stroking but pressed a wet finger up against my hole, imagining that as Noah, teasing me before plunging into me.

"Me too," he said in a husky voice, his toes curling down into the floor. A red flush spread through his chest, catching like fire and spreading up his neck, coloring his cheeks. He opened his eyes, locked them on mine.

And he blew, a jet of come flying up and hitting him in the chin, his legs stretched out and his shoulders twitching, eyes wide and eyebrows dipped. He shot more of his seed, some of it dripping down his side, pooling at his belly button.

It was enough to send me over the edge. I rose up and gave myself one last stroke before I let it all go with a roar, Noah's body covered in sticky wet come by the time I was done. Once the tidal wave receded, the two of us started to chuckle, the laughter a natural reaction to the flood of endorphins and oxytocin that currently made me feel as if I was floating on a cloud. I leaned down and kissed him, tasting some of me on his lips.

"Get me a towel," he said, splayed out like a starfish. "Before I become crazy-glued to your couch."

I stood up, laughing some more, cock still dripping. There wasn't a single cell in my body that didn't feel completely at ease and relaxed, the lazy grin staying on my face as I returned with a towel. Noah reached for it, but I shook my head, crouching down instead and wiping him clean delicately, making sure to get the river that ran down his hips, cleaning out the pool in his belly button and where his chest dipped inward. I kissed him after, the both of us hard again, the smiles going nowhere.

"Want to shower?" I asked.

"Maybe we should get a little more dirty first," he said, playfully tugging on my hard cock.

How could I resist? How could I say no? There wasn't a way in the world. Nothing would get me to leave this man's presence for the night.

Nothing.

I grabbed him, lifting him in my arms and surprising him. He giggled, kissed on my neck as I brought us to my bedroom. There, I laid him down gently on the bed and caged him between my arms, locking him in another kiss. I had no idea what tonight meant or what it would bring, but I didn't want to think too much about it. All I wanted to focus on was the feeling of our dicks rubbing together, both of us as hard as steel. If we had to make a promise in the morning, once the sun came up and the lusty-drunk haze lifted, about never doing this again so that we could keep our friendship intact, then so be it.

But that would come in the morning, and I planned on coming a lot more before then.

The night wrapped us up like a velvet blanket threaded with starlight. We played with each other for hours, interspersed with easy and jokey conversation as our bodies cooled down, only to wind right back up again moments later. And then one cock would be in a mouth and the other in a hand and legs in the air and moans filling the room.

Needless to say, it was a dreamy kind of night. One that I was sure I'd remember for the rest of my life.

Unfortunately, the dreamy feeling was shattered sometime around five in the morning. We'd fallen asleep about an hour before, naked and wrapped up together on top of the covers, our bodies spent and our hearts full.

It was around then, at the crack of dawn, when my home alarm went off, blaring through the house and jolting us both awake.

13

NOAH BARNES

AT FIRST, I thought I was dreaming. That the entire night had been a long and sultry fantasy, confined solely to the time when my eyes were shut and reality faded away.

Then the alarm in my dream got louder, and my eyes snapped open, and Jake shot up on the bed, throwing the comforter off him and reaching for his phone.

This wasn't a dream at all. "False alarm?" I asked, throwing a nervous glance at the door, which was slightly ajar, a slice of the dark hall appearing to shift with shadows.

I knew I should have closed the door before we fell asleep.

"It sometimes gets tripped by a faulty window downstairs. Let me check," he said, speaking loud over the competing sirens. He opened the app to his security system and looked at the screen, eyebrows knitting together. That didn't appear like the face of someone who thought this was a false alarm. Then his eyes grew wider, and he thumbed at the screen, holding it up to his ear and facing away from me.

"Yes, someone tried to get into my home. I need the police here immediately."

It was like someone punched me in the gut. My body entered fight-or-flight mode, my heart pounding so hard that I was sure it would tear through my chest at any moment. Either that or just completely collapse in on itself from exhaustion.

"Okay, thank you." He turned to me, moving to the door and shutting it. Locking it. He turned on the light, allowing me to see his anxious expression in 4K.

"What's going on?" I asked. "Should I be putting on my underwear? I don't want to die naked."

It was a joke. A way for me to rationalize the absolute and utter terror that started to wrap itself around my throat. Jake chuckled, offered me a strained smile. It made me feel slightly better. Even though I had no idea what the hell was going on, seeing Jake manage even the smallest of smiles made me feel like we weren't about to lose our lives in some home invasion. "Put on some clothes but not because you're in any danger," he said. "Whoever tried to get in here was scared off by the alarm."

I breathed a sigh of relief, getting out of bed and rummaging through the bedroom, finding a pair of gym shorts that I was positive weren't even mine, but I pulled them on regardless, finding my shirt on the dresser.

"Is the person gone?" I asked, going over to Jake's side and far from the now shut bedroom door.

"I think so."

That didn't sound very reassuring. I swallowed a lump, looking at the door again with a renewed sense of dread. It was the kind of fear that stole the voice from you, throwing me back to being a kid when my mom and I were home alone on a week my dad had a work trip and a similar situation occurred. I woke up to the blare of alarms, my mom in a panic as she rushed into my bedroom and slammed the door behind her. But we only had landlines back then, so she'd be calling out to the police, and they'd be calling in, and no one could get through. So it was about five minutes of utter panic, with my mom telling me to just stay on my bed and to be very quiet. I listened, crying into my pillow so that I wouldn't make a sound, even though it wouldn't even be heard over the alarm.

Finally, the police got through, the alarm stopped, and they came and searched the place. Turns out, someone had broken in. They smashed through the basement window and took a few meaningless items before they decided to make a run for it. But I always wondered what would have happened if they were more bold? If they came upstairs? Or if my mom decided to go downstairs herself before the cops showed up? Would that night have had a vastly different impact on my life?

This night felt oddly similar to that one. Where one single decision could change the outcome and get us hurt —or worse.

Jake turned off the alarm and looked through the two cameras he had, one on the front door and one on the deck of his backyard. Neither showed any activity or movement, the peaceful scene painted in a brightening orange as the sun started to come up on this chaotic morning. He rewound the footage, scrubbing through it a second at a time.

It was about five minutes prior that the rear camera caught someone running through the yard, wearing a black sweater with the hood thrown over their head. They only appeared on-screen for a couple of seconds and never looked toward the camera, so all we got was their frame and stature, but maybe that was enough?

"Do you recognize them?"

I took a breath, partially shocked at the fact that this was my life right now. I had spent one of the best nights of my entire life with Jake—friend, coworker, walking wet dream—and yet it was capped by the fact that someone was now *following* me. And for what? What did they plan on doing if the alarm hadn't gone off?

"I don't. That could be almost anyone."

"Wait, see that? What are they holding?"

Jake brought the phone closer up to our faces. Sure enough, the person running away was holding something in their hands. "Another package?" I asked.

"Maybe..." Jake said. "But then why try to break in?"

"Unless it wasn't a package and they had other plans with whatever was in there?" My thoughts crashed into a dozen different brick walls. I looked to the door again. Any second now, I expected the hinges to blow off the wall and the door to come crashing inward, whoever was behind this twisted shit standing there wearing a mask and holding a gun. When was this nightmare going to end?

Sirens sounded from down the street, cutting through the quiet of the early morning. Neighbors were likely just waking up, zombie-walking their way to their coffee makers and putting together lunches for their kids, the morning news playing in a dark living room and now police lights flashing through the blinds. Once again, I felt myself at the center of a very fucked-up kind of attention, and what was worse was that I'd brought Jake directly into the center of the storm. Just by staying over his for the night, I had put him in danger.

Maybe that's a sign last night has to be the last...

The thought struck me like a dagger between my ribs. I yanked it out, focusing on the problem at hand instead.

Jake flipped the footage so that it showed his doorbell camera, and he scrubbed through that one with the same intensity. My mind reeled, unable to focus, barely registering a single thing that was on-screen.

Until a car drove past the camera. A beat-up Honda with a sun-damaged green paint job. This angle didn't let me see the decal, but that didn't matter—the entire license plate was in full view. I recognized those letters, having poked fun at Franky once for the plate spelling out BLLZ, which sounded very much like "balls," and for someone deep in the closet, I thought that was a good touch from the universe.

And there it was. Franky and his balls driving down

the street at a speed that must have been illegal, disappearing from view.

Except it wasn't only the decal I couldn't see. "Rewind it," I told Jake, hoping against all hope... nothing. I couldn't tell who was in the driver's seat, even though I was sure that was Franky's car.

"That's him, isn't it?" Jake asked, already reading my thoughts.

"I... it's his car. I just can't see him. But it has to be."

A slash of anger crossed over Jake's features. Pure and fiery, the kind of anger reserved only for someone who proved to be vile, the scummiest of scums. His brow furrowed, and his cheek flinched as he bit down on it, jaw tensed. It was so starkly different from the loving and sensual man I'd experienced for hours on end, his eyes as soft as silk even though his body proved to be as hard as diamonds.

"This ends today," he said, just as the doorbell rang, the police announcing their presence loud enough for the entire block to hear.

"Huh?" I asked, following behind him, walking into the dark hall and feeling my mouth go instantly dry, imagining all kinds of horrors in the shadows. They were immediately banished once Jake flipped on the lights, washing away any fear of the unknown as we continued down the steps and toward the front door.

"I'm going to talk to him," Jake said. "You're giving me Franky's information, and I'm going to speak to him."

My mouth fell into a slant, my head cocked to the side. "I don't think that's a good idea."

"It's the only idea I've got. I doubt the police can do anything without having an actual ID or proof that it was him trying to break in and not just driving through the neighborhood. So I'm going to confront him and ask him why the fuck he's harassing my, eh, good friend."

The pause before the title made me stumble a bit.

"Let's just talk to the police and figure out what they say." I crossed my arms, shaking my head. "I don't want you getting involved in this. At all."

"I think it's a little late for that," he said, hand on the doorknob. "But it's going to be okay, alright? I promise you." He reached out and rubbed my arm, his cool blue eyes swirling with confidence. I believed him, even though I wasn't sure how the hell this would turn out alright. Not unless Franky was in handcuffs and behind bars by the end of the day. That's the only outcome I could see as being a positive one; everything else left me living in a constant state of fear and anxiety.

And now I was wrapping Jake up into it. When we weren't even anything other than good friends. He didn't need to be doing this, opening the door to speak with the grim-faced officers or offering to go confront one of my psychotic exes.

So what did it say about him that he was ready and willing to do all of that and more?

And what did it say about me that I kind of loved it?

14

JAKE PEREZ

I WAS RIGHT. The cops couldn't do much, not without having a clear visual of Franky trying to get into my house. They said they would try and talk to him but couldn't make any promises. All they could do was say to call them if anything else came up, which wasn't at all the answer I was looking for.

So I decided to take matters into my own hands. I convinced Noah to give me Franky's address under the condition that I take him with me. Confrontation wasn't at all my thing, and I normally avoided it at all costs, but this was getting out of hand. We knew it was his car, we had video evidence of him being around the area whenever shit went down, so what else was there to do *but* confront him? Maybe if he realized we were onto him, then he'd stop whatever it was he was trying to do.

It wasn't the best plan, but it was the only one I had, and I was quickly realizing that I'd do whatever I needed to so that I could see Noah smiling, worry-free. The way he smiled when it was just us, wrapped up together under the comforter, his warm eyes speaking volumes without any words being shared between us. It was dangerous—how quickly I was falling for him. Harder than I'd ever fallen for anyone before, and that scared the everlasting fuck out of me. I didn't even know where his head was at, but I was ready to lock it all down after a single night with him.

Dangerous but exciting. A thrill that harkened back to being a high schooler about to ask my crush out to prom. When the stakes felt higher than the Empire State Building itself. It was the kind of buzz that scrambled my thoughts, made crazy ideas seem reasonable and wild fantasies seem like everyday realities.

That's how I found myself sitting outside of a nondescript townhouse with a nervous Noah in the passenger seat, ready to puff up my chest and get this shit over with so we could move on with our lives and figure things out between us without stressing about some crazy ex.

"You sure you want to do this?" Noah asked as he nervously bit his fingernail.

"I am. I just want some answers, but you can stay in the car. I don't want to put you in a difficult spot or anything."

"No, I think I should talk to him, too. I just... it doesn't make any sense. And what the hell are we going to say? Why are you threatening me with a bloody chicken head and following me around?"

"We can start with that, yeah." I reached over and rubbed Noah's leg. "It'll be okay. If things get heated, then we leave, but I plan on keeping everything civil. I'm not a fighter."

"Neither am I. Much more of a lover."

"I could vouch for that," I said with a wink. "Maybe I can get some of that lover side of you after this is done?"

"We'll see," Noah replied, his tone implying that we would most definitely see.

I don't really know what came over me, what pushed me forward, but I didn't really care either. I kissed Noah. Soft and sweet, tasting the reminders of our night together. He smiled, lips slightly parted.

Unexpected, my friend. Unexpected.

I didn't give him a chance to respond. With a deep breath, I opened the door and got out, unsure of how this would go but feeling good that I was at least doing something. Noah was at my side as we walked down the flower-lined path and up the cracked concrete stairs. One of the handrails was missing, which made it very easy to imagine someone tripping and slamming themselves down on the ground. The beat-up green car sat out on the driveway next to a newer and recently washed Mercedes. The candy-blue paint job glittered as if the car was encrusted with diamonds.

Interesting how he didn't drive that one around. It was as if he *wanted* to get recognized by Noah.

I rang the bell, the chime sounding through the house and causing a chorus of dog barks to float through the open windows. Moments later, the door opened, a woman wearing an apron and holding a jug of milk appearing in the doorway. She tucked a strand of brunette hair behind an earring-lined ear, the trail of diamond studs shining almost as bright as the car. "Can I help you?"

"Hi, yes, we're looking for Franky. Is he home by any chance?" I tried to sound as unassuming as possible, even though my nerves were buzzing.

"What is this about?" She sized the two of us up, taking a step so that she planted herself firmly in the center of the threshold.

"We're old friends," I lied, hoping that would get her to relax a little bit. "I know showing up unannounced isn't the most polite thing to do, but we—"

"Susan, who are you talking to?"

She looked over her shoulder. "I don't know. These two guys say they're old friends of yours?"

She stepped to the side, which gave me my first good look at Franky.

He was a stocky guy, clearly lifted weights, and had tattoos going up and down his legs, disappearing underneath a long pair of black shorts. He wore a T-shirt that advertised some kind of cleaning business called Frankly Franky's Cleaning Service, a cartoon representation of himself covered in soap suds holding up the letters. He looked to me first before looking to Noah, their eyes meeting and all the color draining from Franky's face. He stepped in front of his wife.

"I've got this."

Her brow furrowed together, questions clear on her expression.

"Go, get inside, Susan. It's fine."

"Are they really your friends?"

"We know each other, yeah. Haven't seen them in years, though, and I'm not real fond of surprises." He took another step forward, forcing us to move back. Now that the initial shock of seeing Noah at his doorstep was fading, it appeared to be replaced by a growing anger, reflected in the cherry-red color that started to spread across his cheeks like a bad rash. "Go. I'm fine."

Susan gave one last skeptical glare before shrugging and going back inside the house, closing the door behind her with a heavy thud.

Franky turned all his focus onto Noah. "What the fuck are you doing here?" He looked back over his shoulder at the shut door before pointing to the sidewalk. "Explain it down there," he said, moving forward again, nearly pushing us this time. I took the hint, not putting up any resistance and instead going down the steps with Noah, stopping on the sidewalk. The dogs—three of them, all clustered together in a window—continued to bark, getting louder now that they could see us.

"We wanted to ask you a similar question," Noah said, keeping his calm, even though the way he picked at the palm of his hand revealed how nervous he really was. "Franky, I know we ended on terrible terms, but I genuinely thought we were both on the same page. So why are you leaving me threatening packages? Why are you trying to break into my friend's house? Huh?"

Franky's face scrunched up as if he'd just popped a Warhead into his mouth. "What the hell are you talking about?"

"There was a box left at my door addressed to me, and it had a severed chicken head and a Pride necklace in there. There's footage of your car driving away from my community around that same time. Then, last night, we were woken up by an alarm—someone tried breaking in. And, once again, we have footage of your car leaving the area. So tell me the truth, Franky. Why are you doing any of this?"

He should have changed the name of his company to Flabbergasted Franky's Cleaning Service because the guy looked completely bamboozled. He shook his head, rubbing a hand over his face. "Seriously? You show up to my house for this crap?"

"I wouldn't consider Noah's safety and well-being as *crap*," I said, getting the urge to punch this guy's lights out. If not for being a dick, then also for breaking Noah's heart.

"Listen, I don't want my wife asking any questions. You two need to get off my property before I call the cops." Franky cracked his fingers into a fist in a school-yard display of aggression.

"Don't worry," I said, "we already called them. They said they were going to have a word with you. But that can all be pulled back as long as you tell the truth and stop playing these crazy games."

He scoffed, the cherry red spreading down his jaw, onto his neck. "I didn't do shit. I haven't thought about you in years, Noah. Why the hell would I fuck up my life trying to fuck with yours?" He shot another glance back up at the house. I could tell he didn't want his wife hearing any of this. I wondered how she'd feel if she found out this "old friend" of her husband's was actually a long-term boyfriend, the two of them in a secret relationship that could have worked out if Franky hadn't chosen to stuff himself in the closet.

She'd probably be pretty upset, and Franky knew that. It explained why he wanted her back in the house and far removed from this conversation as quickly as possible.

"I... well, I'm not sure," Noah said. He moved a swoop of dark hair that curled down onto his forehead back into place before chewing on his fingernails again.

"Your car was clearly visible in the footage, twice now. I think that's enough to prove you're involved in what's happening to Noah. Here, I can show you the tapes."

Franky clicked his tongue, waving a hand in the air and coming dangerously close to knocking my phone out of my grip. "You don't need to show me shit. I don't care. I wasn't the one driving the car."

"So who was, then?" Noah asked.

"I lent it out. That night you saw me driving it out of your neighborhood was because I had gotten it back."

My eyes narrowed as I tried to read this man. Was he lying? Trying to throw us off his trail? Or was he saying the truth... if he really did lend his car out, then maybe whoever had it was responsible for the threat. "To who?" I asked.

"Come back with a fucking badge if you want answers. I'm done with this shit." He turned and started back up the steps, but I didn't feel like we were finished with this. It was the complete opposite. We were on the cusp of finding another puzzle piece; we just had to get it out of Franky first.

"It'd be a shame if your wife was brought into the investigation," I said, knowing my words might be lighting a fuse and unsure of just how big the blast would be. "Having to hear about the relationship her husband kept secret from her."

Noah looked at me with wide eyes. I couldn't back down now, though. I had to keep pressing, and judging by the way Franky was now frozen midstep, I seemed to have found the right button to push.

"Help us so that it doesn't get that far."

Franky spun around, fast. Too fast for me to react. He practically leaped down the last three steps and was in my face in seconds, fists holding bundles of my shirt. "Don't you dare fucking threaten me." His breath smelled like a mixture of rotten eggs and beer. Maybe his cleaning service needed to be hired out for his inflamed gums before they cleaned any more houses.

"Whoa, whoa, whoa, everyone, calm down." Noah had his hands out like a lion tamer, trying to get the situation under control without having his face bitten off.

"Who the fuck do you think you are?" Franky asked me, ignoring Noah's plea to keep the peace. There was an unchecked rage inside of Franky's beady eyes, his grip tightening on my shirt, so tight that the neckline started to choke me. I realized then that I hadn't thrown a punch in about ten years, going back to a fight I had in college over a roommate's constant loud music. It had been dumb, and no one was hurt, but I had come out as the loser in that fight, with a black eye and a swollen lip that hurt for almost an entire week.

Hmmm... maybe this wasn't a good idea after all.

15

NOAH BARNES

OH NO. This was bad. Worst-case scenario. The nuclear reactor was melting down, and total annihilation was only moments away. I reached for Franky's hands, grabbing his forearms and telling him to stop again, but he ignored me, pushing me to the side instead with a force that nearly made me fall on my ass.

Jake didn't seem to like that. He swiped up, hard, hitting his forearm against Franky's arms, causing him to break his grip.

The physical touch seemed to be all Franky needed to escalate the situation. He started to swing, punching out at Jake's head and chest. But Jake was faster, stepping backward onto the street, fists up. My heart hurt with how hard it beat inside my chest.

Franky went in again, landing a punch to Jake's side. He winced. I cried out, shouting at them to stop. Neither listened. It was Jake's turn to throw a hit. Franky tried to block it, grabbing at Jake's wrist, but Jake had momentum on his side. His knuckles connected with Franky's lower jaw, producing an audible crack and sending Franky spiraling down onto the floor, where he broke his fall with hands and knees.

The door to the townhome opened, and out flew Susan, practically leaping down the steps before crouching over her husband. "What the hell did you do to him?"

I was back at Jake's side. His hand was getting pink from the impact, but other than that, he didn't seem hurt.

"Gave him a taste of his own medicine," Jake said, shaking his hand out.

She looked up at us with anger radiating from behind her glasses. Her eyes bounced from Jake to me, drilling directly through me. "Go. Go *now*. And if I ever see you or Noah here again, I will be calling the police."

There was no room in her tone for arguing. Acid dripped from her gaze, melting holes into the pavement at her feet. Franky groaned but was beginning to get back up. I wanted Jake in the car and miles away before that happened. I grabbed him by the elbow and turned us around, hurriedly getting into my car. As the doors shut, Frank stood up and started toward us, shouting something that couldn't be heard without lowering the windows.

I didn't stick around to figure it out either. I threw the car in reverse and peeled out of their driveway, my foot hitting the gas pedal a little harder than intended. Franky ran into the middle of the street, still shouting profanities, his wife trying to hold him back from chasing after us on foot.

"Are you alright?" I asked Jake as Franky and Susan grew smaller and smaller in the rearview mirror. I realized my grip around the steering wheel was tight enough to snap it in half. I forced in a breath, trying to get my body to relax, to come down from the flood of adrenaline that currently circled around my system.

"Hand's a little sore, but yeah, I'm fine. I didn't want it to get to that."

"I know," I said, looking over at Jake. The afternoon sun slanted in through the windshield and made his perfect complexion glitter as if he were a half vampire pulled straight out of a *Twilight* fanfic. "It was kind of hot, though."

He shot me a wink, lips turned up into a grin. "Well, I'm glad you enjoyed it because there won't be an encore performance."

"Good," I replied. "I got my fix, and it looks like Franky did, too. What a dick. An extremely unhelpful dick."

"I was hoping for some solid answers. But maybe if it is him, this is enough to get him to stop."

I shook my head, something about this still not clicking for me. I just couldn't see a motive, besides the fact that maybe he still hated me for making him confront his sexuality? Was he punishing me for it, or was there something else we were missing? "And what if he was telling the truth about lending his car out?"

Jake huffed out a breath. "That's excuse 101. An easy

lie for him to say without much of a way for us to dispute it. Especially if he doesn't want to tell us *who* he lent his car to. I think he was saying that just to get us off his trail."

I slowed to a stop at a red light. We were now in a more expensive part of the neighborhood, where the homes were further off from the road and circled by tall fences and pristine landscaping. There were political signs on most of their front lawns, making it clear that it was also a primarily liberal neighborhood, which actually wasn't rare for a city like Atlanta.

"We're going to have to look at the tapes again," I said. "There has to be a way to figure out who was driving. We can CSI that shit."

"We can certainly try to," Jake said, keeping his spirits up.

A thought struck me, one that had been teetering on the edge of my focus since we'd started to drive away from Franky's house. "Wait, hold up... when we were leaving, did Susan say my name?"

Jake took a moment to think about that. He nodded, confirming my suspicion. "I think so, yeah. Why?"

"I've never met her before. How does she know who I am?"

He shrugged. "Did we use our names when we introduced ourselves? I can't remember."

"No, I don't think we did."

"Maybe she heard Franky saying it. She was probably eavesdropping by the door the second it shut."

"Maybe..." I tried forcing the puzzle pieces together,

trying to make sense of all this. Franky didn't seem guilty, but his reaction wasn't exactly helping prove his innocence. He clearly still wanted to stay in the closet, and maybe that was feeding some kind of hate-filled monster inside him? It could explain why he was lashing out at me, suddenly fixated on where I was and who I was with.

But what if it wasn't him? Then that meant someone out there was even *more* interested in torturing me than Franky. And we were no closer to figuring out who that person was.

My anxiety started to spiral. I could feel it in the way my chest contracted and my head felt as light as a cloud. "I'm freaking out," I said out loud, keeping focus on the road and simultaneously trying to calm my hammering heart. "Like, legit, I'm starting to really freak out."

Jake must have heard the tremble in my voice. He reached out and put a hand on my thigh, squeezing, his thumb rubbing soft circles. "Right now, you're completely safe. As long as I'm by your side, you're safe. So don't think about the scary what-ifs and focus on the nows instead. Everything is okay."

It was a bald-faced lie. A complete fabrication. A damn fairy tale.

And yet I ate it up all the same. Jake's words struck a chord in me, pushing back some of the waves that had threatened to crest over my head and drag me down into the tide. He spoke with an assurance that sold his lies as fact. I knew he couldn't see the future; he couldn't promise me that everything was, in all actuality, *okay*.

But just having him here, in my car, speaking in that

gravelly tone of his, it was the balm I needed. My lungs filled with air, something they were incapable of doing only seconds ago. My head wasn't light anymore, although my heart still felt like it was lodged somewhere in my throat. "Thank you, Jake. For all of this. For calming me down, for confronting Franky, for trying to figure this all out with me. I'm really glad we bumped into each other at the store that one night."

Jake's smile was effortless, his blue eyes sparkling with the memory. It was enough to silence all of my nervous thoughts, vanquished by the Prince Charming sitting beside me. "It definitely feels like one of those nights that changes things, ya know? So many little things had to line up to make that happen. The smallest shift could have had us barely crossing paths in the store. Maybe one of us took two minutes longer looking for parking, or you chose to go to a liquor store instead of the supermarket. But everything worked out perfectly."

"It really did," I said, matching the intensity of his grin. "And if you weren't a big reader, I doubt I would have told you to come to the book club, which really propelled things."

"*Things*, huh? What do you think got propelled?" He looked over at me, a slight arch in his brow, his grin still wide.

Ah, crap. He got me cornered. "Our, uh, friendship. We went from casual work friends to... really good friends."

"Great friends."

"Best friends."

He chuckled, looking out the window. The streets were widening, and the buildings were growing taller as we drove deeper into the city. "What do you think about walking around Piedmont Park? Maybe we can have lunch on the Beltline. The weather's nice, and I really wouldn't mind some fresh air. Or spending the day with you."

I couldn't tamp down my smile. It stretched up my cheeks, my eyes crinkling. The bubbly sensation made me feel as if my blood had been replaced with champagne. Fizzy. Excited. And all because of the simple prospect of hanging out with Jake for the entire day.

"Yeah, let's do that. I think that's a great idea," I said, looking over and seeing Jake matching my grin. "Bestie."

He laughed, licked his lips, and looked out the window again so that his jawline cut a sharp crease across his face, highlighted by the sunlight. He was fine art. Perfect angles and flawless symmetry. He didn't have a good side because all of them were great. As if painted by a master artist, almost unreal.

And I'm supposed to be friends with him? How is that going to work when all I want to do is climb him like a fucking tree twenty-four seven?

16

JAKE PEREZ

A SQUIRREL SKITTERED UP A TREE, leaping onto a branch and bringing up the nut it had in its tiny hands, stuffing it into its cheek as it eyed everyone that walked underneath his home.

Piedmont Park was packed with people. Families were gathered on blankets, kids ran around the emerald-green grass, there was a game of flag football going on, joggers were doing their laps, and friends celebrating Sunday Funday were riding around on scooters. The skyline was framed by towering office and apartment buildings, their metallic and stone peaks reaching up to a cloudless sky, as if even they wanted to emphasize just how nice the day was.

It was exactly the kind of environment I wanted to be in after the shitshow of a morning Noah and I had. My knuckles were still sore, and disbelief at what happened still filtered through me, but the more we walked and joked around with each other, the more normal I began to feel. There were very few people I'd throw a punch for in this world, one of them being the man currently sipping on iced coffee and telling me a story about his first time out of the country.

"It was pretty wild," he said as we moved aside while a bachelorette party zoomed past us on their scooters, the bride wearing a white-and-pink sash around her chest. "Thankfully, I learned pretty quickly how to drive on the other side of the road. But drinking water without ice? Now, that's where I had to draw the line."

I chuckled, drinking some of my hazelnut-infused coffee. The sweetness swirled down my throat. "Was London a dream trip for you?"

He nodded. I couldn't help but notice the tiny beat of a pulse in his neck, right where I'd had my lips pressed against the night before. "It was," he answered. "I definitely want to go back, but I think my next big trip is going to be to Australia. How about you?"

"Spain," I said. "Australia seems fun, but there's too many animals that can kill you over there. I'd rather go eat some tapas and hang out on the beach. Plus, Spanish architecture is just unbeatable."

"I'd just be nervous since I don't know much Spanish. I can say hi and 'como esta,' but that's about it."

"I can translate for you," I said before realizing what that statement sounded like.

"So you're stuffing me in your suitcase for the trip?" He winked at me, straw sitting in the corner of his mouth, bright white teeth gently pressing down on the tip as he smiled.

"I'd rather have you sitting next to me on the plane. It's a long flight."

"I can practice my Spanish on the way, then."

I shrugged, looking ahead at the curling gates leading into the Botanical Gardens. "Or we can keep ourselves busy some other way."

Noah nearly tripped. He took a big sip of his drink, gulping it down. I watched his Adam's apple move as he swallowed. Another target for my lips, tongue, teeth to graze against. "Are you talking about joining a certain club measured in miles?"

"That's the one. Do you already have a membership card?"

Noah shook his head. His cheeks took on a flush that I was seriously becoming obsessed with. I loved teasing this guy, making him all flustered and rosy pink. And it wasn't very hard to do either. I could give him a wink and a lick of my lips and he'd be morphing into a strawberry with legs.

"Well," I said, "we can become first-time members together, then."

"I can't even imagine how that happens. Those bathrooms are *sooo* tiny."

I scoffed, taking a sip of my coffee. "Oh, I can definitely imagine. All you have to do is push me up against the wall and have your way with me."

Noah's eyes went wide, cheeks catching fire. See? Easy.

"Oh, look, the Botanical Gardens is having a glass-blowing exhibit. Wanna check it out?" I asked, as if I didn't just tell Noah to fuck me inside of an airplane bathroom.

"Uh, yeah, yeah, that sounds good." He blinked a couple of times, as if trying to clear away the surprise from my statement. I laughed and bumped a shoulder into him. His gaze rose to meet me, catching some of the sunlight and making his eyes glitter like two emerald-green jewels. The bright green shirt he had on helped enhance the colors, hypnotizing me. I wanted to lean in and kiss him, right there and then.

But he turned away from me, walking toward the entrance to the gardens, his perky bubble butt bouncing around in his tight khaki shorts. Suddenly, I wanted to do so much more than kiss him. I wanted to explore him with my tongue, burying my face in that juicy ass.

We're going to need to talk about this friend thing between us.

I decided to file away that thought for later. A discussion about what we were to each other could be extremely beneficial or extremely detrimental. What if he decided to keep things as just friends? What if he didn't want to make anything awkward at work between us?

What if, what if, what if...

What if I'm spending the day with my better half? What if this is just the beginning?

We walked up to the ticket counter and got our tickets, along with a map of the gardens. It was deceptively large for being located in the center of a bustling city. An entire afternoon could be spent just lazily strolling through the azalea walk, wandering across the canopy walk and admiring all the blooming roses in the rose garden. I loved spending time here with friends who came to visit from out of state, impressing them with all the natural beauty found tucked inside of our concrete jungle.

I also enjoyed bringing dates here in the past, which was exactly what this was beginning to feel like.

Before we got started on our mini-adventure, we were interrupted by a surprised 'hey!'. We turned to see Mason holding a map in his hands, a camera dangling from his neck along with the multitude of necklaces. "Fancy seeing you two here."

"Mason, hey there," Noah said, offering a wide grin. Atlanta was a big city but still had the magic coincidences of a small town, making surprise meetings like these more common than somewhere like the labryinths that were New York or LA.

"I've been meaning to stop by," he said, putting the map into his back pocket. I noticed his eyes wandered all over Noah, from head to toe, as if looking to make sure he was still all in one piece. "I haven't stopped thinking about you since that night. Everything ok?"

"As OK as it can be," Noah said. He glanced at me, smile flickering a little wider. "There's been a silver-lining to all of this mess."

"Good, I'm glad. I just can't imagine—Not that I can't imagine anyone stalking you. You're clearly an incredible handsome man with a very charming smile and now I'm sounding very weird. Jeez, I need to learn to filter myself sometimes." Mason's papery thin skin took on a flush of rose red, his cheeks turning into bloody spotlights.

"That's fine, I'm never one to turn down a couple of compliments." Noah chuckled. "Or baked goods. Wink wink."

"I'll be around later today with exactly that. The baked goods. Not compliments, unless you still want them. Ok, I'm done. You two go off on your romantic date. I was just heading home."

"Oh we aren't—" Noah didn't finish his sentence and I didn't bother to complete it for him, either. We waved goodbye to Mason and turned, the air between us crackling with a different kind of energy.

"*Ooook*. Where do you want to go first?" Noah asked, looking at the map, which gave me a chance to look at him, devouring him from head to toe, noticing that his bubble butt wasn't the only thing bulging in those khaki shorts.

I brought my thoughts back down to earth. "Want to check out the Cascade Gardens? Then we can make our way over to the orchid center?"

He nodded, smiling at me as he tucked the map into his back pocket. I was surprised there was still room there.

We took a right and started down a path flanked by bushy ferns and perfectly trimmed hedges. Even though it was a random spring Sunday, the gardens were pretty packed, with families pushing strollers and dates walking hand in hand, admiring all the colorful flowers and foliage. The path curved and rose over a tiny hill, opening up onto the Cascade Gardens, which the Earth Goddess called home. She was a living sculpture, massive in scale and covered with hundreds—if not thousands—of flowers that flowed down her long tendrils of hair. Her moss-covered hand was outstretched over a large pool, water falling down from between her fingers like a magical waterfall. It was serene and tranquil, a peacefulness that settled into your chest and made most conversations drift off as everyone stood around in silence to appreciate the beautiful living art.

"This is one of my favorite spots in the garden," I said to Noah, my voice low. He snapped a couple of pictures before lifting his phone in the air and flipping the camera. He leaned into me and smiled. I rested my head against his, matching the grin, both of our eyes gleaming as he took the picture.

"Send that to me," I said, already deciding that would be one of my favorite photos of all time.

"I will," he promised, pocketing his phone and turning back to the Earth Goddess. We soaked in the beauty for a couple more minutes before deciding to move on, walking down toward the azalea walk, which had one of the most stunning blown-glass sculptures I'd ever seen. It rose up at least twenty feet into the air, made of sunny yellow spikes that grew out of an ocean-blue center. It almost seemed like a real plant, belonging somewhere on an alien planet.

"Wow, that's crazy," Noah said, craning his head and shielding his eyes from the sun so he could see the entirety of the towering structure. "How can anyone make that?"

"Lots of dedication and lung strength," I said. "I took a glass-blowing course in college, actually. Thought it would be an easy A. Turned out to be the one class I almost failed."

Noah chuckled at that. He shook his empty coffee cup, the ice clanking around inside. "Where did you go to college?" he asked.

"University of Miami. It was close enough to home but far enough for me to be able to stretch my wings and figure things out on my own. It helped that I had a full-ride scholarship."

Noah nodded, impressed. "Yeah, I crossed that one off my list because of the tuition. And my grades weren't anywhere near good enough to get a scholarship."

"Where'd you go?" I asked.

"Stayed local. I went to the University of Georgia over in Athens. It was a good time, and I went with Eric and Tristan, so it felt like home from the start."

I smiled at that, happy his experience was so positive. "Eric and Tristan seem like really good guys."

"They are. They really, really are. Both of them have hearts of gold, and all three of us have each other's backs until the end. They're like my brothers at this point. How about you? What's your friend group like?"

I pursed my lips, shoulders dropping a bit. "Well, most of my closest friends were from UM, and we all kind of dispersed after college. When I moved back to Atlanta, I started dating, and my friends were mostly my partner's friends, which never really works out after a split. My closest friend here, oddly enough, is probably Ashley, my ex-girlfriend. I turned into her gay guru after she came out to me seconds after I proposed to her. It wasn't great, but it's exactly what needed to happen. I was feeling pressure to pop a question I really didn't want to ask and she was being pressured into staying with me.

After that day, we worked things out. I think I feel closer to her now than when we were dating. Is that weird?"

"Nah, I don't think it is. Sometimes people are just more compatible as friends than as lovers." His voice drifted off toward the end, as if he realized what he was saying could apply to us.

That made my heart skip a beat. Was he trying to insinuate something? Could this be his way of saying that we were better off as friends than as anything else?

Before I could ask him to elaborate, his phone pinged in his pocket. He took it out and read the message, sending back a quick reply before looking to me with a question in his gaze.

"What happened?" I asked, slowing down in front of a series of glass roses.

"I told Tristan we were around. He's at Blakes with his brother and wants us to join. You down?"

Blakes was the local gay watering hole, where people went for strong drinks and good music. I hadn't been in a while but definitely didn't mind showing up with Noah at my side. Hell, he could have asked me if I wanted to walk into the center of an active volcano with him and I likely would have said yes.

"Let's do it," I said, excited to spend the day with the intriguing and smiley man who was quickly capturing more than just my time and attention.

17

NOAH BARNES

BLAKE'S WAS a two-story bar filled with rainbow lights and TV screens playing pop divas on a loop. The first floor had a large bar at the center that served as a great place to post up and chat while sipping on a vodka tonic, with small bar-height tables pushed up against the surrounding walls where more groups of friends gathered. There were two competing kickball teams wearing their blue and green shirts, mingling around the tables next to the wide-open window that faced out to the street.

It was a cool spot and one of Tristan's favorite Sunday hangouts. He greeted us with a wide smile and a warm hug, introducing Jake to his little brother, Malik. He was visiting from Tampa after a brutal breakup, which explained the three empty cups that surrounded his half-full cup of rum and Coke.

"Thanks for the invite," I said to Tristan as I settled in, holding my drink with two hands. "It's been a day."

"Has it?" he asked. "What happened?"

That opened up the floodgates. Jake and I took turns telling the story, starting *after* we were woken up by the alarm (and hooked up multiple times). Tristan's and Malik's faces both dropped in shock once we got to the physical fighting part of the story.

"Damn, man." Tristan shook his head and lifted his drink. "Cheers to fucking that guy up and hopefully stopping this crazy stalker shit."

"Cheers to that," I said enthusiastically, raising my cup and tapping it against the others.

"And you're sure it was him?" Malik asked. He looked just like his older brother, all shiny white teeth and honey-brown eyes, with short dark hair that was usually kept buzzed down. He had a golden dangling earring and a thin gold necklace that popped against his dark skin. A tattoo of an octopus wrapped around his forearm, appearing to dance along with him as he moved.

Both Jake and I slightly deflated at his question. "No, we're not," I answered.

"But he's our most likely lead," Jake said, speaking like a detective. "We've got his car on camera, twice now, around the same time as when the incidents happened. Plus, Noah and Franky have history, which could lead to a motive. Maybe he's upset at the feelings Noah made him confront, and repressing them for these past few years maybe twisted him up."

That got the group nodding their heads in unison. "It does make sense," Tristan said.

I waved my hands over the table as if I were telling

people to stop their bets at a roulette table. "Enough of this spooky shit. Let's try and have some fun today. Malik, how long are you in town for?"

"Just until tomorrow. I needed to get out of my apartment. Too much shit happened there."

"Boy troubles?" I asked.

"Major. I found Peter cheating on me. In our own bed, after he told me he was visiting his sick sister. He thought I was out of town and, and—" Malik choked back tears. Tristan put an arm around his brother's shoulders and pulled him in for a hug.

"It's alright, Mal. You deserve better than that guy."

I nodded my agreement, trying to not let my heartbreak for Malik show on my face. I knew how much he loved his boyfriend, and I knew how much pain that inflicted when the love turned into venom injected straight into the veins. It was a toxic feeling that consumed your every thought, made every what-if moment that much larger, that much more pronounced. It was how I felt when Franky and I broke up, the days after finding me locked up in my bedroom and swearing off boys for the rest of my life.

"Not all men are trash," I said to Malik, shooting a glance at Jake. Tristan cocked his head, but before I could keep going with my pep talk, a firm hand clamped down on my shoulder. I turned, wondering who'd just popped through my personal space. The gay community in Atlanta was large but compact at the same time, and it wasn't unusual to spot friends—or old hookups—out and about.

This one was a friend. A best friend, actually.

"Hey, Eric," I said, going into a side hug. Tristan must have filled him in on where we were hanging out. He looked like he'd just finished working out at the gym with a slightly sweaty green tank top and bright pink Adidas shorts, matching the pink-and-blue sneakers he had on.

"What's up, dudes?"

"Nothing much," I answered after he made his round of hugs. "Just telling Malik here how not all men are complete and utter garbage bins. Some—okay, most—are, but there's a small handful out there that aren't, and it's worth it to keep looking for them."

Eric dipped his head from side to side. "Eh, I don't know. In my experience, every single guy I've dated has had some kind of major flaw."

"Yeah, but you're also extremely picky," Tristan pointed out. "Remember that one time you told a guy it wasn't going to work because he showed up to the first date wearing mismatched socks?"

"It was *one* of the reasons. But as soon as he started talking to me about his obsession with collecting quarters, I knew it was a no go."

"Says the one who collects bookmarks," Tristan shot back.

"It's a *small* collection. And so what? Bookmarks can be works of art. What the hell am I going to do with a rusty quarter from Colorado?"

That got us laughing. Jake jumped in, cutting through the chuckles. "I used to collect teeth."

We all froze. He blinked, seeming confused at our reaction.

"Teeth?" I ask, suddenly concerned about the man who just had me stuffed down his throat.

"What? No, I said *tees*, as in T-shirts. From wherever I went traveling to, either with my parents or with a school field trip or with friends, I'd always buy a T-shirt from there to bring back home. *Teeth?* Jesus Christ, I'm not Jeepers Creepers over here."

That got even more laughter from the group (and a flood of relief washing through me). I dramatically wiped the nonexistent sweat off my brow. "That makes much more sense."

He smiled at me, nudging me with an elbow before taking a drink. I noticed Tristan's attentive gaze picking up on it. I'd likely have some explaining to do later, except there wasn't really much for me to explain. Jake and I were just friends with a couple of great benefits between us. Nothing that deserved a long talk or explanation... unfortunately.

"Alright, now that we cleared that up, I'm going to get us another round of drinks. What do you all want?"

I mentally took down the drink orders and turned to head to the bar, leaving Jake to go into further detail about his T-shirt collection.

What an interesting man he is.

Whether it was discovering his love for *Cats* or his passion for a very specific kind of T-shirt, there was always another facet to him that I found fascinating. His love for his mother, his tenderness in caring for her, his excellent breakfast-making talents, and his vibrantly green thumb.

Then there was the way he made love—able to unravel me with a single touch, making me come undone over and over and over again, only to put me back together with a soft kiss and a gentle caress.

Just friends, I reminded myself as I waved down the bartender. *Just fucking friends.*

I gave my order to the cheery bartender, who danced to the Ariana Grande song as he poured vodka into a brass cup from an impressive height, the liquid flowing down like a clear waterfall. The guy next to me grabbed his cherry-red drink and turned to leave but stopped, catching my eye with his.

"Hey, do I know you?" he asked.

I gave him a quick once-over, trying to do a mental inventory of everyone I knew (or possibly hooked up with) that might have been this guy. He had short, cropped blond hair and a warm, friendly face with bright blue eyes that verged on looking fake. I was about to pretend as if I vaguely recognized him, but I saw the almost fish-shaped birthmark near his left eyebrow and realized I knew no one with that kind of birthmark.

"No, sorry, I don't think we've ever met."

He stuck out a hand, grinning like a Cheshire cat. "Name's Ron."

"Hi, Ron. I'm Noah." I shook his hand, his grip firm around mine. I could feel a couple of rough callouses on his palm.

"There, now we've met."

Smooth. His handshake lingered a little longer than I expected. "What are you drinking?" he asked as the bartender dropped the first drink off.

"I got a vodka pineapple. I like my drinks sweet enough to teleport me to Malibu if I close n my eyes."

Ron laughed at that, a little harder than necessary. "You know what they say about guys who drink pineapple."

"That we're pumped up with vitamin C?" I answered, playing dumb.

"No, it's that your co—"

"Hey, everything good here?" Jake cut in, sliding a smooth arm across my shoulders.

Interesting. "Yeah, everything's fine. Good thing you came—I think I need help carrying the drinks. Oh, and this is Ron. We just met."

Jake put a hand out, shaking Ron's. I noticed this handshake didn't last nearly as long as the one I just had. "Nice to meet you. I'm Jake."

Wait a second... was Jake puffing out his chest? The way he stood like an oak tree that spontaneously grew next to me, an arm still across my shoulders, with his back straight and chin high... *holy shit*, Jake was trying to intimidate this guy. Maybe the fight from this morning got to his head?

It seemed like Ron got the hint. He dipped his head and said a couple of nice things about us before turning and disappearing in the crowd, winding through some people and going past the bathrooms, likely heading upstairs.

"Sorry," Jake said, still not deflating. "I should have figured out if you wanted to talk to him. I just kind of assumed with the way you were standing that you needed some help. Did I fuck up?"

"No," I answered, patting his stomach. "I think it's physically, spiritually, and emotionally impossible for you to fuck up."

He laughed at that, shaking his head. My arm stayed on his stomach so that I could feel the gentle rise and fall of his breath, his firm muscles just a couple of threads away from being against my palm. "You give me too much credit."

"I give you just enough. You're going to have to work for the extra credit."

"Oh yeah?"

"Mhmm," I said. Before he could ask me to elaborate, my drink order was complete, and my tab was paid off. Jake helped me with the drinks, and we came back to our table, where an animated discussion on who deserved the most recent *Drag Race* crown was going on. At first, I was a little worried Jake would feel out of place, considering my friends could be a little domineering, but he slipped right into the conversation with ease.

Soon, hours had passed, and all of us were slightly (okay, *very*) drunk, empty cups stacked on our table. I definitely wasn't ready to call it a night and would have been pretty annoyed if I had to get into my own bed drunk and alone, so imagine my surprise—and utter excitement— when Jake turned to me and asked if I wanted to order pizza and hang out at his place.

The two of us got out of the bar so fast that I was sure there was a dust cloud left in our wake—zigzagging, of course, because I was sure neither of us was walking in a straight line.

Although through the drunken haze, a face did strike out at me.

Mason. He was standing at a bar top by himself, nursing a beer, looking pensive.

At least I thought it was Mason. My foggy beer-goggles made it difficult to register faces. Except for Jake's, of course. His face (along with the rest of him) kept me distracted for the rest of that entire night.

18

JAKE PEREZ

IT WAS difficult keeping my hands off Noah on the Uber ride home. We sat in the back seat, tucked closed to the door and riding in the shadow, only being seen whenever a streetlight would flash through the car. It was enough of a shield to let me put my hand on Noah's thigh, climbing up and finding a hardening surprise between his legs. I rubbed him through his shorts, making sure that if the driver turned around or looked in the rearview, all he'd see was two guys sitting shoulder to shoulder together, possibly holding hands.

He wouldn't be able to see the way my grip closed around Noah's cock, feeling it throb underneath his clothes. He dropped his head back and shut his eyes, a pleasant grin crossing his face. I'd never done this before. And sure, we were both really drunk, but public play was never on my to-do list.

Until now.

That seemed to be the theme with Noah. Shit I never

thought I'd do was now on the agenda. Join a queer book club? Check. Get in a fistfight with someone? Check. Give someone a hand job in the back of a car? Check.

Noah looked to the driver. He was focused on the road, the highway extra busy at this time of night. Music was playing, and his eyes were ahead. Noah took this chance to lower the waistband of his shorts just enough so that he could pull out the head of his glistening cock. I ran my thumb across, spreading the precome that already dripped from the tip. He dropped his head back against the headrest, and I could have sworn I heard a tiny moan escape from his lips.

Fuck. All I want to do is lean over and suck him off.

That would likely grab the driver's attention, and I certainly didn't want our Uber rating to go down because of an on-the-go fellatio violation.

I contained myself, happy with just touching him skin to skin. Holding him in my hands. Feeling his velvet hot heat soak through my palm, enjoying the way he twitched in my grip. He leaned over and whispered in my ear, "You've got me rock fucking hard."

I gave him a playful squeeze. "I know," I responded, my cock pulsing against my thigh just as hard as Noah's. If it were me behind the wheel, we would have already had to pull over and take care of this before I ended up driving us off the road.

"What are you going to do to me when we get to your place?" Noah asked, voice still low so that it couldn't be heard over the music.

"I'm going to rip off your clothes, and then I'm going

to drop to my knees and worship that thick cock of yours until you start speaking in tongues. Then I'm going to bend over the couch and spread myself open for you."

We hadn't really discussed our positions in bed (or on the couch, or in an Uber, or on a train with green eggs and ham), but I was vers, so I figured I'd adapt to whatever Noah wanted, although I did enjoy bottoming more often than I did topping. There was just something about the lack of control, the feeling of being stretched open and used by a man thrusting deep inside me—it was unmatched. And I wanted Noah to be that man. I wanted him pushing at my walls, bucking into me, looking down in my eyes as he filled me with come.

Noah leaked some more. My words must have had a pretty powerful effect. I used my forefinger to wipe it up, then brought it up to my lips and sucked, tasting the salty-sweet excitement on my tongue. Noah's eyes went wide. He opened his mouth. I rubbed his bottom lip, spreading the precome across him before he sucked my finger into his mouth, swirling his tongue around me.

I nearly came right then and there.

Thankfully, the driver was just pulling into my driveway, my busted-ass car sitting there being useless. He parked, and we practically rolled out of the car, ushering some quick thanks his way and hurrying to the front door, where I fumbled with my keys while Noah wrapped his arms around my waist, rubbing into me from behind with his mouthwatering erection. I arched back, pushing my ass into him. The driver was still reversing out of my driveway and surely got a mini show, but I didn't care. We were home, and that meant I was seconds away from getting Noah's naked body against mine.

Our lips locked the second we were inside and the door was shut. I swallowed a moan from Noah, my hand going under his shirt and rubbing his back, feeling the soft skin, which was a contrast to the hard-as-steel cock that pressed against my leg as we stumbled our way back to the couch.

"God, I could barely contain myself in that Uber," I admitted, my hands moving down and going inside of Noah's shorts, rubbing on his firm cheeks. "I nearly straddled you the entire way here."

"That would have been a five-star ride for sure."

"Yeah, maybe for you, but my passenger rating would have probably tanked."

Noah chuckled, leaning up to kiss on my neck. Massive bolts of electricity coursed through each spot that his lips touched. "Would have been worth it, though."

"True, true," I said. "Now, get the hell out of these clothes so I can play with you the right way."

Noah licked his smiling lips, pulling his shirt over his head and then quickly unzipping and dropping his shorts. The black briefs he had on were straining to contain him. I pulled him into me, claiming his mouth with mine as I palmed him over his briefs, feeling the wetness from where he leaked through the fabric. I nipped on his bottom lip, tucking my fingers into the waistband of the briefs and pulling them off, his hard cock springing free, tip glistening in the low light of my living room.

"God, Noah, you're so fucking sexy. I can't get enough of you."

His hands were working overtime to strip me of my clothes, getting us both naked, a graveyard of shirts and shorts and underwear tossed to the side. We embraced again, tongues swirling as our hard lengths pressed together. I ran my hands over his ass, pulling him harder onto me, the two of us falling backward onto the couch. He gripped my face, kissing me like there were a thousand secrets he wanted to share, a thousand stories he wanted to tell, a thousand memories he wanted to impart, all through the kiss alone.

My entire body hummed with an energy I couldn't describe, morphing into a need I couldn't control.

"Come," I said, grabbing his hand and leading him to my bedroom. I needed him to put out this fire. Noah had to give my body what it craved, or I was scared I'd spontaneously combust right there on the spot. It was that intense of a burning desire, scorching my core as if it contained the sun itself.

He sat down on the edge of my bed, cock hard and straight, twitching as he grabbed the base and gave himself a couple of lazy strokes. I walked over to my nightstand and opened the top drawer, taking out a bottle of lube.

"Have you been tested?" I asked.

"Not recently. I haven't had sex either, but do you have a condom, just to be safe?"

I appreciated Noah's honesty and thoughtfulness. Thankfully, I did have a couple of condoms in my nightstand. I took one out, ripping the foil open and going over to Noah, standing between his open legs. Before I could slip the condom on, he leaned forward and took me into his mouth. Instantly, I was transported to paradise. Wet and warm, sensual. He took me all the way in, massaging my balls with one hand and squeezing my ass with the other. I dropped my head back, letting the cloud I was currently on drift closer and closer to outer space.

"Mhmm, that's it, Noah." I threaded my fingers through his soft hair, using it like reins, guiding him further down my cock. I could see him dripping, his shaft taking on a sheen from how much precome he leaked. It was enthralling, watching my dick disappear down his throat while his worked like a broken fire hydrant, proving how much this turned him on.

He pulled back for a breath, looking up at me with sex-drunk eyes, half-lidded and glowing. His lips caught the light, curling at the corners. He lifted my cock and kissed his way down its length, tonguing my balls, lifting them, and sliding his tongue even further between my legs. My cock nearly covered his entire face as he buried himself between my thighs. He took a moment to suck on his own finger, making it nice and wet, before focusing back in on me.

"*Fuuuuuck,*" I hissed out. My hole quivered as Noah's finger found it, applying pressure while his tongue worked on the sensitive flesh between my ass and balls. I ground my ass back, pushing myself onto his finger, feeling myself relax as the tip slipped in.

He looked up at me again, mouth full of my balls and finger beginning to push in deeper. I let out a guttural moan, feeling more aroused than I'd ever been before. It was as if I'd taken a handful of ecstasy pills, every touch and kiss and lick and breath sending jolts of pleasure coursing through me.

"I need you, Noah. I need you inside of me," I said, the words falling from my lips without any restraint. "Fuck me. Take my ass and make it yours."

19

NOAH BARNES

JAKE'S WORDS set me on fire, a lit match falling into dry brush, a scorching inferno consuming me from the crown of my head to the soles of my feet, licking at every single muscle and bone I had in my body.

"Make my ass yours."

I nearly came on the spot. But I had a job to do, and the last thing I wanted to do was get fired on the first day. No, I needed to give Jake exactly what he was asking for.

Me.

I took the lube and spread it up and down my cock, making myself slick for him. Jake got onto the bed, doggy-style, his ass up in the air with a dip in his lower back. He knew exactly how to arch it out for me, giving me the sexiest fucking view on the planet. I reached for his cheeks, massaging them, lining myself up with his crack and rubbing up and down, making him as slippery as I was. He reached back and opened himself for me, spreading his cheeks and making my view all the more mouthwatering.

I leaned forward and spit, making him even more wet. His tight hole twitched as I pressed the head of my cock against him, one hand on his lower back and the other holding his hip. I pushed forward, feeling Jake open for me, taking me inside of him.

"That okay?" I asked, slowly sinking into him.

"So fucking good," he said, head dropped and ass pushing back on me. I watched as I disappeared into Jake's ass, stopping about halfway and leaning forward, holding myself there so that the scarlet-red heat didn't instantly turn me into a pile of horny ashes.

"God, Jake, you're so tight. It feels like heaven."

"Keep going," he said, turning his head so he looked back at me, a smolder in his bright blue eyes. "Fuck me, Noah."

I pushed in deeper, burying myself down to the hilt. We both moaned in ecstasy, the sounds of our sex creating the most mesmerizing song, one I wanted inked onto my soul. His groans, my moans, the slap of our skin, the wet thrusts and throaty oh yeses.

I never wanted it to end. Ever.

"That's it, Noah, oh shit, right there. Right there."

I found my rhythm, sliding in deep before rolling my hips back, nearly pulling out before bucking back into him, earning a breathless gasp each time. Over and over again. Slow at first, opening him and getting him used to my size, then faster, faster, *faster*. My fingers dug into his muscular shoulders as I looked for something to stabilize me, to keep me from floating off into the stratosphere.

"Slow down, slow down," Jake said, reaching back and putting a hand on my thigh.

"Am I hurting you?"

"No, the opposite. You're about to make me come, and I don't want to yet. I want to sit on you first."

I pulled out of him, my rock-hard cock twitching in the air, the condom glistening from the lube. I added some more as Jake rolled off the bed, his cock sticking out like a steel beam. I gave him a couple of tight strokes and locked his lips with mine. Jake wasn't the only one getting close to an orgasm. Just having the tip of his cock rub against mine nearly brought me there.

"Sit," he commanded, the gravel in his voice making my balls tighten even more.

He got onto the bed, straddling me, hard cock aimed up toward the ceiling. I ran my hand over the soft crown of hair, up the trail that led to his belly button. I traced the lines of muscles on his stomach as he lowered himself onto me, his tight, hot heat wrapping around me, sending me right back to nirvana.

"*Ooooh*, fuck," I let out as he sat all the way down, impaling himself with my length. "I don't know how much longer I can last."

He rose up slowly before grinding back down, moving his ass in a way that made me close my eyes and shout for more. Jake repeated the move, over and over, taking the initiative with his power-bottom self and riding me like a professional cowboy, determined to stay on the bucking bull.

I started to thrust, meeting him in the middle, our skin slapping hard. Jake's cock bounced with the movement and leaked precome, a clear string of it dripping down onto my belly.

I gripped his hips, held him down on me, felt him clench. It was like throwing a gallon of fuel into an already lit bonfire. My eyes rolled to the back of my skull as my orgasm came crashing through me. I couldn't even get the words out, a jumbled version of "I'm coming" falling from my lips as I filled the condom, pumping into him. He gripped the base of his cock and let out a hiss of a breath, shooting ropes of come onto my chest, hitting my chin, my lips, drenching me.

Making me the happiest fucking man on earth. I licked some of it off my lips as he leaned down, smiling, cheeks flushed the same firehouse red as his chest was, showing even through his tan skin. His cock hung heavy and dripped onto me as he leaned down for a kiss, my length still plugging him.

"That was intense," he said against my lips. "And insanely good. Where'd you learn to move your hips like that?"

"Same master's course you took, apparently."

"I've got a PhD in grinding, actually."

"Yeah, you've got a PhD in something else, too," I said, reaching for Jake's still-firm cock, wrapping my fingers around the silky-soft shaft.

He kissed me again before getting up, slowly pulling me out. He got me a warm, wet towel to wipe up with before we both went over to the shower, where I nearly got high off inhaling the incredible eucalyptus-scented soaps and shampoo that we used to get clean. We continued to play around underneath the rainfall shower-head, holding each other in between sudsing up, giggling and kissing and touching. It felt right. It was a moment that was tender and heartfelt, something I didn't really think I'd experience after my terrible breakup with Franky and my subsequently empty app hookups. Those were fun, but they weren't impactful. Not in the way our sex had just been.

It felt like a comet had locked in directly—and only—on us, crashing through the ceiling and obliterating any walls or barriers I might have had between Jake and me. Sure, we were friends and coworkers, but tonight proved that we were also so much more.

...

...

But was I the only one who felt that? We hadn't discussed anything, and the last time I assumed something about Jake, I turned out to be a huge asshole.

It needed to come up. I needed to bring it up... but I was scared. I didn't want to ruin this sparkly golden night. I just wanted this feeling to go on forever, for the sun to never come up and for me and Jake to be permanently frozen into this time and place, locked in a shining globe of amber.

Jake and I toweled off as he explained to me the rules of chess, which was something else he was apparently great at. He continued to talk about pawns and knights and checkmates as we went back into his bedroom, but I had a hard time focusing on any of it. All I could think of was cuffing this man to my side. It was made even more intense when we both got into bed, still naked, and he wrapped me up in his big arms, the firm muscles of his bicep serving as a pillow for me. He tucked one of his legs through mine and kissed the back of my neck, and I completely and totally haywired, words coming out of my lips before I could think:

"What are we?"

"Huh?"

"What are we?" I asked again, looking directly ahead at the dark wall. I could feel Jake breathing against my back, his chest rising and falling, our skin pressed together. "I know we're friends. Good ones. But do you feel anything else?"

He didn't even miss a beat. "I do. I feel like I won the lotto over the fact that I get to hold you right now. I don't think I've ever felt this way with anyone else I've been with. This *happy*. This comfortable."

"Me neither," I said honestly. "And that's a little scary."

"Why?"

"Because I'm scared you'll just disappear. Like you'll wake up and decide to keep things as friends between us. We aren't anything official, so it's not that far outside of the realm of possibility."

Jake chuckled, kissed my neck again. "I can guarantee you it is *very* far outside the realm of possibility."

I took that moment to turn over, facing him now. I looped an arm through his, letting my fingertips softly trace random patterns across his back, following the dips and curves of his muscles. "You sure?"

"Very sure," he said, kissing my nose. The lights in the bedroom were off, but enough moonlight spilled in through the partly opened curtains so that I could still see his Tiffany-blue eyes, swirling like two mini-galaxies. "So sure that I'm ready to say fuck being friends."

I arched a brow, licked my lips.

"Forget being friends, and let's be boyfriends," he continued, my heart deciding to do a full-on tap-dance routine against my ribs. "I don't want to tiptoe around my feelings for you anymore. I don't care if we're at work or with your friends or at the fucking grocery store. I want to be able to reach over and hold your hand, kiss you, let everyone else around know that you're mine and I'm yours."

Fireworks went off in my vision, matching the explosions going on elsewhere throughout my body. I couldn't believe that I was scared of bringing this up. "I think that sounds like a great idea to me," I said, unable to hold back a chuckle, produced from the pure bliss that currently bubbled through my veins. "I was scared that you'd want to keep things as just friends, but I've been down to make things official since the moment you walked into the office wearing those khaki pants that showed your ankles every time you sat down and crossed one leg over another."

"Oh, you're an ankle guy? I thought you were an ass guy?"

"Well, I like having your ankles on my shoulders while I pound your ass, so... I guess I'm both?"

Jake and I both started to laugh, kissing through the happiness. I was almost positive that we were seconds away from breaking the laws of physics and simply floating up into the star-blotted sky, turning into our own constellation: the friends to lovers. Right next to the Big Dipper.

Jake leaned over and tapped on the base of his lamp. A dim light flooded the room. He opened the drawer and took out a notepad and a pen. I propped myself up on my elbow and watched him jot something down.

"What are you doing?" I asked him through a yawn.

"Writing this moment down. Date, time, and the fact that you and I are together, officially. It's my way of— well, I know how fleeting memory can be. I just want to be able to remember this moment forever. No matter what. That's all."

He closed the book and set it delicately back in the drawer. The weight of his words settled heavily on my chest, and I was grateful when he turned the lamp off before turning to me because that way, he didn't see the rogue trail of tears that decided to make its way down my cheeks.

I dabbed at them with the pillow and settled into bed,

back to being the little spoon as Jake wrapped me up, encasing me in his body heat and making me feel like I was the safest and happiest guy in the entire world, and it only made me more excited about what this new chapter between us would bring.

20

JAKE PEREZ

"BOYFRIENDS, HUH?" Ashley asked as she took a bite out of her granola bar, leaning on the open door of a shining red Audi. The bright lights in the dealership danced across the candy-coated paint job, reflecting in Ashley's hazel eyes.

"Yup." I nodded, leaning back in the car seat. "Boyfriends."

"And look at that smile you get when you say it." Ashley poked a finger into my ribs. It was undeniable, though. I could feel the strain in my cheeks from how big my grin was.

It had been a few days since Noah and I had made things official, and each one of those days somehow kept getting better and better. I half expected to win the lottery by the end of the week, along with receiving news that I was some kind of Spanish prince who needed to go and get the keys to their grand mountainside castle.

"Where'd you two meet again?"

"We worked together, but what really sparked it was bumping into him at the grocery store and getting invited to his book club. Seeing him outside of work made everything way more intense."

"Do you work closely with him? He's not your boss, is he? That could get messy."

I shook my head as I rubbed the soft white leather steering wheel. "We're in different departments, so he can't fire me."

"Okay, good, because coming from someone who's dating her boss, it does get a little complicated. But it's also a hundred percent worth it." Ashley looked down at me with a glint in her eyes, brought out even more by the turquoise-green gem hanging on her neck. "And he has a book club?"

"Yup. Reading Under the Rainbow. It's him and his friends getting together to read thrillers and mysteries. And you know how I go through those books like candy."

She answered with a nod, running her hand through her long blonde hair with the fresh highlights.

"He sounds like a keeper to me. A guy who likes to read and has a good job? Lock him down with a ring."

I chuckled as I got out of the Audi, walking to the sapphire-blue car sitting near the front desk of the showroom. I didn't wake up thinking I'd be buying a new car today, but when mine didn't start again this morning, I texted Ashley and told her our lunch date was being moved to a used-car dealership. I promised I'd get her a Snickers bar from the vending machine.

"It's way too soon for a ring," I admitted, although the idea didn't sound all that far-fetched to me.

"It's never too soon for a ring. Look at us—we dated for a year and a half before you popped the question. Maybe if you did it sooner, I would have realized I needed to come out sooner, and we could have avoided a whole lot of drama."

I gave her a playful glare. That day wasn't exactly the best, but it left the doors open for future happiness, so I didn't regret it. I was happy Ashely had said no to my beachside proposal, tears in both of our eyes as we realized it wasn't working and it would never work, not in a romantic sense. My proposal had only come because of the extreme suggestions by Ashley's friends, telling me that an imaginary clock was ticking away.

Still, the momentary pain of being rejected didn't last nearly as long as the happiness that came after. And it was obvious in the way Ashley carried herself now, her shoulders a little higher and smile a little easier to come by. Even her way of expressing herself changed as she ditched all the sundresses and floral leggings she'd purchased off a Facebook group (which she told me were moldy anyway and needed to go), swapping them out for some tight jeans and crop tops.

It was exciting to see her find herself, and I supported her every step of the rainbow way. "I'm not taking credit for you being a lesbian. That's all you," I pointed out.

She shrugged. "I guess. Whatever, you get my point. Just live life to the fullest, and if that means going to Vegas and being a little irresponsible, then so be it." She tapped my shoulder, looking very pleased with doling out terrible advice.

"What about you and Xi, then? Why don't I see a ring on your finger yet?"

"Because I've got it in my back pocket right now." She reached around and pulled something from her jeans pocket. A small velvet red box. My eyes went wide, looking up from her open palms to her still-glinting gaze, shining even brighter than before.

"Are you kidding me?" I said, grabbing the box and opening it, revealing a smooth silver band set with a glittering diamond that fractured the light, turning it into a hundred tiny rainbows.

"I'm seeing her after this. It's our sixth-month anniversary, and I already know I want six thousand more of them."

"How are you going to do it?" I asked, handing back the box. I shouldn't have been so surprised. Ashley lived off spontaneity as if it were air, needing it in her daily life to keep her happy.

"We're having dinner at this really nice restaurant on the river tonight. I'm going to have two of my friends ride down there on their boat, with the side of it lit up to say: 'Xi, will you marry me?' And then she'll turn around, and I'll be down on one knee."

"That sounds perfect," I said. "I may need to get some notes from you, then."

She clapped her hands and rubbed them together, her rings clinking against each other. "So you *are* going to propose?"

"Not anytime soon, no," I replied, moving on to another car. None of these were options, as the one I'd already decided to buy was getting washed and ready for me, but it was a decent way to kill time. "He's got too much going on right now to think about a wedding."

"What's he going through?" She crossed her arms, brows inching together.

I sighed, rubbing at the bridge of my nose. "A lot. There's been someone who's fixated on fucking up his life. They left a severed chicken head on his doorstep wearing a rainbow necklace *and* tried getting into my house when he was sleeping over."

"Holy tit balls, seriously? That's some twisted shit. And he doesn't know who's doing it?"

"Has no idea. We confronted his ex-boyfriend, who *might* be connected, but he denied it all. And then we got into a fistfight."

Surprise flashed across Ashley's face. She knew how anti-confrontation I was. She reached for my forearm, eyes wide. "Jeez, Jake, were you and Noah alright?"

I nodded, waved a dismissive hand in the air. "The guy had it coming. It's also been pretty quiet since we talked to him, so maybe he was the one behind the threats."

"Maybe..." Ashley's voice trailed off, but her eyes were pinned to me. "Be careful, Jake. If it's an ex-boyfriend, someone that might still have feelings for Noah, then those threats could end up aimed at you."

A chill crawled down my back. I'd thought of that possibility but didn't allow it to carry much weight. What was I going to do? Tell Noah I didn't want to be his boyfriend because I was scared I'd become a target? That just wasn't even an option for me. I may not have been used to any of this, but I wasn't walking away from one of the best things to ever happen to me because of a crazy ex. No way.

"I'll be fine," I assured Ashley. The firm set of my shoulders and the even tone in my words did a good job of hiding the nerves. "I just want him to be okay, that's all. He's seriously one of the nicest guys I've ever met. You two need to hang out sometime."

"That'd be fun. We should go on a double date," Ashley said, our conversation pivoting but the dark cloud still looming overhead.

Truth was, I likely would continue to keep being worried until whoever was behind this was caught and made to answer for their fucked-up thinking. There was a certain sense of violation to think that someone was fidgeting with my locked window and trying to get inside my home while Noah and I slept peacefully together. I tried to keep hopeful, tried to think that maybe the cops would do their jobs and figure out who was behind this. And if they didn't, then maybe Noah and I could.

One way or another, it had to end. I didn't want Noah to jump at every shadow and second-guess every tiny noise.

"Right?" Ashley waved a hand in my face, pulling me out of my dark thoughts. "Hello?"

"Yeah, yeah. A double date sounds fun."

"But what do you think about my idea?"

She must have read the question on my face. *What idea?*

"To have a *Cats* watch party, Jake. We obviously won't watch the entire thing—I don't have years to spend. But we can play that drinking game you made up. Every time they lick themselves, purr, sing the word 'jellicle.'"

I laughed and nodded. "We got blasted the last time we played that."

"I know, so it's perfect. Or should I say *purrr*fect?"

My eyes practically rolled out of my skull, the two of us continuing to laugh even as the car salesman walked back over to us, a clipboard in his hand and a smile on his face. The day was shaping up to be a good one, and I was excited to share it with Noah, wanting to talk to him about Ashley and the *Cats* drinking game and the way the car salesman tried to get me to buy a dying Honda Civic that Ashley and I were sure was haunted.

I was excited for all that and more, ready to rain kisses on him, every one on him, from his feet to his forehead. I wanted to worship him, spend the evening doing nothing but each other.

Unfortunately for the both of us, life had other plans. Twisted plans. Noah's nightmare was far from over. In fact, from the moment I picked up his panicked call as I parked my new car in the driveway, I knew that this nightmare had only just begun.

21

NOAH BARNES

I KISSED Jake goodbye as he left my place, heading out for a fun-filled day of used-car shopping with his good friend Ashley. It was early in the morning, but I wasn't sleepy in the slightest. Not after Jake woke me up with his lips around my morning wood. I leaned against the closed door and stretched, happy with how this day (and many of the previous ones) started off. I didn't think I'd ever get tired of rolling over in my bed and feeling Jake's firm and naked body next to mine. It was like waking up from a dream only to land in an even better one.

I shuffled over to my kitchen, scratching my belly and pausing for another stretch before I started on making my coffee. While it brewed, I got a clean bowl out of the dishwasher and went into my pantry, grabbing the colorful box of cereal and pouring a generous amount into the bowl.

At my dining table, I settled in by propping my phone up against the napkin holder and sipping on the coffee as I scrolled through the morning news. One head-line made me pause midsip: *Murder of another gay man puts community on high alert.*

I opened the article, picking up my phone and leaning back in the chair.

The death of Alex Torres marks the fifth gay man murdered in Atlanta within the last year, all under similar circumstances. Police have been hesitant to spread panic and have avoided using the term 'serial killer' but after a press conference held yesterday evening, the Atlanta Chief of Police stated they are on the hunt for a serial killer targeting the queer community.

Further details on the murders are being withheld in order to protect the investigation.

... *Fuck.* Gay guys were the targets? That bit of infor-mation was new to me. No one had made that link publicly before, and it was a chilling connection to even think about. Our community was already small enough (and traumatized enough) as it was; now we had to be suspicious of someone picking us off one by one?

I spooned some cereal into my mouth as I searched around for more information, my morbid curiosity getting the best of me. There were unsubstantiated rumors floating around social media, but nothing that came from an official source.

He's a local.

They're cutting off the victim's penis.

I heard he uses chemicals to paralyze and torture his victims.

It was all too creepy for me, especially this early in

the morning. I closed out of the screen and opened up a mindless video app. I tried using the viral dances and trending sounds to scrub my brain clean, but it wasn't working. I kept circling back to the news, and then I started thinking about my own issue—could they be related?

No, absolutely not. I shook off a shiver that traveled between my shoulders. Thankfully, it had been a couple of weeks from that break-in attempt at Jake's house, and nothing else had happened since. It made me seriously consider the fact that maybe Franky was involved, and us confronting him may have worked to scare him off.

It was really the only theory that gave me any sense of comfort, which meant it would be the theory I stuck with until proven otherwise.

I got up and brought my half-eaten bowl of cereal to the sink, where I dumped the rest out after my appetite had been effectively destroyed. The trash compactor whirred and buzzed when I flipped the switch. I turned it off just as my doorbell rang.

Did Jake leave something?

I shuffled out of the kitchen and back to the front door, looking through the peephole and seeing no one. I cracked the door open and peeked outside, spotting a delivery truck driving down my street. I opened the door wider and looked down, my blood turning to ice in my veins.

It was a box. Same shape as the last one left on Robby's door. It only took me a moment to shake off the curtain of fear, this one having a clear shipping and return label on the flap. There was no blood staining the sides either. My fight-or-flight response disappeared, replaced by a simmering excitement.

This was the gift I'd ordered for Jake. I planned on giving it to him at our cabin retreat for the book club. With a relieved breath, I went to close my door but was stopped by a friendly "Hey!" I looked down my steps and spotted Robby waving up at me, shielding his eyes from the sun that beamed directly into them.

I waved back, happy to see my neighbor. We weren't the best of friends, but it was nice seeing a smiling face after that needless scare. "Hey, what's up?"

Robby climbed up the steps, stopping just a couple down from me. "I was just going for a walk and spotted you. I wanted to see how everything was going?"

"Oh, it's going," I said, giving the universal answer to that question. "Just getting ready for my book club's Blue Ridge retreat. How about you?"

"I've been busy applying to new jobs."

"Did something happen at your old one?" Robby was a nurse at a local hospital and had always complained about his job, but it seemed like something pushed him into finally looking for a new position.

"Just the usual drama and lack of support from the higher-ups. It's frustrating when I'm trying to take care of fifteen patients and told I can't even have a snack break. I'm thinking of going to another hospital or maybe private practice." He shrugged, and I could see the exhaustion cracking through the otherwise bright expression. "But enough about my boring life. How's everything been with the—well, you know."

"The horror-movie-type threats? Things have been pretty quiet, actually. I'm hoping I can put it all behind me now."

"And you deserve to. Especially now that you've got someone to spend your time with. Why spend that time worried and looking over your shoulder?"

"Exactly," I said enthusiastically. I didn't tell Robby explicitly about my new relationship with Jake, but I figured it wasn't hard to put two and two together when Jake was coming over to my house almost every other day. "How's your dating life going?" I asked, wanting to get off myself as the topic.

"It's as messy as any other single guy's dating life in Atlanta. I've kind of put it all on hold. I deleted the apps and stopped meeting random guys. I don't know, I feel like my perfect match is right in front of me; I just need to open my eyes a little wider." He rubbed at the back of his neck. A thin gold necklace hung down into his black-and-gray striped polo shirt. "Maybe I'll date Mason from down the street. He seems interested in me."

I cocked my head at that. "Mason? I didn't realize you two were close."

"Mhmm," Robby replied. "So what if he's a little creepy and smells like burnt steak all the time. Maybe he'll give me what I need. I saw him on Grindr before I deleted it, so at least I know he swings for our team."

"Robby, you don't have to settle for anyone," I said, and I meant it.

"Thanks, Noah, but I think I peaked after you." He put an arm on my shoulder and smiled, a sadness reflected in his eyes as he looked at mine.

"I don't believe that." I wanted to be supportive, but I was also a little taken aback by Robby's comment.

"All I'm saying is that Jake is a lucky guy." He put his hands up in the air and smiled. I was about to respond with some kind of self-deprecating joke to lighten the mood, but a buzz in my shorts distracted me. I decided to use that as a way of shifting gears, grabbing my phone and quickly checking the message. I thought it was going to be Jake telling me he was on his way back to my place, or maybe it was another politician talking about their dire need for donations and framing it as if I was the only one who could save the world by sending over ten dollars.

It was none of that. I had to read the message twice— no, *three* times—for it to make sense.

And that was when fear clamped its jagged teeth directly into my heart.

NOAH. This message is for YOU. Break up with Jake or you both WILL regret the day you two met, along with the day you DIE.

I nearly dropped my phone. My hands started to shake, my vision tunneling in so that all I could see were those terrifying words, typed out and sent from a number I didn't recognize, from the person who had become obsessed with me and was now making impossible demands of me. It was like I had opened my eyes to wake from a dream only to step into a nightmare.

My phone buzzed again. Another message. This

time, it was a picture, and it took up the majority of my screen.

It was a photo of needles on a table, all of them filled with some kind of clear liquid.

I couldn't keep my grip tight enough on my phone. It slipped from my hand, falling in a spiral down onto the concrete, landing facedown between a shocked Robby and a paralyzed me.

"What's going on? What happened?" he asked, bending down and grabbing my phone, looking at the screen and letting out a surprised "holy shit." He looked at me, the sadness in his gaze from before being replaced by the same terror that currently threatened to stop my heart. He wrapped me up in a tight hug, which helped ground some of my more out-of-control thoughts, and guided me back into my house, helping me realize that my feet still worked.

Inside, I put my back against the wall and started to cry, unable to stop even once I got Jake on the phone.

"You need... to come... back," I said through frightened tears, knowing that my next words were about to shred me apart. But they needed to be said. I had to get them out. Rip it off like a bloody Band-Aid. "And we... we need... to break up."

22

JAKE PEREZ

NOAH'S WORDS crashed through me like a runaway train without any brakes.

We need to break up.

I asked him what he meant, as if the sentence wasn't simple enough for a fourth grader to comprehend. He wouldn't elaborate—or couldn't, through the tears—and instead just kept telling me I needed to get to his house. I was already in my car and speeding down the highway before Noah got the tears under control, but by then, it was my heart that I couldn't manage to rein in. It pounded against my ribs, as if trying to break free from a prison. This couldn't be healthy. I forced myself to take some deep breaths, but they came up short, my lungs barely filling with air.

I pulled into his driveway, tires screeching on the pavement, and hurried up the stairs to his townhouse. The door was open, and Noah and his neighbor, Robby, were sitting on the couch together. Robby had an arm around Noah's shoulder, but the second I walked in, Noah leaped up from the couch and ran into my arms, burying his wet face into my chest.

"What's going on? What happened?" I asked, holding Noah before he took a step back. I looked him up and down, searching for any signs that he was hurt and finding none.

That's when Noah took out his phone and handed it to me, showing me the message that had come through.

I read it once and felt my stomach do a somersault. The blood drained from my body, pooling in my extremities, fueling my muscles to bolt. This was beyond scary. This was worst-case scenario, a bullseye painted in crimson red directly on my forehead, trailing down into my eyes. All I saw was red, coming from a mixture of fear and anger. I wasn't sure which was more intense.

"This needs to stop," I said, as if that would make a genie blink his eyes and make everything better again. "This needs to end."

"It won't," Noah said through rogue tears. "Not until they get their way."

Robby rubbed Noah's arm, looking at me with his eyes wide. He was likely counting his lucky stars things had ended between him and Noah, or the target could have been painted on him instead. But then Noah and I would never have crossed paths the way we did, and for *that*, I counted every single lucky star in orbit. I wouldn't trade what Noah and I had for the world, even if that was for a world where someone didn't want me dead and in a ditch.

"I won't let them get their way. It's going to be okay, Noah. It will." I held Noah's hand in mine, squeezing it, trying to impart some kind of strength or comfort, even though I didn't have a shred of either of those things in my body.

In truth, I didn't know *how* I would stop them. I tried, back when I thought it could be Franky. I thought a show of force could scare him away, make things calm again. But that clearly didn't work, and we were running low on suspects. Who could want to torture Noah like this? And why turn on our relationship?

"I, uh, should get going," Robby said as he took a couple of steps toward the front door. Fear was apparent in his blown-out pupils. Nothing I could blame him for. "Noah, if you need anything, please call me. I have the keys to my parents' cabin if you need an escape—actually, you said you're having a book club retreat in Blue Ridge, right? Take my parents' cabin."

Noah shook his head. "There's no need for that, but thank you, though."

"It's a two-million-dollar cabin with a three-sixty view of the mountains."

"On second thought," Noah said with a weak chuckle. "Tristan would blow if he found out I said no to this. He likes nice things."

"I'll drop off the keys tomorrow." Robby managed a wink, warm eyes crinkling at the corners in a weak smile. "And listen to Jake. It's going to be okay." He tapped his knuckles on the door and left.

"We have to call it quits," Noah said when the door

was shut, and I could see the seriousness in the way his brows furrowed and jaw twitched. "We have to. I can't be with you if this person is still out there. I can't. I can't."

Noah started to cry again. The sound of his tears made me feel as if I were swallowing glass. It was painful in a way that went beyond just the physical. I reached out for him on instinct, wrapping my arms around him again. He sobbed, continuing to say, "I can't," and I started to realize he wasn't just talking about our relationship.

"You can," I whispered against the crown of his head, his hair soft against my lips. I kissed him. "*We* can, Noah."

He sniffled and patted his cheeks. My shirt was stained with his tears, the light red fabric turning dark around my chest. "No, I refuse to put you in any danger, Jake."

"Danger is a part of life. It can come at you slow, something that takes your mind and body from you at a snail's pace, or it can come fast, in a car crash that turns off all the lights in the blink of an eye. Me being away from you doesn't keep me safe. I can trip down the stairs leaving your house and die from hitting my head, and that's probably way more likely than being murdered by whoever this lunatic is. They're all bark and barely any bite.

"Don't give them this power, Noah. Don't let anyone tear us apart."

"I don't want to let anyone do that, but I feel like they're getting more desperate, and that means that we have to take this threat seriously."

"And we will. We'll be extra careful; we'll make sure neither of us is alone for long. And we'll keep trying to figure out who's behind this so they can be locked up." I took his head in my heads, drawing his glassy eyes up to mine. "Please, trust me. I don't want to lose you."

The words were the most honest I'd ever spoken. They were imprinted on my heart, across my ribs, down my spine. I didn't want to lose Noah. Not now, not ever. He was the best thing to have ever happened to me. The reason why I woke up with a smile on my face. A *smile*. I thought only sociopaths woke up grinning, but I was wrong. There were other reasons to feel thrilled about the day ahead, and all those reasons were looking directly into my eyes. He was a story that I never wanted to end, never wanted to get to the last page. He was my everything. Sun, stars, ocean, and air.

"I can't lose you." I rubbed away a streak of moisture just under his eye.

"I'm sorry..."

He pulled away from me, turned his back to me, his head shaking. It was like getting impaled with a harpoon. A sudden and painful shock spread through me. Had I really lost him? Was this really going to be the thing that snuffed out our growing flame? I didn't want it to be true —I couldn't have it be true. But what else was I supposed to do?

Beg. I'll get down on my knees and beg for you, Noah. Please.

He turned back around, his upper lip quivering. "I'm sorry for dragging you into this."

That gave me a dose of momentary relief. But our relationship still wasn't out of danger yet. "Are you kidding me? My life could use a little extra excitement. I was getting so bored of my routine that I was seriously considering selling my shit and trying out van life." I was able to muster up a wink, trying my damnedest to inject some light back into his situation.

"Really?"

I shook my head. "No, just joking. I can't live without my memory foam mattress and rainfall showerhead."

"Yeah, I was gonna say." He arched a judgmental brow at me.

"What? You don't think I can do it."

"You just said it yourself, you can't do it."

My lips curled into a half-cocked smile. "I can never win an argument with you."

"No, you can't. And that was an argument?"

"It's the most heated we've ever gotten with each other. And I don't see us arguing any more than that, ever, so yeah. Glad we survived it." I reached for his hand again. I simultaneously wanted to burst out into ballroom dance with him and yank him out of the door at the same time so that we could run and run and run, far away from all the bullshit that bogged us down.

"Come on. Let's go to the police station and show them this text. Then we can come back home, shower, and get in bed. I've got some trashy movies we can put on. We can put this day behind us. When tomorrow comes, we'll be rested and ready to hunt this fucker down."

Noah swallowed what appeared to have been a boulder-sized lump of emotion. He nodded, no longer able to produce many tears but still sniffling. His hands squeezed around mine, and his head came to rest on my shoulder, his nose buried in the crook of my neck. We stayed that way for a long moment until Noah's breathing calmed down and the sniffling had stopped. I could have stayed there forever, happy with feeling his heartbeat against mine, knowing that not even a couple of inches separated our bodies.

But we had shit to do, and the main thing on that to-do list: finding the sick fuck before he found us.

23

NOAH BARNES

"GAH DAMN, THIS PLACE IS HUGE," Jake said, looking out the window as he pulled into the driveway, gravel sounding like a rocky symphony underneath the tires. He wasn't exaggerating either. Robby's parents' cabin was something pulled directly out of a movie featuring sparkly vampires and awkward teenage angst. It was a mix of modern with a splash of classic: windows that stretched along the dark black wood, a wraparound deck that sported plenty of hanging chairs and comfortable benches, a white stone trim that blended in with the puffy white clouds that seemed to be touching the tip of the roof from how high up in the mountains we were. It was the only cabin on the road, perched on the edge of the cliff like a queen peering down at her woodsy kingdom.

This weekend was our book club mountain retreat, and *hollllly* crap did I need this escape.

The past week felt like I was living through a daily

nightmare that I couldn't wake up from. Every second that ticked by was another second I expected the axe hanging over my head to drop. The police took down the threat and promised they were trying their best to find this person but couldn't give me any guarantees, only warnings: stay with others, don't go anywhere alone, change my number and my locks, increase security, blah blah blah.

Nothing that gave me any real hope they'd find whoever was behind this. They were basically warning me that I was on my own without actually saying those words. It was disheartening, but more than that, it was terrifying. I had trouble sleeping, even though Jake's comforting presence and soft breaths were right next to me.

Maybe the fear came *because* Jake was with me. I didn't want to give in to the threats; I didn't want to break up with Jake. That was literally the last thing I ever wanted to do. He made me happy. No... happy was an understatement. He made me feel like I was made of fireworks and stardust. An impossible combination that made me wonder if he was working some kind of spell over me. Maybe he slipped me a love potion when I wasn't looking, or maybe he was just that perfect—whatever the reason, it made it near impossible to imagine what my life would be if I pushed him away.

But then I'd start imagining what would happen if I *didn't* push him away. I started picturing all kinds of fucked-up things, fed by the memory of a severed rooster head staring up at me. I couldn't control the images that would randomly pop up throughout the day, and all of them made me want to curl up into a ball and cry until this was all over.

If anything happened to Jake, I didn't think I'd be able to live with myself. It would destroy me, from the inside out. My heart would disintegrate, turning to useless dust in my chest. I was beginning to care more about what happened to him than what could potentially happen to me. My intense worry for his well-being made me forget that *I* was the real target and that this was all happening because someone had their sights set on me. Jake was just an innocent bystander, dating the wrong person at the wrong time.

And yet he still wouldn't back down. He refused to let this sick person win, and for that, I was incredibly grateful. There were defining moments in every relationship that steered the course for what was to come, that would forever shape the way love grew. A singular moment could either snuff out any flames currently crackling and growing in intensity, or it could permanently encase that fire in a protective shell, creating an unbreakable bond that only grows in strength through hardships and through the good times.

I felt like by Jake staying with me, that shell turned solid around us. If he stayed by my side through this mess, then I couldn't see anything tearing us apart in the future.

Jake reached into the back seat and grabbed his backpack before clicking open the trunk of his new car. "You ready?" he asked me, reaching over and squeezing my thigh.

He was so handsome today, even with how casual he looked wearing a backward blue-and-black baseball cap that made his eyes pop. It didn't hurt that a backward cap on a man sent me straight to horny orbit for some reason, and the gray sweatpants he had on were doing *nothing* to help the cause.

Or rather, they were doing *everything* to help.

I nodded, reflecting the smile he wore so effortlessly, mine coming a little more strained these days. "I've never been more ready. Let's go."

We got out of the car and grabbed the two small suitcases from the trunk, rolling them over the crunchy stone and gravel, reaching the door just as another car pulled up.

"Sup, studs!" Tia shouted as she leaned out the window, waving. Jessica jumped out of the passenger side, and Yvette hopped out of the back. They helped Tia with their bags before coming up onto the porch with us, all of them gawking at the cabin that towered above me.

"*This* is where we're staying?" Yvette asked in disbelief. "I might need to be dragged out of here."

"They can't drag all of us out, right? Let's just become a commune of mountain squatters," Tia suggested, an arm thrown around her girlfriend's shoulders.

Jess looked at her, brow arched, the silver ring that looped through it sparkling in the afternoon sunlight. "Let's not and say we did."

Tia shrugged. "We'll see." She leaned in and gave Jess a kiss, which seemed to brighten her face up by about a thousand watts.

"There's Eric and Tristan," I said, pointing to the truck that drove up toward us. "The gang's all here."

The boys climbed out of the truck and grabbed their luggage, both of them bringing only a book bag strapped on their shoulders. "That's all you guys brought?" Yvette asked.

"We're only here for the weekend. What else do I need?" Eric said. "I've got three pairs of underwear and three shirts rolled up in here. Plus my book and my notebook. I'm ready."

"Bathing suit?" Yvette asked.

"That too," he said, his lips quirking to the side as the doubt played off his face, his beard unable to hide it.

"Yeah, he forgot that," Tristan said, smacking him on his chest and bringing out a laugh from the group. "Come on, let's check this place out."

I turned to the keypad on the door and typed in the numbers Robby gave me. For a second, I was scared we had all been pranked, the door taking a short moment to react to the password. Thankfully, the red light turned green, and two heavy locks slid open, and the door slightly pushed forward.

We stepped in and were as equally blown away by the inside as the outside. It was like walking into a movie set, everything laid out with an intention to please the eye and get the most flawless, Oscar-winning shot without putting in any effort. Sunlight poured in through all the windows, making the polished dark wooden floors shine as if they were made of glass. Exposed beams on the vaulted ceilings flowed downward, leading the gaze to the beautiful fireplace that was the star of the show. It was made of white and black stone with a thin border of black tiles surrounding it and was large enough to keep the entire cabin warm if the logs were lit.

"Oh, we're so having our book club around this fireplace," Yvette said, running her hand over the fluffy white love seat that was tilted toward the center table made from driftwood, the table's shape something only Mother Nature could sculpt.

"What about the rooms?" Eric asked.

"Three upstairs and two downstairs. None assigned, so it's a free-for-all," I said, realizing my mistake way too late.

The scramble was immediate, Tia and Jess bolting up the stairs, followed by Tristan on their heels, giggling like a bunch of schoolkids on a race around the yard. Eric took another strategy, running directly ahead and down a hall, opening the first door he found and diving in. Yvette, Jake, and I were left in the living room, looking at each other, slightly dumbfounded.

"I'll take the one that's leftover upstairs?" Yvette asked.

"And we'll grab the one down here," Jake answered, clapping his hands together. Yvette gave a nod and a chuckle as she grabbed her neon pink suitcase and brought it upstairs, the sounds of Tristan and Tia rock-paper-scissoring for the room with the nicest view drifting down to us.

"That was easy," I said as I followed Jake down the hall, trying hard to not stare at the way his ass ate up those gray sweatpants.

Tried and failed. Miserably.

"Let's see what we just signed up for." Jake stopped in front of the door at the end of the hall, a large framed photo of Robby and his parents hanging on the wall. I had to remember to get them a good thank-you gift for letting us stay free of charge in this mountain wonderland.

Jake opened the door, and my jaw dropped. We might have lucked out with the nicest room in the cabin. It was a corner bedroom that somehow managed to be circular, the window wrapping around the entire wall and giving us the most stunning view of the Blue Ridge Mountains, covered in emerald-green trees that climbed up its various peaks and down its dipping valleys. The bed looked like a cloud, the thick white comforter folded with a few chocolates waiting on a small rainbow pillow.

The thank-you gift just got a little more expensive. I hadn't even realized they would make the place so nice for us.

Jake walked over to the window, hands in his pockets as he took in the view. I came up behind him, wrapping an arm around his waist and resting my head on his shoulder. Even though we were an hour and a half away from home, it felt like we had never left. Home for me was no longer a singular roof over my head but instead the heart that beat next to me, Jake's solid presence making me feel safe and comfortable.

"This is beautiful."

I looked up into Jake's glittering eyes. "It really is."

He caught my smile, pressing his lips against mine, the smile spreading.

"Are you ready to host the club tonight?" I asked, my hand sliding under his shirt and rubbing on his lower back, fingers tracing the two columns of muscle that created a small dip leading down to his butt.

"I am," he said, kissing me again. "I've got my talking points ready, questions written down, and drinking game set."

"Awesome." I kissed him again, the temperature in the room slowly rising. But before we got too carried away, I wanted to give Jake a gift I'd been holding on to for a couple of weeks. Now finally felt like the right time to give it to him. I slipped away from his grip and went over to my backpack, unzipping it and taking out a long, wrapped rectangular item. Jake watched me with suspicion creeping into his gaze, brows inching closer and closer together.

"Okay, so I ordered this a few weeks ago, but that's when I got the text and everything went to shit, *sooo* I held off on giving it to you. But I've got a really good feeling about this weekend and think it's the perfect time." I held it out, Jake grabbing it in both hands, the navy blue wrapping paper crinkling in his hands.

"A gift for what?"

"For being so amazing," I said. "My love language is gifts. Just take it."

Jake chuckled, starting to open it from one of the corners. "You really didn't have to get me anything."

"I know, but I wanted to."

His toothy grin was contagious. He stopped being delicate with the wrapping paper and tore off a shred of it, the rest falling down to the floor. He looked at the blank board of wood he held in his hands, slightly confused.

"Turn it around," I said, holding my breath for his reaction.

He turned it around, and his eyes went wide, instantly recognizing us etched into the wood. We were smiling in the photo, the flowers from the botanical gardens behind us and also etched into the wood with incredible detail, some of them even colored in to add an extra layer of depth. There were vines underneath the photo that grew together to spell out the date we had become official.

I heard sniffling and was surprised to see Jake wiping away a tear, overcome by the surprise. I rubbed the spot between his shoulders, and he started to tear up even more.

"This is beautiful, Noah."

"I wanted something we could have forever. That's the first photo we took together, and that's the date we became boyfriends."

"It's—I love it. So much."

He gave me another kiss, this one nearly knocking me over onto the bed. When we separated, I could see the tears welling up so much that more spilled over, one of them falling down onto the wood and darkening it. My own heart swelled with emotion. I hadn't expected this kind of reaction from Jake, who was normally much more stoic and less prone to crying than I was. It melted me. Made me fall even harder for this man, something I thought shouldn't have been impossible. I never wanted to let him go, no matter what was happening outside of our perfect little bubble.

He set the etched wood gently on the dresser and turned, kissing me again, and again and again, until we fell back onto the bed laughing into each other's mouths, hands roaming and my shorts unzipping. "How much time do you think we have before everyone gets suspicious?" Jake asked, already kissing his way down my belly.

"About ten minutes, give or take."

"Should be enough time to show how thankful I am for you," he said, rubbing his face on my shorts before pulling them off with his teeth, smiling up at me the entire time.

Pfft. With how sexy Jake was, I figured we'd only need five minutes for him to show me how grateful he was.

And I was right.

24

JAKE PEREZ

THE CABIN WAS LIKE A LABYRINTH. There were five bedrooms with huge bathrooms and two kitchens. There was one living room at the front of the cabin and another toward the back, along with a neon-bright arcade in the basement and a couple of pool tables. There was a hot tub on the wraparound deck and another lounge area full of comfortable pillows and an outdoor couch that was more comfortable than the one I had in my house. Next to one of the bedrooms was a wall-to-wall library full of all different kinds of books, with an arching window that was flanked by two maroon armchairs.

Yvette wasn't the only one who would need to be dragged out of here.

"Alright, everyone settled in?" I asked as we gathered around the fireplace. We'd already claimed our rooms (while I claimed Noah) and were ready to start the book club, wineglasses in hand and books on laps.

I looked to Noah, sitting directly across from me, his

legs crossed and a pleasant smile on his face, likely brought on by the orgasm of his that I'd swallowed about fifteen minutes ago. I could still taste him on my tongue, a salty-sweet memory of his release lingering on my taste buds. Part of me was still in shock at the gift he got me, one of the nicest gifts I'd ever received. His thoughtfulness, his kindness, his heart—it meant the world to me. It felt like winning the lotto over and over again every time I caught his eye and felt the butterflies in my gut kick up again, creating a mini whirlwind of multicolored wings as they fluttered around in giddy excitement.

He was my guy. And I never wanted to let him go, ever.

I got a cluster of affirmations from the group, and suddenly, the warmth of Noah's gaze shifted into nerves as the attention all turned toward me. I wasn't exactly used to leading a group and always got a little stage fright whenever the spotlight turned toward me, but looking around at the group of smiling friends worked like an antidote, curing the nerves and allowing me to feel a deep sense of comfort. I sunk further into my seat and opened the book.

"Alright, guys, so we're almost done with the book. Tonight, I wanted to talk about Gabrielle and how she still doesn't know the jewelry she ordered is made out of bones. But before we get started, let me explain tonight's game." From out of my book, I took out a bookmark I got custom-made for tonight. It was a glossy bookmark shaped like a rainbow with the book club's name printed across it. "For tonight, we're playing

Drinking under the Rainbow. Every time someone takes the stage to speak, you spin the rainbow first, and whoever the two ends land on has to drink. Sound good?"

Another round of head nodding and excited yeses followed. So far, so good.

"Let me kick it off." I leaned forward and spun the bookmark, the rainbow stopping and landing on Tia and Jess. They both raised their glasses and clinked them together before taking their drink.

I clapped my hands together, looking around the group. "Now, I want to have a vote: who here thinks Archie is the killer and jewelry maker?"

Nearly the entire room enthusiastically raised their hands. Everyone except for Noah.

"Who do you think it is?" I asked, looking at the handsome man across from me and wishing he was sitting on my lap instead.

"I think it's actually Gabrielle. I think she's killing these people and then making the jewelry to sell online, but she's been buying from her own store so that she can have the keepsakes. I think that the abuse Archie did to her was enough to make her lose it."

The hands in the room slowly started to fall. Noah made sense, and he framed the narrative in a way I hadn't thought of before. "So you think the few chapters from the murderer's POV is actually Gabrielle?" I asked.

"I do," he said, looking proud at his detective skills. "Think about it. Both Gabrielle and the killer are obsessed with the color red, while Gabrielle is also obsessed with making Archie's life a living hell. I think he's going to be the final victim."

"Damn," Tristan said, rubbing the back of his neck. "I think you figured it out."

"Too bad I can't figure out the mysteries happening in my own life," he said, shoulders slumping.

That did something to the room. Shifted the mood. Noah was going through a living nightmare, and I was sure that we all wished we could crack the case. Eric, who was sitting next to Noah on the couch, put a reassuring arm around his friend's shoulder. He was a big bear of a man, his frame dwarfing Noah's next to him. "Why don't we put book club on hold tonight and try to use those detective skills on figuring out what the hell is going on?"

"I like that plan," Yvette said, pushing a rogue curl behind her ear. "I'll admit, I've been doing some googling. Trying to figure out how other stalking cases have been cracked."

"What did you find?" Noah asked.

She chewed on the inside of her cheek. "Nothing very helpful. It does always seem like the stalker is someone close to the person. It's not usually some rando online that decides to fixate on you."

"But the only person I can think of that's close to me and would do something like that is Franky..."

"What about any guys you've been with after Franky?" Tristan set his book down and swapped it for his drink. "You hooked up with a couple, right?"

"Just a few," Noah said. He glanced at me, and I wondered if he was nervous about opening up. I didn't care that he'd been with other guys, not when I was the lucky one to claim him.

I leaned forward, feeling like we were onto something. "Were any of them extra clingy?"

He took a moment to think before shaking his head. Jess raised a finger. "Do you still have the messages? Maybe we can compare them to that threat you were sent?"

Noah shook his head again. "I deleted the app. The messages go with it."

"Can I see the text?" Tristan asked. Noah had mentioned how he was a tech savant; maybe he knew how to track where the message came from. "Sometimes, there's ways to get the metadata from it. Maybe I can figure out who sent it or from where."

Noah opened his phone and scrolled to the text message, its words already seared into my brain. Tristan got to work, crossing one leg on the other and sitting back on the couch.

"What about Franky's wife?" Tia pointed out. "Didn't you say that she was pretty angry when you guys went to talk to him? Maybe she found out you dated her husband and she got pissed off enough to torture you and Jake?"

"It's a possibility." Noah pursed his lips and shook his head. "I just don't know why she'd *still* be coming after me and my relationship."

"No, Noah is right," Jess said, countering her girlfriend. "This feels to me like someone that's obsessed with him, romantically speaking. Not someone who's angry with him. Or maybe... is Jake the original target?"

That made me cock my head. I hadn't thought of that being the case, but maybe someone from my past was the one who was behind this vicious curtain? I couldn't imagine it being anyone I dated, especially not my most recent relationship: Ashley. We were still solid friends, and I couldn't see her harboring any resentment for what had happened between us. It was her choice, her decision to own herself and be happy, even if it caused some discomfort in the beginning.

"The first threat was sent specifically for me, though. Jake was there, but the box with the chicken head had my name written on it."

"What about Mason?" I asked. "He was there that night. At your doorstep, he's the one that found the box."

"I don't..." Noah chewed on his bottom lip, turning the pink flesh pale white. "He's always been nice to me. Sometimes he says things that are a little off, but he never gave me stalker vibes."

"They rarely do," Eric said. "What about your other neighbor? Robby? He was there that night. Didn't you two date for a little?"

I looked to Noah, slightly surprised by the news. I didn't know all of his past relationships and didn't have an expectation to learn them, but the neighbor sounded like one relationship that should have been brought up, at least in passing.

"Dating is a *very* strong word. I saw him on Grindr once, and we hooked up after each having an entire bottle of wine. It happened a couple more times until I told him I wasn't feeling it. We weren't compatible at all in the bedroom, so I told him to just stay friends."

Ah, that must be why it was never brought up. It barely even registered as a blip to Noah, who had severed any kind of sexual connection with Robby long before I entered the picture.

"And he was okay with that?" Yvette asked. She had the eyes of an eagle, penetrating and powerful, likely honed from her years working as an in-demand lawyer. She didn't have her own firm yet but was well on her way to tacking on her last name to the side of a skyscraper in Downtown Atlanta.

"Yeah, he said he understood. Honestly, he was into some pretty intense stuff, and he said he gets that not everyone was into it."

Tristan looked up from the phone, his attention catching on the conversation. "Dark stuff? Like what?"

"He liked pain play and wanted to role-play some intense things. It just wasn't for me."

"Robby? The twink that crashed his car twice into the same stop sign at the entrance to your community? That Robby?" Tristan looked skeptical, but Noah answered with a nod. Tristan's forehead wrinkled in surprise before he turned his gaze back to the phone glowing in his hands, the light from the screen catching on the shiny silver chain he had around his neck, the links thick.

"*Alsssoo,*" Jess said, "he's the reason why we're in this mansion in the woods, right? He can't be that bad."

"True, true," Tia said. "Although that would be twisted as fuck if he lent us this place to like watch us or something."

Jess clapped her hands and stood up. "Uh-uh, this is where I call it a night. I'm sorry, but I'm way too big of a scaredy-cat, and I don't want to have to sleep with the light on." She turned to Noah, putting a hand on his shoulder. "I love you, Noah. You're like my little brother, and as the honorary big sis, I refuse to let *anyone* hurt you. I think all of us here can say that. So don't stress out too much, okay? We're going to figure it out."

Noah sucked in a deep breath. He managed a smile, although I saw a quiver in his lips. Tia stood, grabbing Jess's hand in hers. "Let me go tuck Jess in. If you guys are still out here plotting and theorizing, then I'll come back and join."

The two disappeared to their room upstairs. The sound of the door shutting and the shower starting filtered down into the now silent living room. We were all tossing around our own theories while Eric looked through some kind of database on his phone, likely given to him by the connections he still had in the police department.

But nothing was coming to me. I couldn't put the pieces together, and that made me angry and frustrated, like I was banging my head against a brick wall over and over again. All the while, Noah was suffering, and our lives were both threatened. How the hell did we get here? And why? Why couldn't my time with Noah just be smooth sailing? Instead, it was like we were steering a rickety sailboat into the Bermuda Triangle while there was a category five hurricane ripping through it.

That was when Tristan said, "Hmm, hold up, I think I've got something," and threw a life raft directly toward us, giving me hope that maybe we could make it out of this storm in one piece.

25

NOAH BARNES

ALL EYES TURNED TO TRISTAN. My heart raced, unsure of what to expect but my hope growing alongside Tristan's widening smile.

"I was able to dig into this text a little bit. Turns out it was sent through a burner app, so someone can get assigned a random number and have the message sent without linking it to themselves."

"Is there any way to see who sent the text, then?" I asked, my mouth as dry as the pot of dirt holding a variety of succulents on the coffee table.

"All I can see is that someone scheduled the text. There's two time stamps attached to it. One when it was written and saved and the other when it was sent." Tristan looked closer at the phone. "Wait, actually, there is something here... It was sent from somewhere in Georgia."

"Great, that really narrows things down." I couldn't keep the sarcastic bite out of my disappointed comment.

"Sorry, Noah, I wish I could give something more solid."

I shook my head, rubbing my face. "It's not your fault. You did more than I've been able to do, so thank you."

Tristan leaned over and nudged me with his shoulder, handing back my phone. "Come on. How 'bout we all get in the hot tub and talk about it some more with fresh beers and a nice view?"

That actually didn't sound too bad. "Let's do that. But no more talking about—*this*." I wagged my phone in the air from the tips of my fingers as if it were infected with something. "Not tonight. I want to try to have at least *some* fun, and I don't want to drag you guys down."

"You aren't dragging us down, baby," Jake said, his gaze pinning me to the couch from across the table. He had his legs spread and planted firmly on the ground, his hands hanging loosely between them, his lips cocked into a half smirk. This was the first time he'd used a pet name with me in front of my friends, and it sent a quiver shooting straight down to my core.

God, he was so damn sexy. Even when the conversation swirled around stalkers and threats, he still somehow managed to cut through the fear and anxiety with a smoldering look.

"Ready to get wet?" he asked.

Tristan scoffed, rolling his eyes. "Okay, you two need to stop. Not in front of Eric."

"What? What did I do?" Eric asked, leaning over to look at Tristan with an arched brow.

"I just know you're a little relationship deficient right now. I don't want you to pass out or anything."

That got a laugh out of us. "Being single is not the same as an iron deficiency," Eric tried to clear up.

"Yeah, but for your dramatic ass, it might as well be," Tristan shot back, standing up and taking his book with him up the stairs to his room.

Eric was left with his jaw on the floor, looking around at Jake, Yvette, and me. "Am I really—"

"Yes," Yvette and I answered in unison. More laughter spread through the room as we cleared out to get ready for the hot tub portion of the evening. I needed this palate cleanser and felt myself getting excited at the idea of getting drunk in a hot tub overlooking the star-dusted mountains.

Being in the same room as a naked and changing Jake *also* made me excited but in an entirely different way.

———

JAKE, Yvette, and Eric were the only ones who made it into the hot tub with me. Jess and Tia both decided to call it a night, and Tristan stayed in his room, likely sexting one of his many conquests. He was definitely the player of the group, constantly juggling three or four different guys with no sign of ever slowing down, no matter how many times we told him he deserved something serious and long-lasting.

Eric and I were the complete opposite, Eric even more monogamy-centered than I was. He rarely hooked up with guys unless he knew there was the prospect of a real relationship between him and the guy, having avoided most of the apps but not being able to avoid major heartbreaks.

We sat in the bubbling hot tub with beers and wine in hand, discussing Eric's latest breakup. "I don't know. I think I'm going to become a monk, live in a mountain somewhere. Maybe here. Are there monks in Blue Ridge?"

"There'll be at least one." Yvette chuckled, taking a sip of her wine before leaning back on the rim of the tub. The mountains opened up behind her, as if they were a rocky cape that draped off her shoulders. A bright and unobstructed full moon hung in the sky and gave a ghostly glow to the peaks and valleys.

"I think we can find you someone before you turn into a man of the cloth," I said.

Jake cocked his head at me. "I think that's the term for a priest, not a monk."

"Right, well, you get what I mean. Although I do think you'd look fabulous in whatever kind of robes you choose to wear."

Eric laughed and took a swig of his beer. "The only robe I plan on putting on is a bathrobe." He let his legs float up, toes breaking through the bubbles. "I'll be fine. I'm feeling okay being alone, actually. It's weird to say— I've been used to being with someone constantly, but being alone has helped me get back to, well, me."

"This is your eat, pray, love moment," Jake said, "except you're loving yourself."

I looked to Jake, smiling. My legs were crossed over his under the water, our sides pressed together. I also used to enjoy being alone, but ever since Jake entered the picture, the thought of being alone actually terrified me. I had found my one, my other half, no doubt about it, and I never wanted to let go.

"Such a good book," Yvette said.

"And movie," Eric added. "Didn't read the book."

Yvette put a scandalized hand to her chest, doing a soap-opera double take in his direction. "In front of your book club?"

Eric dropped his head, shamed.

"I didn't read the book either," I said in a stage whisper.

Yvette laughed and sent a splash of hot water in my direction. Eric rolled his neck and stretched, covering his mouth for a yawn that quickly spread throughout the tiny group. Yvette glanced at her watch before she leaned out of the hot tub to grab her towel.

"Alright, boys, I'm heading to bed. That was just too much for me to handle," Yvette said, shaking her head as she looked between Eric and me like a disappointed mother. Eric stood up, water dripping from his hairy chest.

"I'm going to bed, too. Maybe I can read some chapters before Yvette excommunicates me from the club."

We told our friends good night and were left alone in the hot tub, the star-filled night sky serving as a twinkling canopy, the sounds of bubbles breaking through water mixing with the sound of cicadas and crickets singing their last notes before clocking out.

"Did you want to go to bed?" Jake asked me, arm around my shoulder.

"Nah, I can stay out here a little longer."

"Good. Me too." He kissed the side of my head as his leg slipped through mine. His arm dropped under the water, going around my waist and pulling me onto his thigh. "Have you been having a good night?" he asked, and I couldn't help but sense a suggestive note in his tone.

"I have," I answered. A smile spread across my face as I let my head drop back on Jake's shoulder. "You?"

"Same." He kissed me again, this time on my cheek. "Any night with you is guaranteed to be a great night."

I let that sink in, allowing the words to nestle somewhere inside my chest. Even in my longest relationship and most recent relationship, I'd never really heard words like those. Franky was so busy hating himself and what we were doing that he rarely—if ever—let me know how much he enjoyed his time with me. I didn't realize how *good* it would feel to hear those kinds of words, especially when they were coming from Jake's lips. I felt high. Giddy and floaty, like I was being lifted by the bubbles breaking all around me and pushed straight into the galaxies above us.

"We should do this more often, go on little escapes. I like traveling with you," I said, letting my heart speak before my brain did.

"Let's do it. Where do you want to go next?"

I considered his question, a dozen different picturesque destinations gliding across my mind. "We've got the mountains covered. Want to do a beach next? Maybe Costa Rica?"

Jake's brows shot up at that. "I've always wanted to go. My mom actually used to go a lot when she was a kid. My aunt used to live there but moved to America sometime after I was born, so we never ended up going."

"Let's do it, then. We can explore the jungle and maybe take some surf lessons."

"We'll book it tomorrow," Jake said, and just like that, we had another vacation scheduled together. That giddy feeling only grew more intense. I loved this moment. I loved tonight.

I loved—no. Nope. Too soon to go there. Even though the L-word wanted to shoot from my throat and land directly on Jake, I had to swallow it down. It would change everything between us. And what if I said it and Jake didn't feel it back? We'd only been together for three months; even though it felt like three lifetimes already, he could potentially shut me down.

"How's your mom?" I asked before I could let my head drift too far up into the clouds.

"She's okay. My aunt's actually staying with her this weekend, just in case. This is probably the farthest I've been from her in a while. It's tough, not gonna lie. But at least she isn't alone."

I nodded my head, cuddling in closer to Jake. "Do you think she'd want to go to Costa Rica with us?"

Jake looked at me, his eyes catching the moonlight,

his smile as soft as the diamond-white glow. I was surprised when I saw a tear slip from the corner, falling down his cheek like a stray jewel. "I don't think she can," he said, his voice hitching. "But God, I'd love it if she could. Us three together, that would be incredible. But... she's already forgetting some major things. I don't think taking her out of her comfort zone would be good." He closed his eyes and swallowed a lump. "Fuck, I can't even talk about her without getting choked up."

"It's okay," I said, rubbing the back of his neck. I'd come to learn that was one of his favorite places to be touched. "I can't imagine how hard this must be. I'm lucky enough to say I'm close with both my parents, and they're both in good health. I honestly dread getting any kind of call with bad news from them. And you've been so supportive of her, too. You've been a really good son, and that's what matters."

Jake's bottom lip quivered. Seeing him crack like this made my own emotions swell like a rising tide. "It just really fucking sucks. I'm twenty-six, and I'm already losing my mom after I already lost my dad. And it's all happening in—in slow motion. I have to watch her forget about me. I have to watch—" He couldn't continue, his lip shaking beyond his control, more crystalline tears dripping down his cheeks. I turned away, hiding my own tears, not wanting to feed into his sadness.

"And there's nothing I can do," Jake continued when he felt comfortable enough to speak again. "There's nothing that can give us hope. I've tried getting her into a few experimental trials, but nothing is guaranteed. It's such a monstrous disease. Cruel."

"Even if she can't remember, those moments you've shared with her aren't going anywhere. They'll always make up the fabric of you and her. History can't be erased, no matter how flimsy memory can be. And then when we all make it to wherever we're going in the end, we can reminisce on them."

Jake licked his lips and managed a smile. His eyes bounced between mine like he was searching for something. What it was, I wasn't sure, but I let him look, digging through my soul for whatever it was he needed.

"That's a beautiful way to think about it," he finally said. He leaned forward and kissed my forehead, his lips lingering on my skin for a couple of heavenly moments. "Maybe there is a way to keep the hope alive after all."

"There's *always* a way," I said. It was my turn to kiss Jake, this time finding his lips, feeling them softly part against mine. I held his face in my hands, breathing in the same air, his arms wrapping around me and encasing me. "Always."

"Promise?" he asked me, long lashes blinking away rogue teardrops.

I answered him with another kiss, and another, and another. The heavy moment began to shift, the two of us getting closer and closer. "And whatever you or your mom need," I said between kisses, "just ask. I'm here now. I can help. Even if you just need to talk."

"Thank you," he said, the smile working its way back

onto his handsome face. "Let's do a little less talking right now, though."

"That's fine with me," I said, pressing my lips back onto his, moving my body so that I straddled him underwater, sitting on his lap as the kiss grew into an all-consuming wildfire that licked its way up my legs, past my core, straight up to my head, where it melted away any other thoughts except for one that was strong enough to resist the flames:

I'm so fuckin' in love with this man.

26

JAKE PEREZ

I LET myself sink into Noah's kiss. His lips and tongue were like a balm, working to soothe the burns that marked my soul. His kiss was a teleportation device, picking us up and sending us directly to nirvana, no layovers and no stops. Just a direct flight to paradise.

I opened my legs wider, giving him a better seat. Water bubbled all around us, splashing up onto my neck. Noah's hand wrapped around my nape, fingers digging in a little tighter as his kiss grew hungrier. I matched the intensity, my blood starting to warm as much as the water that surrounded us. Noah's excitement twitched against my stomach, pushing against his shorts and making my own cock throb with a rising need.

"Is everyone asleep?" I asked, looking around Noah to the closed door leading into the cabin.

Noah gave a breathy reply. "I think so." His hand dropped from my neck, going under the water and rubbing my hardening length through my swim trunks.

He kissed my neck and stroked, sending me even further out into orbit. Noah's grip around my cock never failed to make my toes curl. I loved it. My body was his to use, to please, and *fuck* did he do a good job of pleasing me.

I rubbed Noah's sides, running my hands down toward his perky ass. I pushed my hands under the waistband of his shorts and felt those soft globes against my palm, opening him, running a finger across his sensitive hole. He bit his lower lip, looking down at me with puppy eyes that only managed to fan the flames that crackled inside my core, the heat spreading to between my thighs.

He started to grind on me, straddling me, rubbing his ass on my hard cock. I slammed my mouth against his, holding him closer to me. The pressure on my cock was delicious, but my body cried out for more. There was a shouting desire in the forefront of my brain: get him naked, and get his twitching cock in my ass.

But first, I wanted to taste him. "Can you stand on the seat?" I asked, needing all the willpower I could muster to break from the kiss.

"Let's see." He put his hands on my shoulder and pushed, water cascading off him as he lifted up and stood on the small ledge that wrapped around the hot tub. I looked up at him, barely able to see from the massive tent of multicolored fabric that blocked my vision.

He lowered his shorts, and out sprung that thick cock of his. I immediately started drooling, leaning forward and licking the tip before I went down his shaft, my hands on his thighs as I buried my nose under his balls.

Water dripped down his body, making him glisten like a rare jewel.

I palmed myself under my shorts as I took him in my mouth, slow at first, tasting every inch of him and watching as his eyes rolled back in his skull. I worked to take all of him down my throat, my body thrumming with an electricity reserved for a power plant.

Coming up for breath gave me a chance to appreciate Noah's beautiful cock. I held him by the base, admiring the heft of it in my hand, the way it twitched, how a drop of precome slid from his tip. I stroked him, slow, watching as his balls tightened, his pink cock head swelling. I kissed it, his salty-sweet precome coating my lips. "Fuck, Noah, you have such a perfect dick."

He smiled down at me, hands twining through my hair. "So do you," he said. "I think we both lucked out."

"We really did," I said, going back to my worshipping. I just loved Noah's cock, even when he was soft. The way it hung between his legs, tucked inside his foreskin—it was a work of art. Many people (likely straight) didn't consider the male anatomy as attractive as I did, but my fascination with dick went far beyond just sexual. I loved them in all their shapes and sizes, loved how hard they got and how wet they got and how they tasted and smelled and felt inside of me. It was a long, long list of things I loved about cock, and Noah's checked off each of them.

He groaned as I deep-throated his entire size, swallowing him down whole. He coated the back of my throat with precome as I swirled my tongue around his shaft, earning a deeper groan, one that made my cock harder than iron. I plunged a hand into the water and jerked myself off. The night was chilly, but the water kept us warm, steam rising and curling into the air. We were on the corner of the wraparound deck, away from any windows while having one of the best views of the Great Smoky Mountains.

Although I certainly wasn't concerned with the view of the mountains at that moment.

"God, Jake, you've already got me close."

I stopped sucking him off, licking my lips, smiling up at the sex-drunk man with his cheeks flushed and nipples hard. His eyes smoldered with the same heat I felt coursing in my veins. It was in that instant that I realized this man had claimed me. I wasn't exactly sure of when, but I was sure of how, his cock still hard in my closed grip. He looked into my eyes with a possessiveness to him that made me throb. Noah gave me a look that imparted a message: It was just us two, us against the world, and nothing would be able to tear us apart. Nothing and no one. His thumb traced a soft circle on my cheek, trailing over my bottom lip, as if that was the signature to his proclamation.

You are mine, and I am yours.

Noah stepped off the seat, and I rose to stand with him in the hot tub, grabbing his face in my hands and giving him that same possessiveness but through my kiss. It was a kiss that had no brakes, nothing to hold it back. I wanted him to know how much he meant to me, how happy I was that we'd bumped into each other in that grocery store, and how excited I was for everything that was yet to come.

Underneath the water, our cocks rubbed, battling for space, the smooth friction sending bolts of lightning through my nerves. Noah reached down and grabbed my ass in both his hands, opening me, pulling me harder onto his body as the kiss between us grew hotter.

"I need to have you," I said breathlessly, hungry. My entire body ached to be filled by Noah. To have him stake his claim, over and over and over again. Harder and harder. I needed him inside me.

"Can I fuck you?" he asked in a husky whisper. The question did almost as much for me as having Noah's stiff cock between my lips.

"Yes," I answered, turning and lifting up so that my knees were on the seat, my ass out of the water. Noah's grip closed around my hips as he lined himself up behind me. I could feel the pressure of his cock head pushing at my hole, followed by the sound of Noah spitting, adding some extra lube even though I was so horny for him that I wasn't sure it was even needed.

Although it was appreciated, Noah's cock sliding into me with a smooth thrust. I propped my forearms on the hot tub and dropped my head, arching my back so that Noah had the best angle. He slowly rubbed my lower back, his cock filling me up. I moaned as he slowly pulled back, getting me accustomed to him before increasing the pace.

"Oh, Noah, fuck that feels so good. Keep fucking me."

"Yeah?" he asked, spreading apart my cheeks as he started to thrust harder, spurred by my increasingly loud moans. "I love watching you take my cock."

The words nearly fell from my lips, pushed out by the rhythmic thrusting. "And I love you—" I caught myself. Too soon. Too scared. Just because Noah was currently scrambling my brains with his cock didn't mean I had to lose all sense of logic and reasoning.

"Love you giving it to me," I said. It was the truth, but not entirely what I meant to say.

He seemed to have been spurred on by that, bucking into me harder, faster, as if he wanted to become one with me, fused together. With every thrust, his cock pressed against my prostate, making me leak, sending me on a collision course with my orgasm.

"Keep going," I pleaded, "keep going, Noah, oh fuck, that's it."

"I'm going to come," he warned.

"Give it to me." I pushed back, my hold around him tightening. He let out a primal sound as his fingers dug into my hips, and his thrusting stopped, his cock buried deep inside me as he came.

I followed right after, shooting ropes of come out onto the deck, my entire body quaking and my muscles melting and my heart skipping about three dozen beats. I leaned forward to try and catch my breath as Noah slowly pulled out of me, leaving me pleasantly sore and still ready for more.

"God damn, you nearly made me pass out," I said, climbing out of the hot tub and wrapping a towel around my waist, my semi-hard cock hanging out of the front. Noah's smile reached from ear to ear as he climbed out of the hot tub, the water making his lithe body shine as though there was a spotlight aimed directly at him.

He looked like a prince who stepped out of a story-book. Handsome and charming and hung. The holy trinity of traits for a fairy-tale prince. Noah had it all. I couldn't even dream of a man who would compete with him.

That's when it hit me. Hard and fast, just like Noah's thrusts. It slammed into my brain, pushing aside every-thing else, the words tattooing themselves across my heart: *I'm in love with Noah.*

The words bubbled back up to my lips, forming on the tip of my tongue. Before I could get them out, Noah came over for another kiss, pressing his body back against mine. He wrapped his arms lazily around my shoulders, nipping on my bottom lip and looking up into my eyes with that same possessiveness from moments before, but softened somehow. As if his eyes had taken on the velvet qualities of a rose petal plucked straight from my garden.

I let the moment take us, getting lost in the comfort-able silence, happy to just hold him and kiss him and feel his heart beating against mine. This was all I'd ever wanted, a love that made you feel like you were on top of the world, even higher than the mountain you were currently standing on. Noah gave me wings, invisible but powerful enough to carry us both into the sky.

I couldn't hold it back anymore. The emotion grew in me, a seed sprouting and thriving, pushing up through my throat and nearing my mouth. I had to tell him. Had to let Noah know how much I loved him.

A series of vibrations threw us off, the thin silence between us getting severed. It startled Noah, who jerked backward, looking at the still-shut door. We both had towels around us, so no one could tell we were naked, but maybe it wasn't Noah's friends who scared him.

"Who the hell is texting me this late," Noah said, going over to his phone.

Before he even picked it up, I already knew it would be bad. An icy chill slipped into the space in my chest that was fiery hot only seconds before. Dread wrapped around me like a thorn-covered vine, snapping tighter the moment I saw Noah's face blanch, fear making his eyes bulge as he read whatever messages had landed in his inbox.

27

NOAH BARNES

THE WORLD SPUN on its axis. I went from feeling on top of the world one moment to being crushed underneath it the next. As if the sky had flipped and the ground had fallen in all around me. I started to shake, so much that Jake took the phone from me, reading the words that sent me on a terror spiral:

"I SEE you didn't listen to me. You must really not love Jake, HUH?"

Jake's eyes widened, pupils blowing wide like saucers. The moonlight reflected off of them, magnifying his fear. It was the same raw fear that gnawed at my ribs like a bunch of caged rodents desperate to escape, visceral and painful and breathtaking.

The dark woods that surrounded us were no longer romantic. Every shadow belonged to a bloodthirsty monster, eyes peering at me through the branches and bushes.

I dashed for our clothes, throwing mine on and

tossing Jake his. This was too much. Way too much. I had somehow managed to lull myself into thinking that everything was fine, that someone out there wasn't maniacally obsessed with making my life a living hell.

Eric was inside the living room, having a midnight snack, when we burst in. I was sure I looked like someone who'd just come across a dead body: pale and wide-eyed and shaky. Eric stood up from the couch, the bag of chips dropping to the floor as he came over to my side.

"What happened out there?"

Jake handed him the phone as I made my way to the couch on trembling legs. I collapsed onto the seat, using the armrest to support me. I couldn't peel my eyes off the wide-open windows that looked out into the dark woods.

Where were they? Was the person watching me right this very moment? Could they see me and I couldn't see them?

My spine shook like the tail of a rattlesnake. I clenched my fists and tried to keep myself from passing out.

"Jesus Christ." Eric handed the phone back to Jake. He didn't even take a second to put on his shoes, going straight to the door and throwing it open, walking out onto the deck even though I offered a couple of weak protests.

He came back in five minutes, concern magnified across his bearded face. I didn't think I'd ever seen Eric this shaken up. He was always the stony and solid support for the group, having consoled me and Tristan through a variety of different problems and crises. He never cracked, his face never showing fear.

Until tonight.

"I didn't see anyone or find any signs of anyone being around. It's a big property, though..."

Jake was sitting at my side, an arm around my shoulders. He pressed his lips gently against the side of my head. It wasn't really a kiss, more like a silent sign of comfort, a life raft thrown into the middle of these turbulent waters. I leaned into him, but instead of finding comfort, I turned icy-cold, my entire body turning into a taut wire ready to be snapped by the slightest movement.

This was my fault. Because of exactly *this*, of leaning on Jake and calling him my boyfriend. He'd be safe and sound in his own bed if he had never met me. If he'd never shown up at our workplace, if he'd never pulled into that Publix, if he'd never— I swallowed back a sob.

"Maybe Tristan can track this one?" Eric suggested. "Let me get him."

"Wait, wait, we might have to wake everyone up." I looked at the clock on the wall. It was already pushing close to one in the morning. "I don't know if we can stay here. Not if this person can see us."

"We don't know that for sure," Jake said. His grip around me grew tighter, which I was thankful for. It helped to keep me from feeling like I was unmoored and drifting out into dark and open waters.

"The message said 'see,' and it was all caps."

Jake looked at me, but I could recognize the unchecked anxiety that rattled around in his skull. He chewed nervously on his bottom lip, nearly drawing blood, turning the skin around it white underneath the five-o'clock shadow that seemed to be growing darker by the minute. I closed my eyes and tried to wake myself up from this nightmare.

"We have to go," I said, my eyes snapping open, the nightmare continuing on. "We can stay at the cabin I originally got us for the retreat. I think it's still available. Let me check." I went for my phone but remembered the message that sat inside it like a deadly viper curled up and waiting for the right moment to strike again. I put my phone back down on the couch.

"The Eagle Rock cabin? That's like forty-five minutes from here. Once we wake everyone up and get going, it'll almost be sunrise." Eric cracks his knuckles. What he said next clearly took some work to get out. "And if this person really does have eyes on you, Noah, they'll know if we leave tonight. I think we stay here and then regroup in the morning. I'll sleep down here in the living room, just so I can wake up every now and then and keep an eye on things."

"Want to do it in shifts?" Jake suggested. I looked to him, a slash of guilt and sadness cutting across my chest. This man, he was perfect in every way and didn't ask for any of this—didn't *deserve* any of this.

"I've got it," Eric said, offering a somber smile. "But thank you, man."

"Yeah, of course."

"What about the police?" I asked, needing to stand up from the couch so I could begin pacing, trying in vain to burn off the excess anxiety that made my bones vibrate. "Shouldn't I call them?"

Eric used to be a cop. He'd know.

"We can call them, make a report, and get it recorded. They could do a search around the property, although I doubt they'll find anything. I think this person's just trying to fuck with you, Noah. I've seen stalker cases like these, and they either end up with the stalker getting caught or burnt out. Usually, once they see law enforcement is getting more heavily involved, then they step back."

There was the stone-faced and logic-spewing Eric I'd come to love. He cracked his knuckles and glanced at the door.

"Okay, let's call them." I went to grab my phone but froze as I leaned over the couch. "Actually, Jake, can you call them? I still don't want to grab my phone."

Jake immediately had his phone in hand and 9-1-1 dialed. I could hear the dispatcher on the other line, asking about the problem and promising to send out a car in the next few minutes. I settled back into the couch, accepting that this was going to be a very long night.

———

I WAS RIGHT. Last night had been one of the longest of my life. The police arrived and talked to us outside so that we didn't wake anyone else up. We handed over the message and watched as they did a full sweep of the surrounding property. It was two older guys who must have been Blue Ridge natives with how they navigated around the tree-covered and sloping land with nothing but their flashlights.

They came back with neutral news: no one was there, and they couldn't find signs of anyone having been there recently. It wasn't great that they didn't find anyone, but it also let me feel a modicum of comfort over the fact that no one was standing out there and watching me through the heavy shadows.

Still, sleep wasn't happening for me. Jake fell asleep sometime around two in the morning, but I continued to stay awake, staring at the ceiling, rolling around and trying my hardest not to look into the dark corners of the room. I kept going through a mental Rolodex of people I knew in my life, wondering who the hell would have such an obsession with me. I kept landing on Franky, but then I'd start thinking about his wife—she knew my name, she likely knew our history, and she was upset at how that meeting with Jake and Franky had gone. But was that all enough to make her want to destroy my life? Couldn't she just leave me the hell alone?

I watched as the room became lighter, the walls of the cabin painted a soft blue by the early morning light that crept in through the thick beige curtains. I stretched under the covers, my feet brushing against a sleeping Jake. He stirred but didn't open his eyes, allowing me a moment to look at him, finding some peace in the way he slept. How his blond hair looked messy but perfect, his lips slightly pouty and parted, his lashes long and his breathing soft.

If anything happened to him, I'd be destroyed. I wouldn't be able to live with myself.

My stomach twisted into a series of knots. Anxiety seeped back into my bones, making me twitchy. I had to get up, had to move.

I slowly pushed a leg out from under the comforter and stepped on the floor, trying my best to be as silent as possible. I managed to get both feet on the floor before Jake stirred again. I didn't want to wake him, not this early in the morning. His eyes remained shut. I stood and tiptoed my way out of the bedroom, opening the door as slow as I could so that the hinges didn't creak. I did the same as I closed it, walking down the hall and toward the kitchen, where I could hear some low chatter.

It was Tristan and Eric, both of them holding water bottles and looking like they were about to go for a run. "Morning, Noah," they said, echoing off each other.

"How ya feeling? Eric told me everything."

I sighed. Exhaustion from this all-nighter would likely hit me in a couple of hours, but for now, I was still running on some leftover fumes. "Not great. I barely got any sleep."

"Come on, let's go for a walk and get some fresh mountain air," Tristan said, hand on my shoulder. He offered me a sympathetic smile, which I tried to return but failed midway.

"Let me grab my sneakers."

Tristan, Eric, and I headed out of the cabin and started down the curving gravel road that led to the more populated parts of the mountain. Rocks and twigs crunched under our feet, mixing with the chorus of birds belting their morning songs. It was getting chilly; the shorts and T-shirt I had on would soon be needing a jacket and sweatpants to keep me warm. Tristan had already beat us to the punch, wearing black sweats and a long-sleeved shirt.

He always ran colder than most people.

"What a fuckin' mess, you guys." I looked to either side of me, flanked by my closest friends, and I started to laugh. It was likely fed by delirium, but at least it made me feel a little better. The laughter spread, both guys joining me, Tristan shaking his head and slapping me between the shoulders.

"Only you would land yourself the man of your dreams at the same time as you get the stalker of your nightmares," Tristan said.

"Well," Eric said, "there was that one guy you dated, Tristan. Who you thought was stealing your used underwear while also being a reincarnation of a Greek god."

"Oh yeah, that's right. I still don't know what happened to my underwear... or how he got that eight-pack."

Eric and I chuckled. We took a turn down the road, sticking to the main path and avoiding any of the hiking trails that branched off into the woods. The mountain sloped downward at a steep incline, making us have to do a slight shuffle to keep balanced. There were a couple of cabins appearing through the thin trees, none of them as large or as modern as the one we were staying in.

"Seriously, though, you and Jake are a really solid

pair. I don't think I've ever seen you this happy with someone," Tristan said.

I shook my head. He was right—I'd *never* been this happy with any of the guys I'd been with. "Jake is special. I can't even explain it. We just get along so well; it's easy with him. I never have to second-guess anything or worry about what I'm saying or how I look. It's not like with Franky, when he was scared to even be spotted in the same car as me in case people recognized us and started talking. That shit hurt. But I can't imagine anything ever hurting with Jake."

"You give me hope, man." Eric put his hands into his shorts, the water bottle strap tight around his big wrist.

"What about me? I don't give you hope?" Tristan asked with an offended glare.

"No, you give me fear. Fear for all the hearts you're breaking."

"I'm not breaking hearts. I'm *healing* them. With my dick. I'm basically providing a service and for free. I'm a saint."

"Ah, yes, the patron saint of penis," I said with a roll of my eyes. The guys started to laugh, and the question got tossed out: was there some kind of saint that over-looked sex? We joked around some more, the mood feeling infinitely lighter than earlier. This was why I loved these guys. We were able to turn any situation around into something positive, so long as the three of us were together.

Friends for life, brothers forever. I loved these two.

"Should we start heading back?" Eric asked as we

reached the bottom of the gravel road before it turned into pavement, a large lake opening up in front of us. There was still a delicate cloud of morning mist hanging above it.

"Let's do it," Tristan said, clapping his hands. We turned to walk back to the cabin when Eric's phone started to ring. He went to answer it, but the call dropped. Then Tristan's phone began to ring. Weird. He answered his phone, but the service still wasn't great, the call dropping before he could get a "hello" through.

Then *my* phone started to ring. Tristan and Eric both looked at me, worry knitting through the wrinkles in both their foreheads.

It was Yvette. I answered, and a couple of words managed to break through. "Come back—cameras." And then the call ended.

"We have to get back. Let's go." The boys likely picked up on the fear in my voice. We broke into a run, fighting against the sloping hill, none of us sure of what the hell we were running toward.

28

JAKE PEREZ

THE ENTIRE CREW was gathered outside of the cabin, bags packed and frantic faces on each of them. Tia held Jess in her arms while Yvette walked in circles as she spoke rapid Spanish to someone on the phone, her words flying like bullets. Noah came right over to my side, looking like he'd just thrown on a pair of gym shorts and a T-shirt, his dark brown hair still messy from lying on the pillow.

"What the hell happened?" he asked, and I could tell he was already expecting the worst. Another threat made, another chicken head found, something else to fuel his endless night terrors.

"Yvette found a camera in her room," I said. "And when we started to look, we realized they were everywhere."

Noah's jaw dropped, and the color drained from his face. "Seriously?"

"They were everywhere," Jess said, her lashes wet

and eyes red. "They were in the bathroom, Noah. In the vents."

"Robby never said... what the fuck? What the fuck. What the *fuck*."

Eric and Tristan went into the house, only taking a couple of minutes before they walked out with one of the cameras in hand. "Jess is right. These are everywhere. Jesus Christ." Eric went to drop it on the floor and crush it with his boot, but Tristan stopped him.

"Hold on. If we save them, then we could possibly delete the footage. Even if it's stored online somewhere." Tristan grabbed the camera from Eric's hand and pocketed it.

"Can he still hear us through that?" Noah asked, looking down at Tristan's pocket as if a cobra were about to slip out of it and strike him at any moment.

"No, I made sure it was disconnected before I brought it out here."

Noah looked up into my eyes. His upper lip quivered as tears welled up. "Jake—that means... if Robby didn't say anything, and after that text message last night—" Noah choked on a cry. I wrapped him up in my arms and held him as tight as I could.

Noah didn't need to finish his thought. I already knew what he was going to say, what this morning implied. It started to fall into place, the picture becoming clear.

It was Robby. Noah's neighbor, his onetime fling, and his obsessive stalker.

Robby had eyes on us. He had made sure to keep

watch, and he'd made sure to keep the pressure on. He'd been obsessed with Noah since they hooked up but likely didn't decide to act on it until I entered the picture, increasing the heat on our relationship in hopes that we'd break up and Noah would go running to him.

"We need to tell the police," Noah said, sniffling and rubbing at his face. His cheeks were pink, his pupils blown wide with fear. I didn't have to have my hand on his chest to know his heart was beating at an unhealthy pace. "Is that what Yvette's doing?"

"She's calling her sister. She's the lawyer," Tia explained. "She wants to sue Robby into the ground."

Noah shook his head. "That won't work. This guy's crazy—he's insane. He needs the law, not the legal system."

"Those are one and the same," Eric said. "The cops won't be able to arrest Robby without any cause. We willingly stayed in his parents' cabin. He can say he wasn't even aware of the cameras, and the police would have to thank him for cooperating and leave."

"But if I sue that fucking asshole, then maybe he can learn a lesson," Yvette said, steam rising off her shoulders from how angry she was.

Noah rubbed at the bridge of his nose. I could see him spiraling. He started to bite at his nails, something he only ever did when his back was up against the wall. I rubbed his elbows, but I knew that nothing I could say or do in this moment would help ease his worries.

"I'm going to call him," Noah suddenly said, pulling out his phone. "I'm just going to have to call him."

"Wait, hold on, hold on." Tristan had his arms raised as if he were negotiating with someone who'd threatened to blow a bomb. "Let's not give the crazy and unhinged stalker a heads-up that we're onto him."

"Tristan's right," Eric said.

"Then what the hell do I do? Just lie down and wait for him to abduct me?" Noah's face turned cherry red. A vein in his forehead throbbed, his eyes snapping shut as he rubbed his nose again.

This hurt. Watching him suffer like this tore me apart. I may have not said it out loud, but Noah was the man I loved, irrevocably and powerfully. The kind of love that binds two souls together. When he hurt, so did I. And the fact that I couldn't do anything to fix it only made it a thousand times harder, turned the twisting knife into a rusted blade, making every breath more painful than the last.

"You might be able to get a stalking protective order," Eric said. "If we can get the parents to say they never put in those cameras, then maybe a judge can see that Robby wanted you under surveillance. That would be enough. And if he violates the order, then he goes to jail."

"And if we can't get the parents to cooperate?" Noah asked.

Eric didn't need to answer. His silence was enough.

Noah would be fucked. Robby had been careful with his tactics, keeping himself out of the picture as much as possible. He must have been wearing a wig when he tried breaking into my house, although I still wasn't sure how he had gotten Franky's car. Either way, it didn't really matter. None of it proved to law enforcement that Robby was the one behind the threats and break-in attempts.

"I need to go home, I'm sorry," Jess said, looking back at the cabin as if it were a cougar poised on its haunches and ready to launch. She had an arm around her stomach. "I feel sick." She started to cry, and no amount of comfort from Tia seemed to help soothe her. "I'm so sorry, Noah. I'm just so scared."

"It's okay, it's okay." Noah took Jess in a hug. She cried into his shoulder, triggering a couple of sniffles from Noah. She turned and hurried into the car, Tia giving Noah another hug before promising that she'd meet up with them later.

"I'm not going home," Noah said. "I can't. I can't go back there, not with Robby next door."

"We don't have to," I said.

"Can you stay with me? We can go to the other cabin?"

I nodded, certain that nothing could take me away from Noah's side. "Of course."

He grabbed my hand in his, squeezed. My heart hammered, my fingers locking around Noah's. It was in these dark moments that gave us the chance to prove ourselves to each other. I wasn't about to let him go through any of this alone.

"I'm going to go meet with my sister," Yvette said with her keys already jingling in her hand. She came over and wrapped Noah up into a hug, but he didn't let go of my hand. "Stay strong, Noah. We're going to figure this out."

He nodded. His bottom lip twitched, and I could tell he currently had his molars clamped down on the inside of his cheek. She got into her car and drove down the gravel road, kicking up a small dust cloud in her wake as she pressed down on the gas pedal.

It was just Noah and the boys left. Tristan sighed, his brows dipping downward in the same direction as his frown. "Are you two good? Want one of us to go with you?"

"I think we'll be okay," Noah said. "Thanks, though. I'm sorry any of you even have to worry about this. I hate it. So much."

"We hate it for you," Tristan said, giving Noah a friendly pat on the shoulder. "Let's just stay positive. At least we have someone to point to now. We know who to be careful with."

"Tristan's right." Eric stepped forward. He was about five inches taller than both of them, his shoulders broad and his beard thick. They were all in their midtwenties, but Eric carried himself like someone much older. It was likely all the shit he had seen when he used to be a cop, which got me wondering why he gave in his badge at such an early age. "We've got a clear suspect. Maybe he's made a mistake already, and now that we know it's him, we can tie those two things together. Just hang out in that other cabin you've got for a couple of days. Let's see if we can sort this out. Tristan and I can do a little drive around your block and see if we can spot anything suspicious."

"You don't have to do that. I really don't want either of you guys getting hurt."

"The only person who's at risk of getting hurt here is Robby." Eric's light brown eyes lit with anger, his nostrils flaring. He turned to me, a hand on my elbow. "Keep him safe, alright?"

I nodded, although Noah huffed next to me. "Jake asked me to kill a cockroach last week. I think you should be telling me to keep *him* safe."

"Wait, and you killed it?" Tristan asked with an arched brow.

"Of course not. Jake ended up throwing a shoe at it from across the room and managed to hit it. But still."

That got the four of us laughing, some of the icy fear that had coated us beginning to crack. Laughter had a way of making the sun shine bright, even if there was an active rainstorm pouring down on you.

We said our goodbyes to Eric and Tristan, the mood slipping back into somber as we got into our car. I'd already gotten all of Noah's bags from inside and had put them in the trunk, not wanting him to have to step foot in that place again. It made my skin crawl. Such a beautiful and picturesque home now looked twisted and monstrous, as if the ever-spanning glass windows belonged to the eyes of a hungry spider, spinning a dangerously elaborate web while its fangs dripped with venom and its hairy legs rubbed together in excitement.

"Come on," I said, putting a hand on Noah's shaking leg. "Let's get the fuck out of here."

"Please," he said and dropped his head back on the headrest, eyes shut but tears leaking from the corners.

29

NOAH BARNES

THE OTHER CABIN was a forty-five-minute drive away, although I wished it were further. As in countries further. I couldn't shake the feeling of being watched, even as we drove in a heavy silence through the winding mountain roads. The window was cracked open, a hiss of fresh air circulating through the car. Outside, the day appeared to be one of the prettiest ones yet. The sky was a sapphire blue and dotted with a couple of clouds, looking as if they were placed there with a paintbrush. The trees still had most of their summer leaves, although some were already started shifting into orange and brown, adding another splash of color from the brush.

It served as an extreme contrast to the storm that raged inside me, with lightning bolts striking at my spine and hurricane-force winds rattling through my ribs.

"This it?" Jake asked as he drove up a small driveway, the cabin tucked between two larger ones.

"It is," I said, looking out the window at the quaint

place. Robby's mansion in the mountains put this one to shame, and yet I wouldn't trade it for the world. I didn't care that it didn't have a view or a hot tub or a hundred windows. It wasn't Robby's, and it wasn't full of cameras, so I was happy.

"Come on, let's get settled," Jake said as he put the car in park. He looked my way, and I could tell he was worried for me. The wrinkles in his forehead give him away, his eyebrows doing origami work with how much they folded together.

"I'll be fine, Jake. Don't get too stressed-out." Now it was my turn to offer empty reassurances.

"It's just... if he saw us in the hot tub. I'm wondering what that would make him do."

I swallowed a ball of acid. "I thought about that, too. But there's nothing we can do about it right now."

"We need a plan. Some kind of way to prove that he's the one doing all this. Making our lives a living hell."

"Maybe we can bait him?" I asked, sitting up a little straighter. "It might be dangerous, but it could be the only shot we have at ending this before he does something even more unhinged."

"Bait him how? I'm not doing anything that puts you in danger."

I shook my head, my hand on the door handle. It was beginning to feel stuffy inside the car. "No, but maybe I can call him. We can record the conversation, try to get him to admit to stalking me." I took a deep breath and pulled on the door handle. "But let's talk about it outside. I'm getting claustrophobic."

We got out of the car, the scent of dirt and wood drifting over from a construction site across the street, where the skeleton of another cabin was beginning to form. Jake got our bags from the back of the car and walked with me to the front of the cabin, the door painted a bright blue. There were a couple of potted ferns hanging from the awning that seemed slightly singed at the tips of their leaves. A "welcome home" wreath hung on the door, a couple of spiders having decided to do just that and set up their webs in the fake leaves.

"Do you think talking to him might just make him more unpredictable?" Jake asked as I unlocked the door with the code I was given.

"Maybe," I said with a shrug. "But I'm running out of options here. Then there's the possibility that it's *not* Robby. Maybe it was his parents who set up cameras in there? Or maybe my stalker beat us to the cabin before we did and installed the cameras." Frustration bubbled up inside me, mixing with the already toxic oil spill of fear that coated my gut.

I opened the door and stepped inside, thankful to not have a line of trees at my back.

"It makes sense it's Robby, though. Think about it." He dropped our bags on the leather couch, hands slipping into the pocket of his sweatpants. "Who was the one that discovered that initial box with the chicken head inside of it? It was him. And it wasn't put through the postal system, so we thought it might have been hand-delivered. But who would get the address wrong on a package that important? No one. Because all Robby had to do was step outside his door and put the box down and then yell as loud as he could. The windows were open, the blinds were open—I'm sure he saw us inside your house. He knew how to get your attention. He thought you'd be a damsel in distress that night, and he was ready to bring you in. He just wasn't counting on me being there."

"What about Franky's car? And the attempted break-in at your place?"

Jake's lips quirked to the side. "I don't know. I'm assuming he was wearing a disguise when he tried to break in, but I don't know how he was able to use Franky's car as a getaway car."

I locked the door and put my back against it. The cabin was warm and cozy, with plenty of thick blankets thrown over armchairs and spilling out of wicker baskets. A fireplace was framed by two tall windows that looked out to the back of the property, lined by trees. There was a small trail of smoothed-over stone that led from the cabin and through the trees. Walking the five minutes down that path took me to one of my favorite spots and one of Blue Ridge's best-kept secrets.

Maybe that's what I needed to clear my head. I went to Jake's side, my hand fitting into his. I tugged him toward the side door. He gave a confused "huh?" as he followed me out into the back porch.

"I can't think about all this right now," I said. My throat tightened. If I hadn't already cried so much, I was sure more tears would have made an appearance. But I was as dry as a husk. "Come with me. Let me show you this cool spot down the way."

I led Jake down the stone path, the trees creeping in on either side for a couple of minutes before they suddenly opened, the path ending on a large outcropping that looked down onto a bubbling river. Mountains climbed on either side of it, a natural-made border that turned sunsets into works of art as the blues and purples of dusk painted the natural canvas. A few wildflowers broke through the rocky dirt, reaching up toward a bright and ever-present sun.

"I'd come here sometimes just to read," I said, going up toward the edge of the ledge and sitting down. It wasn't very high up, so it didn't trigger my fear of heights, but it was high enough to create a weird tickle in my core. I let my feet dangle, and Jake did the same, sitting next to me, his hand coming to encase mine.

"It's peaceful here," Jake said. His eyes turned forward, following the curving river as it disappeared around a bend. Evergreen pines grew on either side of us, dancing slightly in the gentle breeze. A squirrel fought with another one as they spiraled up the trunk, chittering and chattering to each other.

"*Peaceful*. As if I even know what that is right now."

"It's whatever I feel when I'm with you. I know that much."

I smiled at Jake and was surprised at how genuine it felt. It had the effect of turning a light in on a dark room, erasing the cobwebs and imaginary demons that lurked in the corners. "I seriously don't know how I would have gotten through all this without you," I said, allowing the honest emotions to rise to the surface. "You could have turned around and left at any moment. A lot of guys probably would have, but you stayed. And you keep me from losing my mind on a daily basis."

"Anyone who would have left when you needed them most didn't deserve you in the first place." Jake's hand squeezed around mine. His thumb traced soft circles against my skin. It created another sense of warmth and comfort that I wasn't really ready for. It blew down any defenses or barriers I had left between us, if there had even been any left.

"Franky wouldn't have stayed past that first night at the book club."

"Pfft, Franky wouldn't have even *been* at the book club. I thought we agreed that guy was trash?"

I chuckled, leaning into the solid column of man that sat next to me. "Very true. Thank God the trash has been taken out."

"It has," Jake said. He kicked his leg out, twining it around mine. I picked up a rock in my free hand and lazily tossed it toward the river, landing painfully short of it. Jake wore a thin gray hoodie that made him look more handsome than he already was, even though it hid some of his more muscular attributes. I had a feeling Jake could wear a trash bag and still make it look good.

"How did I get this lucky—well, and unlucky, I guess."

Jake's chuckle was soft. "Let's focus on the lucky part. Because I keep asking myself that same exact question. I really didn't think I'd find someone this perfect for me, not after the road bumps I had in getting to you. From a failed engagement to cheaters to a couple emotional abusers, I've dealt with it all, and I was getting to my breaking point.

"Then you come along, buying wine for your book club, and my entire life changes. My perspective shifts, my heart fills. I feel like happiness is attainable again.

I know it sounds poetic and dramatic, but it's all true."

Did it sound poetic? Yes. Did it sound dramatic? Maybe.

Did I love every single fucking word he was saying? Absolutely.

"I think we were both in the same spot, relationship-wise. I didn't think it was worth putting myself through all that again. I was about to just go on without any strings attached, messing around and seeing what happens. But you came along, and any desire to mess around completely vanished."

Jake batted his long lashes at me. "So you don't want to mess around with me?"

It was my turn to laugh. "Not what I meant."

"I know," Jake said, leaning in and giving me a kiss that landed on the edge of my lips.

"You're special," I said as I turned to fully face him, resting our foreheads together. I could see the specks of diamond dust that made his eyes glow as bright as the sun. The gentle touch of his breath gliding over my lips and down my chin sent a tingle down my spine. My hand closed tighter around his. "I'm so—I..." The words started to race out of my mouth, becoming tangled in a tongue-tied mess. "I just—" had to get it out. Had to say it. Jake needed to hear it, and I needed to say it.

"I love you, Noah."

He beat me to it, nearly knocking me over in surprise. I blinked a couple of times, just to make sure he didn't fade away into a dreamy mist.

"I love everything about you," he continued, smiling. "I love your heart, your brain. I love how courageous you are and how loyal you are and how funny you are. I love every little thing about you. I'm in love with you, Noah, and I never want to let you go. Ever."

"I love you, too, Jake." I was surprised I was able to get the words out past the swelling knot of emotion lodged in my throat. For the first time since this day had started, I felt like myself again. Happy and carefree and light as a damn feather. I drank in this feeling, knowing it would be fleeting once our serene little bubble was popped and the real world came back into focus.

But for now, all I cared about was the dreamy man pressing his lips against mine, whispers of "I love you" crossing between us, and my head floating directly up into the cloud.

This moment was huge. Monumental. It cemented something between us. It verified every single feeling I had, and it made them all the more stronger. My body flooded with a serene sense of warmth and calm. I thought back to being scared at even thinking those three words, and here we were, saying them out loud, smiles on our lips as we kissed over and over again. It was beautiful.

"Come on," I said through one of the breaks in the kissing. "I think this place has champagne in the fridge. Let's pop one open."

"Let's," Jake said, kissing me one last time, a gentle hand on my cheek as he looked into my eyes. This was as close to the top of the world as I was getting.

"God, I'm so glad we didn't stay just friends," I said, standing up and brushing some dirt off my pants.

Jake laughed, his hand finding mine. "Yeah, that would have sucked. Not that being your friend is a bad thing, but I'd much rather be able to do this," he leaned in for another kiss, this one feeling even more passionate than the rest, "whenever I want."

We walked the short way back to the cabin, every step lighter than the last. Laughter and smiles and flirty comments filled the air. I almost forgot about the circumstances that lead us to this cabin in the first place.

Almost.

30

JAKE PEREZ

NOAH LAY DOWN IN BED, *Just Beneath Her Bones* open on his chest as he shook his head, jaw slightly dropped open. He looked up at me as I came into the room, towel wrapped around my waist.

"You finished it, right?"

I nodded. He must have gotten to the reveal. "It was Archie the whole time? And he was speaking to the killer and jewelry maker because he was having a psychotic break? Twisted. Damn." He shut the book and sat up a little higher on the bed. "He was obsessed with her from the start, and that divorce broke him. He knew what kind of jewelry she'd buy and went to work. What a fucked-up story."

"Plus, how Gabrielle finds out is pretty messed up, too."

"Oh yeah! That was wild. Archie doesn't kidnap her, does he?"

I shrugged. "No spoilers from me."

"Damn, I want to know what happens, but suddenly, my mind keeps going elsewhere." His eyes traveled up and down my still-damp body. I walked across the freshly polished wooden floor, leaving wet footprints in my wake. The bedroom was toward the back of the cabin and featured a queen-sized bed with a tall black headboard. A long rectangular window looked out to the yard, where that stone path disappeared into the trees and led to one of the most scenic spots I'd ever been to. Noah had taken me there again to watch the sunset from our perch, from the spot where I'd spilled my heart out to him.

That wasn't always easy for me. I had trouble sharing my truest emotions, and some of that probably came from being broken up with by Ashley while I was down on one knee. It didn't ruin me, but it certainly did affect my willingness to be vulnerable.

Not with Noah, though. He made me feel safe and protected. I could trust that he wouldn't hurt me, same way as I'd never hurt him. That mutual comfort made every moment I spent with Noah a special one.

And I was determined to make these next few moments some of the most special.

"Come here," I said, dropping my towel and getting on the bed, grabbing his legs and pulling him toward me. He chuckled as I pressed my lips to his, stealing his breath away. His hands immediately started to roam around my body, focusing on my ass, his fingers kneading into the firm globes of muscle. I moaned into his kiss. I could feel him getting hard in his boxers, his cock battling for space with mine.

I gave a thrust, rubbing myself against him. It was his turn to moan, and I greedily swallowed it, kissing my way down his chin, over his jaw, settling on his neck, where I sucked on the tender skin. "Fuck, Noah, I love how you taste. How you feel. I love how hard you get." I rubbed him through the boxers, the steel rod twitching in my hand.

"How hard you make me, you mean?"

I grinned down at him, his cheeks already getting rosy pink. "Well, I love everything about you," he said, raking his eyes over my chest, down toward my stiff cock. He reached for it, grabbing me in both hands and giving me a delicious squeeze. "Especially love this." He licked his lips, eyes glued to me as he stroked, starting at the base and working his way up, increasing the pressure. A drop of precome oozed from the tip. He rubbed his thumb over it, spreading it.

I dropped my head back, letting every muscle in my body relax. He jerked me off, both hands working to worship my cock.

But I still needed more. I always needed more when it came to Noah. "Take these off," I said, tugging on the waistband of his boxers. He was already shirtless, so at least that cut down on the overall time it took to get him completely naked.

I got off his lap and watched him pull his boxers off, his hard dick flopping out with an audible slap against his stomach. He had the body of a runner, lean and muscular, even though he only did sporadic at-home workouts and never watched what he ate.

He also had the cock of a horse. It was impressively thick but not uncomfortably so. I could sit and ride him for hours and never get tired. When we fucked, he hit me in all the right spots, and my entire body lit up like the sun at the sight of him.

I went to my backpack and opened the front zipper, taking out the small bottle of lube. Noah's eyes drank me up as I walked back to the bedside, one hand wrapped around my hard dick and the other popping open the cap to the lube. I spread it on him, a single line down his shaft. I set the bottle down and spread it, watching his eyes roll to the back of his head. He opened his legs, but instead of me climbing onto him, I got onto the bed instead, with my face down and my ass up.

"Fuck me like you love me," I told him.

He got behind me, the mattress dipping where his knees pushed into it. Noah lined himself up. A warm pressure pushed against me. I arched my back a little more and took a deep breath, pushing back against him. He opened me up, sliding in with a single smooth stroke.

There, just like that, we were one. "Yes, baby, make that ass yours."

Noah listened to my command. He bucked into me, slow and strong, his cock filling me up in a way that scrambled my brain and made my dick leak like a broken faucet. Every thrust made a new string of precome drop from my tip, wetting the white sheets underneath me. "That's it. Harder, baby, fuck me harder."

His hands came to rest on my lower back as he drove himself into him, thrusting hard, our skin slapping. Beads of sweat formed on my chest, my body flushing with an inferno's worth of heat. I fisted the sheets, moaning with every thrust, loud, uninhibited. No one was around to hear, and so I let it all out, grunting and moaning like a wild animal.

"Lay down, Jake. That's it." Noah laid me down on my side and lay behind me. He lifted me for easier access as he slid back into me. I grabbed my rock-hard cock and jerked myself off as Noah fucked me, hitting my prostate, making me see stars as my balls grew tighter and tighter. Noah began to get more vocal, nipping at the back of my neck as he whispered how much he loved my tight hole, how much he loved being inside of me, loved me.

I couldn't take it. My orgasm tore through me. I gripped the base of my cock and shot rope after rope as Noah continued to grind into me, milking me for every last drop. His fingers dug into my hips as he gave one final thrust and buried himself deep inside me, unloading. He pressed his head to the back of mine as his breathing became ragged. I could feel him filling me up, his ropes of come coating my insides.

It was one of those orgasms that made you light-headed and wonder how close you were to passing out.

"Holy fuck," Noah said as he slowly pulled out of me. I could feel some of his come dripping down my leg.

"That was incredible," I said. I rolled over, seeing a drunken glaze roll over Noah's eyes. He smiled as if he'd just gotten the best news of his life. Noah and I always had great sex, but something about tonight felt *extra* special, *extra* hot.

"God, I'm so fucking in love with you," I said, unable to stop myself. My brain was full of glittery stars and bright rainbows and singing bluebirds. I was in a musical without any music (which was likely for the best, considering I was a terrible singer). This was my happily ever after, and we had only just begun our story. It made me excited for our future together.

Noah kissed me, both of us still working to catch our breath. "You're my soul mate, Jake. My other half. I'm so fucking in love with you, too." He laughed through another kiss, the bubbly ecstasy from our shared climax still working its way through us.

"You make me feel invincible," I told him. "And *damn* is your dick magical. Seriously, you should have to register that thing for being a lethal weapon. I'm sure it could give me a heart attack one day."

Noah laughed some more, the sound adding to my musical theory. "Let's stick to just giving you orgasms."

We shared a couple of lazy kisses between us. Jokes and giggles continued to flow until my thigh got uncomfortably sticky. I begrudgingly got out of bed and gave myself a quick sink bath, giving the bathroom over to Noah, who still hadn't showered that night. He entered the bathroom with phone in hand, his eyes glued to the screen.

Instantly, my heart dropped. "Everything okay?" I asked. I didn't want tonight to be ruined by another threatening text.

"Yeah, yeah. Eric was just texting me. He and Tristan are about to stake out Robby's place." He filled his lungs with a deep breath, letting it whistle out. "I really don't want them getting involved."

"Eric's an ex-cop, right? He'll be fine. He knows how to do those things."

"I guess." With a sigh, he put the phone on the counter and came over to me, wrapping his arms around my waist and resting his head on my chest. "It'll be okay, right?"

"It will," I said, believing it with everything I had. How could it not turn out okay? There was no other choice, not in my eyes.

Noah stayed in my arms for a few moments longer before he pried himself off and went to turn on the shower, turning the knob to as hot as it went. He loved his steaming showers.

"Hey, where are the sheets kept? I'm gonna swap ours out."

Noah leaned out of the shower, shampoo already foaming in his hair. "There should be some in the laundry. It's in that closet in the living room."

"Got it."

"Thanks, babe."

I put on some boxers and took off the sticky sheets, bundling them up. That was one (of the only) drawback of being bi—the amount of come sometimes meant midnight trips to the laundry room. Still, it was a very small inconvenience. Especially considering how much I enjoyed shooting that come, getting rammed by the love of my life.

Yeah, I'd make ten midnight trips to the laundry room and still be down for an eleventh.

I walked through the dark living room. This place was much smaller than the last cabin and had a fraction of the number of windows, which I actually preferred. I wasn't much of a mountain man, and a lot of that had to do with a ton of horror movies my father had me watch as a kid. Looking out into dark woods never gave me a sense of comfort, so I actually liked the lack of windows in this place.

Oddly, one of them was brighter than the rest. The motion-activated light must have been flipped on by a squirrel. It turned off quickly, meaning whatever was out there had skittered off into the trees.

I went to the laundry closet, dumping the sheets inside the washing machine. I reached up for the detergent, hearing the floor creak behind me.

"That was a quick shower," I said, uncapping the detergent. I was slightly surprised. Noah enjoyed taking long showers, even when they were late at night.

I felt the needle plunge into my neck. For a moment, I thought I'd been stung by something. I went to swat at whatever bug had stabbed me but could hardly raise my arm. I stumbled forward. The needle fell to the ground. I turned, my vision blurring, my words slurring.

The world went black, curtains dropping over my vision as my legs gave out.

31

NOAH BARNES

I TOOK my time in the shower, enjoying how the steamy hot water felt against my skin. It was a tiny bathroom, which meant it was easily converted into a sauna. I scrubbed and let myself relax under the showerhead, enjoying how all my limbs felt like wet noodles. Sex with Jake never failed to be explosive, but tonight was an entirely new level. It was the kind of sex reserved for your wildest, steamiest, hottest dreams, shared with someone you connect with beyond just the physical.

And now that our true feelings were out and laid bare, it only made the sex that much more magical. I could fully let go, and I knew that Jake could do the same. It was an exciting stage in our relationship, and I couldn't wait to see where it took us.

I turned off the shower and reluctantly stepped out onto the plush gray rug, grabbing a thick white towel off the rack and drying off my hair before rubbing the towel over the rest of my body. The mirror was fogged up, so I took a wet hand across it, my handprint dripping at the top of the mirror.

I dried my hair off some more and ran my hand through it so that it didn't look too wild. I needed to get a haircut soon. With everything going on, I neglected the simple things. Haircut, gym, dentist. All added up on my to-do list, underneath the one major task: figure out how to get Robby to stop.

Tonight wasn't the night to deal with that. We'd have time tomorrow, once the sun came up and things didn't feel as hopeless. There was always something about the night that amplified all your worries and anxieties, turning molehills into actively erupting volcanoes, and I just didn't want to put myself through that right now. Instead, I planned on going for round two (and three and four) with Jake.

I finished toweling off and put on a sexy pair of black Armani briefs that barely held all of me inside. I gave myself one last look over the mirror, feeling a giddy rush of butterflies kick up in my chest. Jake had made it clear he liked—no, loved—me in all my iterations, whether it was waking up from an hourlong and reality-altering nap or after I spent an hour in the bathroom getting ready for our date night. He always looked at me like I was special, even when I may not have been feeling that way.

He was my everything, and I was over the moon happy that we got over the L-word speed bump.

A loud thump sounded from behind the closed bathroom door. "Jake?" I called out, opening it.

He didn't answer. It sounded like he'd dropped something in the living room. I grabbed my phone and saw I had a text from Eric. Before I could open and read it, another loud thud grabbed my attention. My eyebrows inched together as I cocked my head and looked to the bedroom door, a light from the hallway leaking in underneath the threshold. The nightstand lamps were on in the bedroom, which gave the perfect ambiance lightning but didn't really make me feel comfortable in that moment.

I flicked on the overhead light and opened the bedroom door. "Jake? Babe, are you in the kitchen? I could use some champagne." I went down the hallway. Why the hell wasn't he answering me? The silence began to take on a physical form, pressing against me, almost willing me to turn back. The hairs on the back of my neck raised. This didn't feel right.

I paused at the end of the hallway. The living room light was off. I could only see a corner of it, where a large bookcase stood in the shadows, its glass facade reflecting a dim picture. It appeared like someone was sitting down in the center of the room. I could only see the dark outline of the back of someone's head. Had Jake come to the couch and fallen asleep? It had been a long day, and Jake did have the near supernatural ability to fall asleep anywhere and at any time.

That's when I heard a groan. It sounded like a pained groan, like someone was struggling.

Jake.

Oh no. No, no, no.

My phone. I had left it in the bedroom. I needed to call the police. I needed to call for help.

I needed to run.

I turned, bolting down the hallway. Immediately, I heard the sound of echoing footsteps behind me. Someone breathing hard, running fast. I tried to run faster. It wasn't a long hallway at all, but it felt as though it stretched on for infinity. My blood turned to pure ice. I was near the door. I could reach it; I could stretch out and touch the doorknob. If I got inside, I could slam the door and call the police, get us help.

A cold hand snapped around my wrist and yanked me backward. I gave a shrill shout, my shoulder threatening to pop out of its socket at the angle my arm had been twisted. I looked into Robby's dark eyes, the glasses on his face appearing to magnify the dual black holes, sucking in any and all light. He grinned a wicked smile before driving his knee up into my stomach.

I curled over, dropping to my knees. I coughed and sputtered and tried getting up. Another kick landed against my ribs. I cried out for help, but the kicks continued to rain down on me. He started to laugh; I started to cry. I curled up into a ball and covered my face with my forearms to try and get some cover from the barrage.

Jake... he's—he's hearing this. He—needs. He needs me.

"That's what you get for running away from me," Robby said, blows still raining down on me. The pain blurred into one massive throb, radiating through every single bone in my body. I gasped.

I need to get up— for Jake.

The thought of him being hurt was more painful than the kicks. I found a buried well of strength and reached forward, latching onto a leg and pulling it to my mouth.

I bit down, hard. It was the only thing I could think of doing. An admittedly savage move that also admittedly worked. Robby shouted, "What the fuck!" before stumbling backward, holding the back of his calf. It gave me enough time to get up.

"It was you this entire time." My lungs felt like they were on fire, but I still managed to get the words out.

"Surprised?"

"Not really," I said, that well of strength growing. This was it. This would be the end, one way or another. No more looking over my shoulder, no more being scared of shadows and noises. Everything would be brought out into the light.

He lunged at me again, but I was ready this time. I used my shoulder as a brace, hitting him in the chest before he could land a punch on me. That seemed to have surprised him, knocking him back. His fist flew through the air again, this one connecting with my jaw and sending a stinging pain across my face.

"I don't want to do this to you," he said, coming at me again like a rabid dog.

"Then stop," I said, blocking a hit with my forearm. "Stop. Please, stop."

"I can't. It's gone too far. I messed up."

I pushed him up against the wall and managed to land a knee directly into his groin. He closed his eyes and clamped his arms around his gut. I took this as my chance to run, going down the hallway, forgetting about my phone and needing instead to get to Jake.

There he was, tied down to a chair in the center of the room. Plenty of moonlight came in through the open windows. He looked at me with wide and scared eyes, a rag stuffed into his mouth. He had a towel wrapped around his waist, his chest bare. He didn't look hurt.

I undid the knot on the gag, dropping it to the floor and kissing him. "Jesus, are you okay?"

"My wrists. Untie them."

I nearly tripped moving to the back of his chair. I tried to untangle the knot, but my hands were shaking, and the knot was made from a thick rope that looked like it was used for anchoring ships. I could only undo a single knot before Robby came back into the room. "Get up. Now."

I looked around Jake and realized Robby was no longer unarmed. He held a gun, which shone in the moonlight, the jet-black weapon appearing to glitter in his grip.

That changed things. A fear like I'd never felt before gripped me by the throat. I stood on wobbling legs, using the chair Jake was currently bound to as a brace.

"This was *not* how I envisioned all this going," Robby said, stepping into the living room. He flicked the light on with the barrel of the gun. He stood there, wearing a stained white T-shirt and black pants. I'd never seen him this disheveled, this undone. His hair was wild, growing down to his shoulders in oily tendrils that clumped together, and his glasses were cracked, sitting lopsided on his nose. Acne clustered around his cheeks, and his eyes had heavy bags that made it clear he'd been running low on sleep. The way he sniffed and rubbed at his nose with his free hand gave away what substance he'd been using to keep himself up.

Robby was unhinged, and that made this all extremely unpredictable.

"How did you envision it going?" Jake asked, his voice surprising me. How could he talk without crying? I doubt I could get any cohesive words out. "You stalked and threatened us both, for what? To kidnap and kill us?"

"No, no," Robby said, a hand covering half his face. "Oh, that's not it at all. I didn't want things to get to this. I just... I wanted you, Noah. I've wanted you ever since you showed me the true meaning of happiness. I connected with you on a level I've never felt, not with anyone. But I knew you'd need more work to see it. You'd need something to push yourself into my open arms.

"So when I started seeing Franky—well, I got an idea."

That admission made my head spin, as if a bucket of ice had been dropped from above me. "You and Franky were together?"

That explained how he got Franky's car, how he was able to shift some of the suspicion in the opposite direction.

"Oh yeah. I caught him one day after he was leaving your place. Even when you two were secretly together, he was fucking around with other men. So much for being in a closet—Franky's hiding out in a warehouse. And he's still angry about it. He's still very resentful, more so now that he's with his wife. And he'd also always talk about you, to the point that it made me jealous. But not because he still wanted you, but because I wasn't the only one who fell for your spell."

I swallowed, my mind racing to process this information while trying to come up with a way out of this. How the hell were Jake and I going to make it through tonight in one piece? I had little to no fighting skills, and neither of us was armed.

But maybe I could talk my way out of this...

And if that didn't work, maybe me secretly working at undoing Jake's knot would help.

"So you made up that fake threat with the chicken head. You thought you'd pin it on Franky and I'd come running into your arms for support that night. But you weren't counting on Jake being over."

"No, I wasn't counting on Jake at all. When he entered the picture, I thought I could cut him out of it. Leave you mourning after your boyfriend overdosed on a bad batch of fentanyl-laced coke. Injected into the system, it would show up the same as if he snorted it. I thought that would do the trick."

I avoided the urge to look down as my fingers dug into the thick rope, trying to find the areas with the most amount of slack, tugging and tugging without moving a single muscle in my arm, only my hand.

"That was the night you tried breaking into my house?" Jake asked.

"And still, that didn't work. Nothing worked.

Nothing is going to work. But I can't keep going, Noah. Not without you. I can't explain it. You treated me right— you treated me like a human. You were like my father, the only other man in my life who ever loved me. I only had him for nine years before he died of a heart attack. A monster took his place. My stepdad messed me up, Noah. He would lock me in the bathroom for days, telling me to drink from the toilet like a dog until I decided to come out acting like a man.

"He hated me for being gay, for being flamboyant. And I hated him. And I hated myself. And now I hate you both. I hate all of this." His hands were shaking, but mine were now steady. Adrenaline sharpened my focus, turning it into a diamond's edge, sharp and lethal. I just had to untie Jake, and then maybe the two of us could overtake him. As heartbreaking as Robby's story was, I knew I couldn't let it affect me. The innocent Robby was gone, transformed by the hatred he'd been fed as a kid.

"What are you doing back there?" Robby asked, eyes dropping to Jake as if he could see right through him. "Step the fuck back."

"Robby, listen to me," I said, my voice proving to be not nearly as steady as my hands. "You can still walk away from this. We all can. Just put the gun down and let us go. Please, Robby. What your stepdad did to you was wrong, but it—"

He aimed the gun at the ceiling and let out a shot, the explosive sound making my entire body vibrate. My ears rang. He trained the gun back onto the two of us. He was about five feet away from us, way too far for me to try and make a grab for the gun.

Shit, shit, shit.

"Don't talk about him. Just step away from Jake. Step away, there. Stop."

I had to listen to him. But with each step I took, I could feel the hope I had for getting out of this alive slipping further and further out of my grasp.

"Please, Robby, please." I entered into the begging phase. Would dropping to my knees make a difference?

I looked to Jake, and I realized one thing: if I couldn't make it out of this, I needed to make sure he did. "At least let Jake go. Please. You want me, don't you? Then take me, but let Jake go."

"No, no," Jake said, looking at me now. "I'm not going anywhere, baby. Where you go, I go. It's a done deal. I love you, baby. I won't leave you here. Never."

"You're right," Robby said, face twisted with a rage-filled grimace. "It is a done deal."

He lifted the gun. He took aim. His finger twitched on the trigger. My eyes closed.

I wanted to shout and cry and fight and run and fly. Instead, I lurched sideways, pushing into Jake. A gunshot rang out. I fell through the air, landing with a devastatingly sharp pain radiating out through my body. I blinked, I breathed, I was sure I was dead.

But my heart still beat. The sharp pain had come from landing on my bruised ribs against Jake's chair, now broken and in splinters across the living room floor.

Among the splinters was a gun. Robby's gun. It had

fallen from his hands, sliding to the center of the room. I crawled for it, grabbing it, looking to the left and seeing him crumpled on the floor, a hand pressed against his bleeding shoulder. He cried out a random string of expletives, and only when I heard the door open did the situation start to make sense.

Eric walked in, gun in hand. The window next to the door had been shattered from the gunshot. Behind him was Tristan, already on the phone with the police.

My best friends, my brothers, they were the ones who had saved the day.

"Noah, Jake, fuck, are you two okay?" Eric was towering over a still-whimpering Robby as Tristan helped me and Jake up onto our feet.

"We're okay, thanks to you guys. Holy shit. Thank you." I embraced Tristan in a weak side hug before I went to Jake, kissing him on the lips and telling him how much I loved him, how scared I was.

"How'd you guys get here?" I asked, shock still filtering through my system, mixing with relief.

"When you didn't answer my text about finding out Robby was headed to the mountains, I knew something was up. I called a couple of times, and still nothing, but by then, we were already halfway here. All the lights being on let us see everything. I just needed a clear shot to take."

"Thank you, both of you," Jake said, leaning on me as he held his bruised chest. "And thank you, Noah."

"It's over," I said as the police sirens grew louder, drowning out Robby's grunts and curses. "That's all that matters. It's all over. We don't have to be scared anymore."

We could finally wake up from this nightmare and embrace the dream that our love had foreshadowed. We were together, we were whole, and we were both ready to put this behind us so we could move toward our happy ever after, shining just over the horizon.

EPILOGUE

Jake Perez

IT WAS DATE NIGHT. My favorite night of the week. Always full of surprises and fun, no matter how many times we did it. We'd been together for a year and a half now, and every date night had somehow been better than the last. They weren't all extravagant nights out on the town either. A lot of them were staying inside my house, eating home-cooked meals and watching some fun movie before devolving into a tangle of limbs and dick.

Tonight *was* a night out on the town, though. We were going to a place that had a special place in our relationship: the Atlanta Botanical Gardens. They were having an evening light show for their Spring Nights and Lights at the Garden event. The entire place was supposed to be decked out in colorful and coordinated lights, giving the illusion that all the plants and trees and buildings came alive once the sun went down, shifting and dancing with music that played through invisible speakers.

Just walking through the main entrance took us about ten minutes as we watched the tunnel of twinkling lights ahead of us shift like a living rainbow.

It might have been ten minutes, could have been two.

"How strong was that brownie we had?" I asked Jake as we walked through the tunnel, eyes wide like a pair of kids admiring

"Not too strong," Noah answered with a giggle, which told me that the brownie was indeed *very* strong. Both our phones buzzed in unison, drawing our attention to the news alert that had just been pushed out.

"Damn," Noah said, shaking his head before putting the phone back in his pocket. I did the same, not needing to read any more of the CNN article that had appeared.

"Another killing, and it's another gay guy. What's going on?" Noah asked, shaking his head. "The Midnight Chemist is apparently what they're naming the killer."

"They'll find them," I said, wanting to reassure Noah as much as I wanted to reassure myself. We'd already dealt with one lunatic; why did we have to be scared of another one stalking the streets? Robby had left us both with a lot of shit to deal with, and thankfully, after doing some solo and joint therapy sessions, the two of us had found peace with how the situation unraveled. Noah still remained a little jumpy but was getting better by the day, especially last month, after Robby was sentenced to thirty years in prison for attempted murder and aggravated stalking charges with no chance of parole.

It gave us some peace, let us breathe a little easier. The world was still a fucked-up place, evident by the alert on our phones, but that didn't mean we couldn't enjoy the good parts either. Being together was one of those good parts. One of the best parts, honestly. Noah was the best thing to have ever happened to me, no matter what we had to go through to get to where we were. I would have done all that and more if it meant getting to wake up next to Noah every morning of every day, telling him how much I loved him while spending nights like these together.

"Come," I said, leaning in and kissing him. I felt good about tonight. There was a certain magic in the air (and it wasn't because of the brownies). "Let's get lost in some lights."

I held his hand as we walked down a path that had lights dangling down from the overhanging branches, making it seem like we were swimming through an ocean of stars. On the other side of it was a glass-blown fountain where dozens of lit-up benches were placed around it, each bench shining under bright white light, shifting as a wave of blue went through the circle.

We sat there for a couple of minutes, watching as a column of light shot up from the center of the fountain, fracturing the light into a hundred different colors.

"You're seeing this, too, right?" I asked, suddenly becoming paranoid that the brownie had been *too* strong.

"Yes, yes I am." More giggling, chuckling. I put my arm around Noah's shoulders, and he laid his head down against me. I smiled, my fingers making soft trails on his arm.

"I love you, Noah." I kissed him, his lips fitting perfectly against mine.

"I love you, too, babe."

We drifted in a relaxing silence as people came in and out of my periphery, admiring the prism that appeared to be floating in midair, circled by a continuous wave of blue light. It hypnotized me, lulling me.

That was when Noah looked at his watch and shot up from the bench. "Crap. Crap, crap, shit." His outburst startled a couple sitting on the bench across from us.

"What happened?" I asked, worried at the sudden barrage of curses.

"I totally lost track of time. We're going to miss the special show at the Earth Mother. Come on." Noah grabbed my hand and tugged me up onto my feet. Before I could ask another question—mainly: there was a special Earth Mother show?—Noah already had us running down the path, nearly tripping over a child who was trying to break free from the leash that was wrapped around his mother's wrist.

"You know, I always wonder if kids shouldn't be..." My train of thought trailed off as we turned a corner, coming up on the Earth Mother's garden.

It was breathtaking. I'd never been at night, with the entire garden lit up, so I'd never seen how stunning the huge floral sculpture could look when the tendrils of bright green hair were glowing with light, subtly changing colors. Her eyes were lit up as well and appeared to move, giving her an entirely new sense of life, something that not even being draped in living flowers could have done. Water cascaded from her open palm and fell into the pond, shining like the rest of the garden.

"Wow," I said, Noah and I finding a spot by the railing and squeezing in between two other lovestruck couples. I could only get that singular word out before we both became entranced, falling under the Earth Mother's spell.

There was a dark wall of ivy behind her, conspicuously lacking any kind of spotlight. Across the wall, words started to appear as if written by an invisible hand in curving, white letters. I cocked my head, surprised. None of the other exhibits had a written element to them. It started off in a slow scrawl, drawing everyone's attention.

The first three letters had me cocking my head.

J.

A.

K.

That was weird. The strokes of light were spelling out my name. Was there some kind of interactive thing going on tonight? Did they take my name from my ticket purchase? Or maybe it was another Jake... wait a second.

The rest of the words filled up the wall of trailing ivy:

"Will you marry me?"

I blinked a couple of times, trying to get the words to make sense in my head. This had to be a joke, had to be for someone else. It couldn't be... I turned to Noah, and—he wasn't there.

He was behind me, down on one knee, smiling up at me with tears welling in his eyes, shining like jewels from all the glittering lights. Everyone else faded away. The entire world disappeared as Noah spoke.

"Jake, you're my everything. I want to spend the rest of my life with you, listening to you quoting *Cats* and *sometimes* snoring in your sleep." He gave me a wink.

"I never snore," I said in a hushed and shocked whisper.

Noah continued, his smile growing, the velvet box in his hand slightly shaking. "We may have started off as friends, but it wasn't long at all before we realized we were soul mates. So, Jake, my soul mate, will you marry me?"

I didn't skip a beat. "Yes, Noah. Yes, a hundred times yes."

He slipped the band onto my finger and stood to a round of cheering and applause, the people fading back into reality as I took Noah into the most meaningful kiss of my life, holding his head in my hands and saying yes over and over against his lips. I didn't even realize I started to cry until Noah rubbed away a teardrop from my cheek, looking up at me with the entire star-filled sky captured inside his eyes.

A hand came to fall down on my back, and soon I was wrapped up in a tight hug. It was Eric congratulating us. Tristan had picked up Noah and swung him around in a circle, nearly hitting Jess and Tia, who were holding a bottle of champagne while Yvette held the plastic cups.

The entire book club was here—my people, Noah's family.

My previous assumption about tonight had been totally wrong. It wasn't magical at all. That would imply that it was fake, that it was a made-up fantasy. Except this was all real. The intense warmth and floaty happiness that turned the concrete into clouds wasn't fake at all.

Neither was my love for Noah, and I intended on showing him exactly that tonight.

———

Noah Barnes

WE BARELY LASTED a couple of seconds once we got into the house before all our clothes came off and we were butt-ass naked in the living room, hands flying over bodies, gripping and tugging and stroking and kneading. I kissed Jake—my fiancé. The ring on my finger felt like it weighed a hundred pounds while also making me weightless at the same time. It was like attaching a new limb to my body, my senses hyperaware of the metallic coolness that clung tight around my ring finger.

It was perfect. Tonight was perfect.

Jake was perfect, and now he was mine, forever, to have and to hold.

And to suck.

I dropped down to my knees, unable to hold myself back any longer. I had to taste him. His cock was easily my favorite thing to put in my mouth. He was girthy and long and uncircumcised and always dripping with precome. He fit perfectly between my lips as I took him in, looking up at the man of my dreams, the glint of my silver band against his tan thigh catching my eye.

My heart skipped a beat, my dick throbbed, and my entire body lit up like a freshly born star.

"You look so good with my dick in your mouth," Jake said, a teasing grin playing on his big lips. He had trimmed his beard, shaving it along the neck to make his jawline even more prominent, making him look as sharp as a high-powered executive.

I swallowed more of him down my throat. He took that as a sign to push forward, thrusting into my mouth. He kept going, my fingers digging harder into his thigh. The sounds of my wet mouth gargling around his thick cock filled the room. He face-fucked me right there, balls pushing against my chin as his hands gripped either side of my head.

He took complete control, and I let him, my throat a pleasure tool for him, my body now his.

He pulled out. His cock shone under the bright light, dripping with my saliva. I rubbed my mouth, the back of my hand now soaked. I smiled up at him as I caught my breath. That wasn't all I wanted to taste tonight, though.

"Bend over the couch," I said, my turn to take the reins. He licked his lips, a smoldering glare in his eyes as he listened, bending over the back of the leather couch, hands on the seat and ass in the air.

I stood behind him and spat, the wet glob landing on his hole, sliding down over his taint. I thumbed it, spread it around his crack, and then I dove in headfirst. He responded with immediate moans of pleasure as I tongued him, rubbing up and down over his sensitive hole, burying my nose between his cheeks, his natural and intoxicating musk sending my senses into overdrive. His moans became louder, his grinding more powerful. He pushed back onto my face, giving more of himself to me.

Jake's back dipped, and I could see the rivets where the muscles formed and rippled underneath his tanned back. His shoulders spasmed as I tongued his hole, eating his ass like it was a five-star buffet. Jake started to grunt, calling my name. It drove me wild, the fire in my veins burning hotter.

"Eat my ass just like that, fuck, Noah, oh fuck. Finger me."

His words drifted back into moans as I slid my finger inside him. His velvet-soft walls gripped me, pulled me. I probed, pushing in deeper, rubbing against him. It was like pressing on a nuclear button, over and over again. His body squirmed on the couch.

My fiancé, my soon-to-be husband.

My soul mate.

I continued to work him with my finger, using another to stretch him open. It wasn't long before he cried out for more of me. More than just my fingers.

I spat into my hand and stroked it over my stiff cock. It pulsed in my hand as I looked down at Jake's ass. "Spread it open for me," I told him, watching as he reached back and grabbed himself, opening himself for me. I lined my cock up with his hole, relishing in the moment just before penetration. That delicate moment right before the world turned upside down from the pleasure.

I pushed in. He didn't resist me, his hole stretching to take me in. He gasped as I sunk into him. The sensation of being inside him was one that even nirvana couldn't compete with. I slowly rubbed his back, holding myself there, letting him feel every single inch of me.

"Oh, Noah, I love you. I love how you feel inside me."

I answered him with a thrust. He gave another gasp, crying out my name. Over and over again, getting louder as I fucked him harder. It felt like being on a tight wire strung up high between two skyscrapers. We were teetering on the top of the world, getting higher with every thrust. I could feel Jake's body tightening around me, feel his walls clenching.

He cried out, and I knew I'd fucked him right over the edge. He pushed back, coming hard onto the floor as I buried myself balls-deep in his ass. The way his orgasm made him convulse sent me over my own edge. I unloaded, emptying all I had, filling him with my seed, grunting with every shot. The world spun. Had we really fallen off the tightrope? Were we barreling through an empty sky? I couldn't quite tell, not with how fried my circuits were.

I leaned forward, closing my eyes and kissing Jake's neck. He still held me inside of him. Both of us were gasping for breath.

And then came the laughs, the giddy little chuckles

that turned us both into a sweaty pile of come and bliss. I kissed him again as I slowly pulled out of him.

"Fuck," Jake said, turning around so he could look me in the eyes with his sex-drunk gaze. "Is that what I've got to look forward to for the rest of my life?"

"It definitely is," I said, smiling as we kissed, and I gave his softening cock a playful tug. "Why, are you having second thoughts?"

"No, the opposite. I'm wondering how I could live forever so that this never ends," he replied, pulling me into his arms and pressing our spent bodies together, kissing me in a way that melted me.

We somehow managed to walk to the bed, using our mushy legs to carry us there, where we talked about possible wedding venues and honeymoon locations. It was a conversation I never imagined having with Jake on the day we were introduced back in the office.

It was all so... unexpected.

Thank goodness that day hadn't been the end to our story. It proved to have only been the beginning.

The End.

THANK YOU.

Thank you for reading LOVE AND MONSTERS and going on this ride with Jake and Noah. This book was one that poured right out of my heart and I'll forever be proud of their story.

Keep a look-out for the next book in the series which will be following our perpetually single Eric as he finds his better half with help from the book club. Things won't be easy—especially when the Midnight Chemist strikes close to home—but the friends have each others backs and that should be enough to get them through.

Hopefully.

Sign up for my newsletter for all the updates and follow me TikTok, Instagram, and Twitter: @maxwalkerwrites

Happy Reading!
Max
max@maxwalkerwrites.com

ACKNOWLEDGMENTS

Thank you, Camille, for creating the cover of my dreams. I'll never forget our afternoon coffee in Paris and can't wait to do the same in your city!

Thanks, Dalton, for beta reading and making this story shine brighter than a big gay rainbow.

Thank you, Vania, for using those hawk eyes and catching the little things that slip right by me.

Sandra, thank you for always taking my books to that next level. Working alongside you has been a true highlight of my entire career.

And thank you, reader, for going on this wild ride of mine.

ALSO BY MAX WALKER

The Rainbow's Seven -Duology

The Sunset Job

The Hammerhead Heist

The Gold Brothers

Hummingbird Heartbreak

Velvet Midnight

Heart of Summer

The Stonewall Investigation Series

A Hard Call

A Lethal Love

A Tangled Truth

A Lover's Game

The Stonewall Investigation- Miami Series

Bad Idea

Lie With Me

His First Surrender

The Stonewall Investigation- Blue Creek Series

Love Me Again

Ride the Wreck

Whatever It Takes

Audiobooks:

Find them all on Audible.

Christmas Stories:

Daddy Kissing Santa Claus

Daddy, It's Cold Outside

Deck the Halls

———

Receive access to a bundle of my **free stories** by signing up for my newsletter!

Be sure to connect with me on Instagram, Twitter and TikTok **@maxwalkerwrites.** And join my Facebook Group: Mad for Max Walker

Max Walker

Max@maxwalkerwrites.com

CPSIA information can be obtained
at www.ICGtesting.com
Printed in the USA
BVHW032208220123
656882BV00003B/107